REDNECK REBELLION

BWWM ROMANCE

JAMILA JASPER

VISIT WEBSITE

Copyright © 2020 by Jamila Jasper

ISBN: 9798467616056

All rights reserved.

No part of this book may be reproduced in any form or by any electronic or mechanical means, including information storage and retrieval systems, without written permission from the author, except for the use of brief quotations in a book review.

Thank you to my Patrons:

Join the Patreon Community.

Created with Vellum

DESCRIPTION

Sharing her is easy. Protecting her? Not so much.

Caroline's political dreams require dreaming big...
Especially in her small town.
Especially when she's in an unconventional relationship with three strapping country boys.

As Caroline takes her congressional campaign on the road,
Dark secrets and shady pasts keep their small town on edge.
This race won't be easy...
Especially not with an opponent who stirs hate.

Her three hot boyfriends love her...
But can they keep her safe from the redneck rebellion about to break?

Book #2 of 3 books in an interconnected steamy small town RH trilogy.
Click here to read Book #1 first.

ACKNOWLEDGMENTS

Thank you to all my readers, new and old for your support with this new year. I look forward to making 2020 and 2021 an INCREDIBLE year for interracial romance novels. I want to thank you all for joining along on the journey.

Thank you to my Patrons:
- Join the Patreon Community.

THE COMPLETED SERIES

Redneck Rebels
Redneck Rebellion
Redneck Retribution

CONTENT

A steamy black woman white man reverse harem novel. Themes include: three men, one woman love story with three Southern men loyal to one black woman.

Some other content includes violence, mention of racism, police brutality and other subjects that may be upsetting.

This book is not for the faint-hearted. The scenes in this book are for adults looking for WILD romance between a white man and a black woman.

This is an adults only read sitting at around 50,000+ words for billionaire romance readers who enjoy black woman/white man love stories with no cliffhanger and a Happily Ever After ending.

1
THE THREE MEN

CAROLINE GASPED as rough lips caressed her neck. Bud lay on top of her, his large muscular body firmly planted between her legs. Chase gingerly ran his tongue over her shoulders while Travis massaged her nipples, pinching them between his thumb and forefinger as she moaned. Caroline groaned as Bud's beard tickled the wet spot on her neck.

"We gon' spend the rest of the day testing this damned bed out," he murmured, rubbing his hands over her waist.

Caroline giggled.

"No," she whispered, "We have to… We have to…"

She lost her train of thought as Travis traded his fingers for his tongue. His tongue tickled her sensitive nipples as Bud hiked her thighs up.

"Bud," she whispered, "Not now…"

"Oh yes, Caroline," he whispered, "Welcome to your new home…"

Caroline responded with a loud moan as he slid inside her. Travis and Chase weren't naked yet. They'd taken their shirts off, which gave Caroline quite the view. Chase still had a sunburned neck, despite all her warnings about sunscreen while he repaired the porch. Travis heeded her warnings about sunscreen, but his time in the sun turned his blond hair so light it was nearly silver.

Bud buried himself inside her to the hilt and Caroline squeezed her eyes shut as he ardently thrust into her. She reached over his broad, farm-boy back and duck her nails into the thick muscles. Bud groaned and grunted, rutting between her legs like an animal.

His body warmed hers right up. January in Old Town didn't get freezing cold like towns in the North, but it was cold enough to be uncomfortable without three warm bodies in her bed. Once she got used to the three of them, she couldn't live without them. Better than blankets, that's for sure.

Bud tensed up and let out a half-moan, half-growl as he emptied himself between Caroline's legs. He was big. Enormous. And as he withdrew his staff from her sex, Caroline couldn't help but moan as juices erupted from her thighs and her yearning mounted.

Before the three boys: Travis Montgomery, Chase Owens and Bud Landry, she would have never assumed she was that type of girl. The type of girl to let three firm, well-built rednecks have their way with her. Especially not in a town like this one.

They'd hooked her in. More accurately, she'd hooked them in. And once she'd accustomed to having all three of them, her urges grew to match theirs. They were all three insatiable. Bud liked to have her first thing in the morning. Sweaty and gross and smelling of sleep was how he liked her best. Travis enjoyed her in the shower.

He'd murmur, "Let's get a little dirty before we get clean." Then he'd drop to his knees and spread her lower lips with his tongue before sponging her clean with ferocious vigor. Chase had her after work. He'd get back from the factory smelling like grease and sweat, having had some big argument usually, and he'd pin Caroline against the wall and plead with her to help him work out his pent up tension.

This time, all four of them joined in bed, a rare occurrence these days, but important on such a special occasion. The bed was new. And they'd spent the past few days sleeping on couches on sleeping bags until Bud finished stitching up the mattress.

As Bud rolled away from Caroline's split thighs, Travis hurried out of his pants, crumpling them at the base of the bed as he flipped Caroline onto her stomach and took her from behind. Travis celebrated with slow, deep strokes, whispering into her ear. If it weren't for Chase kissing her on the lips and Bud trailing kisses down her bare, spread legs, she might have forgotten that she and Travis weren't alone in the room.

When he finished inside her, Caroline didn't think she could stand any more of them. But Chase wouldn't let her off that easy. He flipped her onto her side and entered her right where he lay, his trousers only halfway down his thighs. The delicate curve of his hardness hit all the right spots. Bud and Travis sucked on her breasts as Chase moved between her legs. Her hair came unraveled from the tight bun and Travis wrapped some of it around his fingers as he pushed his tongue into her mouth, kissing her deeply.

Chase finished inside her after she came two or three more times. By then, the four of them were a mess. But very satisfied.

"Looks like the bed works fine," Bud said. His broad chest rose and plunged. Caroline predicted they would only have a few minutes before he wanted her again.

"Told you we could make it," Chase answered, drawing Caroline's naked body into his so her butt pressed against his groin.

The boys made the bed custom for their new house. The boys were good with their hands. Chase drew up the plans, Travis bought the supplies and Bud spent all his time out of the office hammering away. Caroline sat up, hair spilling over her breasts as Chase joined her in leaning against the soft velvet headboard.

"Do you think people suspect we aren't really roommates?"

Bud grinned, stroking his chin and running his hand down his flat stomach.

"I'd like anyone with suspicions to come talk to me about it."

Caroline giggled.

"Mayor Landry, we suspect you're living in sin with a woman and two other men," she mocked a potential citizen complaint and Bud chuckled.

Travis didn't find it so funny.

"We have to be careful," he said, "Caroline's right. Especially with the campaign coming up."

Chase folded his arms behind his head and sighed.

"Has anyone checked the mail yet?"

Caroline folded her body up nervously. They'd waited for the past three weeks for the letter. She'd spent ages gathering signatures and convincing residents of both sides of Old Town to sign her petition. They'd get news soon if they'd allow her to run for congress. She'd represent Old Town, Virgil and Moravia in Congress if she won the seat. Before all that, she'd need approval to run.

Bud rolled off the bed and groaned.

"I'll get it," Chase filled in, "I need to take a walk down the street and check on Ma, anyway."

Travis got up and stretched.

"Fine. I'll get supper started. Do we have anymore pork chops?"

Caroline searched the crumpled pile of clothes in the bed for a t-shirt.

"You three spoil me."

Bud grinned, "Ain't that what every Southern man wants? A little lady to spoil. I'm takin' a leak."

He ambled off to their en suite bathroom while Chase and Travis bustled off to busy themselves with various chores. Caroline slipped into one of Travis' white shirts. It smelled like sweat and magnolias. She found her underwear, a tight pair of black cotton panties and then a pair of Bud's sweatpants. She pulled the drawstring tight, so they'd fit around her waist without slipping down.

As she finished dressing, Bud emerged from the bathroom, naked except for a pair of red boxer briefs that hugged his tree trunk thighs. He hung onto the top of the door frame and bit his lower lip as he stared at Caroline.

"Too sore for me to take you again?"

Caroline's cheeks warmed.

"Bud…"

"Just joshing. How'd'you like the house?"

"It's strange. Living in Buchanan's old place. It feels… somehow wrong."

"I know. I know. It ain't exactly what you wanted, living in a plantation house and all that. But I'm the Mayor of this town and you're my girl. It's my job to care for you."

He nodded and gestured to Caroline, beckoning her closer. She obliged, tiptoeing across the large room before wrapping her arms around Bud's thick neck. He gazed down into her eyes, and she noticed a smattering of freckles across his face. Her thighs melted together. Bud was attractive. And up close he smelled like aftershave and hay.

"I love you," he murmured, "We all love you."

"I know," she sighed, "I hope I make it. I don't want you

three working your butts off to take care of me while I sit around doing nothing."

Bud flicked the tip of Caroline's nose with his thumb.

"You could always have babies," he said, grinning from ear to ear like this was the most brilliant suggestion in the world. Caroline reached up to peck him on the lips. Crazy Bud.

"Babies? Would the three of you want that? I mean... it's one thing to share me, but what about kids...?"

Bud shrugged.

"I'm a simple guy. Ain't gonna complicate things. If you have a baby... we'll share the responsibility. Like we share you."

Caroline teased the nape of his neck with her fingers. Talking about babies gave her the powerful urge to have Bud again. Between her thighs. Inside her. Touching every inch of her...

Before they could continue their discussion — or escalate it — Chase and Travis bounded upstairs, thrusting the door to the bedroom open. Travis held up an envelope, his cornflower eyes wide with excitement.

"It came," Chase said.

Bud spanked Caroline on the ass, encouraging her to grab the envelope, egging her on like one of his horses. She grabbed the envelope from Chase.

"You didn't open it?"

"We thought you ought to do the honors."

Caroline bit down on her lower lip and ripped the envelope open fiercely. She intended to make a big show of it, slowly opening the envelope and reading each word out loud to her three boys. Once she'd fished the thin sheet of paper out, she couldn't help herself.

Caroline screamed. Loud.

"I'm in! I'm going to run for Congress! Holy shit!"

Bud lifted her off the ground as she screamed. Once he set her down, Travis threw his arms around her waist and kissed her. Chase set his hands on his hips, patiently waiting for Travis to finish.

"Don't forget the little guy once you make it to Washington," he said, a cocksure grin spread across his sunburnt face.

"There's no way I'm getting to Washington without your help," she said, "I've got to run a good campaign. Do you have any idea who I'm running against?"

The boys shrugged.

Chase said, "Dixon's retiring this year so whoever it is will be fresh. Someone young."

"If it was someone in Old Town, we'd know about it right?" Caroline asked, wracking her brain for anyone she knew who might run for Congress.

Their town's election for Mayor had been tough enough on Old Town tensions. Her parents even moved away at her brother Caleb's behest to get away from everything. He was staying up in the house now, alone.

"Maybe it's someone from Virgil?" Travis suggested.

Bud stroked his beard and shrugged.

"Don't matter. We'll make sure you kick anyone's ass."

Caroline's heart fluttered as the reality set in. A part of her didn't think they'd accept her running for Congress. She'd tried, but she didn't expect to make it this far. She was a black candidate, running for Congress in a rural county with three segregated towns. She couldn't win on the black vote alone. She'd have to win over voters from both sides of the tracks. Her head swam with the complexity of what she'd gotten herself into.

"Care?" Chase whispered, holding onto her shoulders and bending at the knees to meet her eye, "You okay?"

"Yeah."

"She's nervous," Bud said, "like a skittish mare."

Caroline rolled her eyes.

"You're comparing me to a horse now?!"

"She has every right to be nervous," Travis pointed out, which didn't help Caroline, but at least softened Bud and Chase. Chase pecked her on the lips.

"We'll stand by you. We promise."

"I know. I guess I never thought I'd make it this far. It's time for me to saddle up."

Chase's facial expression changed, and he glanced at Bud. Caroline noticed an entire conversation exchanged in that glance.

"We have news," Chase blurted out.

Travis nervously chewed on his fingernails. Bud remained calm and nodded slowly, urging Chase to continue.

"What?"

"My brother's back and he's on the force."

Zach Owens. Caroline's skin crawled when she heard the name. She'd gone several weeks without thinking of Zach Owens. She couldn't help thinking of Buchanan. Bud bought the old Mayor's plantation house with his new salary and some of Travis' savings, and they'd spent all their free time fixing the place up.

Caroline couldn't help thinking of Buchanan as she sanded wooden railings in what had been his house.

But Chase's brother had been far from her mind. And his return wasn't good news.

"Do you think he'd run for Congress?" Caroline asked.

2

THE OPPONENT

ZACH OWENS WASN'T RUNNING for Congress. But thinking about her opponent made Caroline realize she had to do this. Buchanan waltzed into the mayor's office and access to that much power nearly got most of them killed. Caroline shuddered at the thought. The very next day, she submitted her ultimate confirmation: she'd run for Congress.

The boys insisted they have a celebratory dinner. Chase couldn't get the afternoon off until Wednesday. Bud cleared off his schedule and Travis had all the time in the world since he quit the police force, a situation he wasn't particularly happy about.

Chase bought the ingredients for their celebratory dinner. Travis got an old family recipe out for pecan pie and Bud grilled the pork ribs out back using a special "meat rub" he'd invented. Caroline tried to help, but the boys would swat her on the bottom of with their spatulas or other implements, so she got stuck hovering around while they prepared dinner.

Travis poured Caroline whiskey and ginger ale and had himself a glass while he waited for the pie to bake.

"So. I'm taking the LSAT again soon."

"You're going to do this?"

"I believe in this justice system, Caroline. It's served us well for many many years."

"It's served some people well," Caroline muttered.

Before their conversation could take a more negative political turn, Travis reached for her fingers, intertwining his hands with hers.

"I need to provide for you, Caroline. I know you're a powerful woman and you can handle business yourself but... the Montgomery family takes care of their own."

His eyes were so blue you could swim in them. You could drown in them. Caroline ran her thumb over Travis' large veiny hands.

"I never thought I'd end up here," Caroline said, sipping on the strong whiskey.

"Neither did I. But we're here. And we're going to get you to Congress. All of us."

"Aren't you worried?"

Travis shook his head.

"If Bud Landry can end up in the Mayor's Office, we can get you to Washington."

"Maybe Old Town isn't ready for a black Congresswoman."

Travis shrugged.

"It doesn't matter if they're ready for the future. It's coming."

Travis got his pie out of the oven. The sticky, sugary smell of pecans filled the room. Chase carried side dishes into their dining room from the kitchen with Caroline's help, and Bud hauled in the meat.

"Good food, good meat, good God, let's eat."

"Was that your idea of grace?!" Caroline squealed at Bud.

He winked and dipped his finger in barbecue sauce before sticking it in Caroline's mouth. She wrapped her lips around his finger, tasting the tang of honey and tomatoes with a healthy dose of mustard and black pepper. Bud pulled his finger out of Caroline's mouth and smirked. She playfully smacked his bicep, and they dug in.

Chase gave a toast. He would have stood right on the table to do it, but Travis talked him into standing on the chair.

"To Caroline, the woman who brought us together and the woman who will take us to Washington. A brilliant woman, well deserving of sitting in the House of Representatives."

"Hear, hear!" Bud responded in a sonorous voice that might make you think he was calling to a crowd.

"Now, Mister Mayor," Caroline whispered, "Can we dig into the pecan pie? Why don't you cut the first slice?"

Bud cut the first slice, and Travis apologized profusely on the off chance he'd messed up his family recipe. There wasn't a chance of him spoiling it. From the first bite, Caroline wanted to devour the entire pie herself.

The boys crowded around the sink and wouldn't let Caroline so much as rinse off a spoon.

"Am I supposed to stand here doing nothing?"

"Get more whiskey in you," Bud growled, "You'll need it."

Caroline's thighs melted together. She knew exactly what it meant when Bud used that tone. He meant business and normally the kind of business that made it difficult to walk the next day. Tonight was about celebration and tomorrow, she'd meet with the paper and the party mentor helping to run her campaign. Caroline appreciated the boys' support, but she knew the chances of her winning this Congressional election were slim to none. In three months as Mayor, Bud made some changes around town, but he was still one of them. He was a Southern man who rode horses and played football.

Caroline was still an outsider. And Old Town was still segregated. And the other towns in the county were even worse. Chase broke away from the boys early and grabbed Caroline by the waist, pressing her against the wall in the hallway to their bedroom, a precursor of what was to come. Their high school portraits hanging on the wall rattled as Chase manhandled Caroline with a necessary kiss.

Caroline raked her fingers through his copper hair.

"What's that for?"

Chase grinned.

"A precursor to bad news. Zach's back in town and living with my ma. It's nice she has someone to take care of her but... he's different. Worse somehow."

"I'll stay out of his way."

"If you want me to run him out of town, say the word. I'll get one of Landry's guns and scare him off."

"No," Caroline whispered, "No guns. No fighting him off. We're doing things the right way now."

Chase buried his nose in Caroline's neck and came up for air, stiff and eager for her.

"Travis rubbing off on you, huh?"

"Maybe," Caroline answered.

"Yeah, well, he used to be a cop. It scrambled his blond brains."

"Chase..."

Chase took her lower lips between his and kissed her again, pinning her hands over her head. The floorboards creaked as Travis wandered down the hall, shirtless, with his jeans unbuckled.

"Heating up dessert?" he teased Chase.

"I'll leave that to you," Chase murmured, breaking eye contact from Caroline and twirling her down the hall into Travis' arms.

Travis dipped her dramatically and pulled her up for a

Redneck Rebellion

kiss. Caroline's fingers danced over his broad shoulders. Caroline rested her head against Travis' shoulders and he scooped her up and brought her to their custom-made bed — perfect for exactly four.

By the time Caroline lay on her back, Travis pulled her clothes off and Chase crawled in beside them. He patiently kissed Caroline's neck and shoulders as Travis eased his trousers off and thrust his hardness into her. Caroline moaned, digging her fingernails into Travis' back, moaning as he entered her. Travis made love to her tenderly, taking his time thrust deep inside her, eagerly diving into every sensation of making love. Her tightness wrapped around him and Caroline crossed her ankles over his taut buttocks.

Her fingers clutched the back of Travis' head as her skin lit up with pleasure from Chase's tongue sampling every inch of her bare flesh. Travis pressed his forearms into the bed, his bicep tense next to her cheeks as his hips swiveled slowly between her legs.

His cheeks grew pink with each thrust, his skin holding a rainbow's range of shades as he took his pleasure from her sex. A climax surged in Caroline's core and she moaned, tilting her head back and causing her breasts to spill on either side of her chest where Chase eagerly wrapped his lips around her nipple and sucked so hard that she came. Her tight heat wrapping around Travis' invading member pushed him over the edge and he spilled thick spurts of hot cum between Caroline's eager legs. The three rednecks knew how to make her lose control. The moment Travis rolled off her, Chase pulled her on top of him. She raked her fingers through his hairy, masculine chest and kissed him as she lowered herself onto his protruding tumescence.

Chase moaned, as he steadied Caroline's hips, bringing her warmth down over his cock slowly. Once her wetness enveloped his dick, her fingers gripping his masculine chest, and she rode him nice and slow, taking her time to draw her fingers along Chase's muscular chest, sculpted by brutal factory work and daily passionate lovemaking.

Chase groaned as she moved her hips in an unusual swivel shape and he reached for her nipples, pinching them between his fingers as Caroline moaned and rode him faster. Chase's cock hit all her deepest spots at this angle, and when she came, her pussy gushed with her juices and the remnants of Travis's cum between her legs. The heat and wetness proved too much for Chase and he erupted inside her, a thick glob of cum coating the back of her tightness as he shudders and squeezed Caroline's hips desperately. Caroline removed her sticky entrance from Chase's hardness and rolled onto her back.

Travis emerged from their bathroom with a warm washcloth. Chase hiked her legs up and Travis wiped her clean. The warm rag tickled her inner thighs and once her thighs were cleaned, her legs and pussy tingled. Bud's thudding footsteps came down the hall.

"Bud…" she whispered desperately, grabbing one of their pillows and curling up.

There was one more enormous cock to take before the night ended. Bud stood in the doorway grinning at the two men naked in bed with Caroline.

"Y'all tuckered her out."

Travis stole Caroline's protective pillow away, and Chase pushed hair out of her face.

"Our girl can handle it."

Bud whipped his belt off and cracked it like he planned to use it for a spanking. Caroline squealed and Bud tossed the belt aside with a grin.

"Not tonight, buttercup."

He undid his shirt and gestured at Chase and Travis. By now they could communicate their bedroom needs without words. Chase flipped Caroline onto her stomach and held one of her legs down. Travis held down the other leg. They pinned her down good. She felt Bud's knees sink into the bed. Then she felt his tongue. His large, flat tongue felt almost too big to be a human tongue. He licked her until she was soaking and until she'd cum three or four times.

As she recovered from her fourth (or third) orgasm, Bud thrust his cock into her hard and pressed his enormous weight into her. She gasped for air as Bud took her hard from behind, grunting and rutting into her with animal fervor until he spilled his seed inside her and instead of rolling off Caroline, he collapsed.

"Bud!" she squeaked, "You are killing me!"

He pulled his hips off her a bit and flipped her over onto her stomach before kissing her.

"Not yet, little lady. I'm ready for round two."

Bud fucked her three more times. Then Travis had another round and then Chase woke up from a power nap and fucked her twice again. Caroline didn't think she could cum anymore than this. Were other women really satisfied with only one guy? Three insatiable Southern men changed Caroline's sex drive permanently.

Tonight, she slept cradling Bud's giant body, fingers on one hand interlaced with Travis' while Chase spooned her from behind. They slept like puppies after a good feeding.

Their good night's sleep wouldn't last. A crash came downstairs. Then another. Caroline woke with a start.

Bud was already out of bed, and he had his shotgun.

"Bud!"

"Someone's knocking," he said, "Let's find out who it is."

"Don't jump to shooting them!" Caroline protested, searching for a t-shirt to slip over her naked body.

Bud didn't care about greeting anyone at the door stark naked apparently, but the other boys had the decency to slip their pants on while Mayor Landry stalked through the house bare ass cheeks sliding past each other. Caroline wore Bud's oversized shirt as she tiptoed behind him.

Chase grabbed an ax from the top of the stairs and Travis pointed to the kitchen, indicating the pistol he stashed at the bottom of the sink — and left Caroline to discover with a shriek one day. Caroline flicked on the porch light and they all lowered their weapons.

Nothing to worry about. It was only Caleb. He pounded on the door again.

"Caroline, open the damn door!"

Caroline thrust the door open and Caleb's eyes dropped to Bud's... pistol. Bud cleared his throat and stepped behind Caroline so his genitals were no longer in view.

"Y'all need to hurry up the road. We got a problem."

"What? It's three in the fucking morning, Caleb."

"Zach Owens was on patrol. He shot Ezra Mayfair. The Mayfair boy... He's dead."

3

WE MUST COME TOGETHER

CAROLINE FROZE when she heard the words. Zach Owens shot Ezra Mayfair.

"He's dead?"

"You need to come. Now. All of you."

Caleb tipped his hat and muttered, "Mayor Landry."

Bud became conscious of his indecency and turned tail to pull on his clothes. And the other two men set down their weapons. Caroline froze in the doorway. Her brother grabbed her shoulders.

"Caroline," he said, drawing her in with his voice, "You need to watch yourself tonight. People are angry. Furious. And it's a complete mess. This is it. This is the spark that will light this town on fire. Do you understand?"

Caroline didn't. A faint ringing in the back of her ears distracted her and her tongue hung heavy in her mouth. Ezra Mayfair and his sister lived across the street. He was a good boy. He always had a smile that cracked open his cinnamon-colored face and a warm demeanor.

He'd joke with Caleb sometimes about getting out of Old Town. He'd stop and stand in the middle of the streets to watch the sunsets. He'd seen his last sunset. Had he known it would be the last? Caleb tore up the street, and Caroline flinched when firm hands touched her shoulders. Chase.

"You okay?"

"No."

"We're ready to go up there. Bud's taking the truck."

Mayor Landry bought himself a new truck to go with his new house. Bud hurried past Caroline and Chase to fire up the engines. Chase sat in the backseat with Caroline. Travis sat in the front. Neither Travis nor Bud spoke. Caroline could imagine what Travis was thinking, so she didn't bother saying anything. He believed in the law, and he couldn't understand a world where the people he grew up with might act unjustly.

Chase was different, at least. He didn't see a reason someone ought to shoot a man in cold blood without rights to a trial or a jury of his peers. Caroline laced her hands with his. Chase pressed her hands to his lips, rough stubble prickling her knuckles and warm lips sending a shiver through her arm. Hot tears rose in her lower lids and Caroline pushed them back.

Don't cry. Don't cry yet.

When the Mayor's truck pulled halfway onto the sidewalk, a crowd formed around it. Police officers. Bud got out of the truck and the world disappeared around him. Caroline knew he'd impress as Mayor, and now she watched him in action. Bud Landry towered over all the men. Their uniforms and guns holstered on slender hips didn't carry the same intimidating power when they stood next to gigantic Bud Landry.

"What the hell happened down here?" Bud growled.

"We've got Zach Owens to safety, sir. The medics are over there with the body. They're taking him to the hospital but... he's dead, Mayor."

"How the hell did this happen?"

Caroline's mouth went dry. She felt an arm around her waist. Travis. He never touched her like this in public. And she wasn't sure she wanted him around. Ezra Mayfair could have been anyone she knew. He could have been Caleb. But Zach Owens... Zach Owens could have been Travis, and somehow Caroline felt worse.

"I need to... I need to..."

She pulled away from Travis and propelled by emotion rather than better judgment she ran toward the crowd surrounding the ambulance. She saw all her neighbors huddled together on one side of the ambulance and on the other side, people from the white side of town, the part of town where Caroline now lived. I'm betraying them, she thought. I've been enjoying myself living in an enormous house with three attractive men, and I thought that was improving my circumstances, but what I've really done is I've betrayed them. She burst through the caution tape and ended up on the other side before anyone noticed her. And not knowing what else to do, she flung herself onto Bianca Mayfair, who stared at the white sheet covering her brother's body and gasped when Caroline's weight fell into her.

They only knew each other in passing. But Caroline needed to hold someone. She needed to hold another black woman and mourn. Ezra Mayfair's life ended, but grief wouldn't end there and they both knew it. This sadness would ferment and grow, and it could sour every bit of happiness from their lives if they let it. Bianca emitted a shuddering sob, like she knew everything Caroline was thinking, like she'd had the same thought herself.

"He's gone," Bianca whispered, and the two words split Caroline's heart in two. By the time she pulled away, the light-skinned woman's face turned purple and Caroline held her hand. They heard another sound. Cars. Trucks. And then chaos. Two news vans.

"Go," Caroline whispered to Bianca, "Go to the hospital before they find you."

Bianca nodded. Caleb found his sister and grabbed her by the forearm.

"Travis is looking everywhere for you."

"Okay."

"You need to get out of her, Caroline before it gets crazy."

"Okay."

"Bud's staying behind to talk to the news trucks. Chase and I will walk you home."

"What about Travis?"

Caleb patted Caroline's back and pursed his lips.

"Don't worry about Travis."

The next forty minutes blurred past. Chase sat on the arm of their parlor couch and passed a mug of tea over to Caroline before he took Caleb to the door and they spoke to each other in hushed voices. When Chase shut the door, his boots thudded against the hardwood and he leaned in the parlor's doorway. His eyes met Caroline's and her throat tightened.

"Baby..." Chase said, and the anguish on his face reflected her own. Caroline sobbed. How many years would they have to fight?

"Don't," Caroline whimpered, "I don't have time to be weak right now."

"You ain't weak. You ain't weak for feeling. Goddammit, you don't have to be a soldier all the time."

"Don't I?" Caroline whispered.

Chase stroked her hair. He wasn't as soothing as Bud. He had rough, workman's hands and little delicate about him.

"The cops are protecting their own on this one. But there weren't any reason for it as far as I can tell. Zach... my brother... he shot an innocent man."

Caroline gazed up at him again. His mother was out there. His brother killed someone. But he was here. With her.

"Your mom," Caroline whispered, "I'm so selfish. I didn't even think about her."

"Don't," Chase responded sharply, "Travis will look after my ma. He's... he's talking to my brother."

"Shouldn't you look after them?"

"Caroline. If I have to see my brother tonight, I'll kill him. And I won't do us any good behind bars."

He was earnest about killing his brother. He'd come close, Caroline knew that. And Chase didn't have that ability to stop himself from acting on his impulses. He was brash. And crazy. And Caroline didn't want to love that about him, but she did.

Chase settled next to her on the couch and wrapped Caroline in his arms. He was warm and eventually she cried herself to sleep pressed against his chest. They slept through the night on the couch together. Caroline woke to hushed voices. Travis's slow drawl and Bud's gruff grunts in response. Chase shifted beneath her, rousing Caroline from sleep. He'd lost his shirt in the night and her bare cheek pressed against the hair on his chest. She ran her fingers through it before sitting up and yawning.

For a few moments, before she was properly awake, it was like a normal morning. Then she remembered, and her shoulders slumped.

"G'morning," Travis said, pushing a plate of eggs and toast across the coffee table.

"We made breakfast. I ate already."

"Great."

Caroline stared at the plate. How could she eat at a time like this? Chase didn't have that problem, and he crudely plopped eggs onto toast with his fingers. Bud kept the mood light that morning. Caroline could tell he was trying his hardest not to burden them all but his eyebrows knitted together seriously between his wisecracks and she knew he hadn't forgotten.

They spent a quiet morning together until Caleb dropped by around 11. Chase led him into the living room while Travis studied for the LSAT upstairs and Bud hollered on the phone. Chase cleared his throat and exchanged a knowing glance with Caleb.

"You two are planning something."

"Yes," Caleb said, "A protest. What happened to Ezra Mayfair wasn't right. We can't let Old Town continue like this. Not anymore. Zach can't get away with this. No offense, Chase."

"None taken. I'd be the first man in line to kill that sonofabitch."

Caleb flashed Chase a prohibitive look but dismissed his rough talking as Chase being Chase.

"What do we do, then? Make signs?"

"Yes," Chase replied, "Against my inner desires, we are going to organize the people non-violently to protest the unlawful killing of Ezra Mayfair. No weapons. Nothing but silently showing our disapproval."

Caroline shook her head.

"What? You're not onboard?"

"It doesn't matter how we protest. They'll make us look like the bad guys."

"We have to do the right thing," Chase urged, "We know the cops in this town. I mean…"

He lowered his voice and whispered, "Sherriff Montgomery had KKK affiliations. We had proof."

"I'm running for Congress. Won't this affect my campaign?"

"Look," Caleb said, "You're my sister. I want you safe. I

won't begrudge you avoiding the front lines. But there's Bianca Mayfair to worry about. Ezra provided everything for her. And what's going to happen if she doesn't have two pennies to rub together to provide for their family? We need to get justice for them. For her."

Caleb had a point. Caroline remembered holding Bianca, how numb she felt. How they both cried about a shared pain that they didn't realize they had. Only last year, Caroline thought she'd been in the same position with her brother. She would have wanted people to protest. She would have wanted justice for him.

"The story's picking up speed," Chase pointed out, "The goddamned internet finally knows about Old Town."

Caroline wondered if that would become more of a curse than a blessing.

"So. A protest. Where?"

"The park, the mayor's office, maybe the police station."

"You want to protest outside of Bud's office?"

"He'd support us. He does," Chase pointed out, "That might count for something."

"Some folks from out-of-town want to come here and help us organize," Caleb said.

Travis appeared in the doorway.

"A protest?"

Caleb's expression changed. He'd never liked Travis as much as Chase. Caroline couldn't imagine the rage her brother felt for him now. Travis was one of them. Even if he'd taken off his uniform. He thought like a cop.

"Yessir," Chase responded with a grin.

He and Travis disagreed often. He was better at diffusing situations than Caleb. Travis shook his head.

"That ain't the way to get your message heard in this town. You protest, it'll seem like you have a problem with the cops. Is that the message you want to send out here? I mean... Zach Owens doesn't speak for all of us."

Caroline wanted to sink into the couch. She could feel her brother's mood changing. He was too angry to listen to Travis. To hear him. He was like Caroline: grieving. And he had every right to grieve. Chase rose and clapped Travis on the shoulders, perhaps more rough than friendly.

"Travis, buddy? My brother shot an innocent man. Protesting ain't illegal. First Amendment rights protect it. So until we get that boy the justice he deserves, we'll exercise those rights."

Travis shrugged, but his cheeks were pink and Caroline sensed their conversation had not finished.

4

PEACEFUL

TRAVIS DIDN'T APPROVE. Caroline sensed his disapproval. What was wrong with a protest exactly? Chase was right. They had rights, and they had to get justice for Ezra Mayfair.

"When they bring Zach to court, they'll handle him. If you go out there in the streets, it'll be like looking for war."

"It's a peaceful protest," Caroline snapped, "Peaceful."

"Yeah, well. Those things have a way of not staying peaceful," Travis responded.

Caroline glanced over at Chase, who patted her on the thigh.

"Listen, man. How about we discuss this when we've all cooled down? I'm thinking about Caroline."

"So am I," Travis snapped, "And she doesn't need you going off half-cocked ready to cause more trouble in this town than she can handle."

Bud ambled into the room.

"Y'all fighting?"

"No!" the three responded sharply enough for Bud to assume they had more conflict than they let on.

"We're protesting. Landry knows about it. That's all there is to discuss."

"Bud..." Travis reddened and turned to his old friend.

Bud shrugged and responded with a grunt.

"You can't grunt your way out of this, Mayor Landry," Travis insisted.

"They got rights. You got rights. From what I've heard, Zach Owens had no right to fire a weapon on that boy. He wasn't in uniform. The boy wasn't doing anything wrong. He shot him in cold blood."

Caroline bit her lower lip to stop it trembling. How could Travis stand there and not see plain as day what she saw? Ezra could have been her brother.

"It could have been Caleb," Caroline whispered.

Chase kissed her cheek.

"Travis. Maybe you ought to give her space."

"No," Travis insisted, "She's my girl."

"She's our girl," Chase corrected him.

"Exactly, which means she's mine too. And I won't have you two leading her astray when she has bigger things to worry about than Ezra Mayfair."

"Shut up!" Caroline yelled.

All three boys stared at her.

"I'm sick of listening to you all arguing. I'm going for a walk. Don't follow me."

"Caroline..." Chase pleaded.

"Reason with him," she snapped at Chase before storming out of the house.

Caroline didn't want to go back to the crime scene. She needed to get away from the boys and their incessant arguing. She appreciated Chase standing up for her, but he ought to know better than picking a fight with Travis. Bud never involved himself in arguments. He cared too much about being liked, Caroline thought. And Travis...

Caroline's eyes pricked with tears. Her relationship with Travis had always been different. He was more protective. More gentle than both Chase and Bud. And now.

"He doesn't mean it," Caroline whispered, "he's just looking out for me."

After all they'd been through, there was no way Travis sided with Zach Owens. He thought about the world differently. Caroline had always known that. And she'd never let these differences tear them apart. But this was different. Ezra Mayfair didn't live far off. Caroline entered a cafe on Old Town's Main Street. The two blonde girls behind the counter stared at her too long.

"Um... may I have a black tea?"

The one at the cash register left to grab the tea without saying a word. Caroline wondered if she'd imagined their coldness. The girl behind the counter looked like Augusta Abernathy. They might have been related. She handed Caroline the tea and Caroline winced as she grabbed onto the cup. Too hot. She sat at a table outside and sipped the tea, thinking of nothing and everything.

Did this count as grief? She hadn't been close to the Mayfairs. They were neighbors, which meant you had someone to wave to, someone to grab your trash can lid when wind dragged it halfway down the street. A flicker of recognition when you crossed them downtown. And Ezra... well, he'd been a flirt. Too young for Caroline. Way too young. But he was one of those young men who would grow up handsome, with a string of broken hearts left behind when he finally left Old Town.

Caroline's hands shook. He wouldn't grow up, though. He'd never flirt with another shopkeeper. He'd never smile. Didn't Travis get it? Didn't he get how badly it hurt to know that Zach Owens shot him in cold blood and because this was Old Town, nothing would ever come of it. That was the unspoken truth of the matter. Without marching. Without nationwide attention. With none of that, Ezra Mayfair would fade and they'd forget him. Only the Mayfairs would remember and twenty years from now, Old Town ladies would pull their friends close and whisper, "Remember their son? They shot him all these years ago and things were never the same."

Caroline didn't finish her tea. She left the cup on the table and wandered away from town onto one of the dirt roads leading to Virgil. Trees hung over the road, softening the sounds of the parallel highways to the bigger cities. Caroline kicked a few loose stones.

Caroline lost herself when she heard footsteps in the gravel. She whipped her head around. She couldn't hear anything except her own loud breathing, which she suddenly perceived as far too loud.

"Hello?"

It could happen again. Zach Owens popping out of the trees, armed. Or someone else.

"Hello?"

Caroline folded her arms and yelled, "I know you're following me."

A pair of legs dropped from the tree behind her. And then she saw him... Zach. No. Not Zach.

"Chase! You scared the hell out of me! What are you doing in that damned tree!"

"When I heard you call, I shimmied up there."

"You little monkey," Caroline grumbled, "Why are you following me?"

"I'm looking after you."

He reached into his Carhartt pants for his box of American Spirits and stuck one in his mouth. He struck a match and lit his cigarette. Caroline rolled her eyes.

"I don't need you looking after me."

"I know. That's why I hid."

"I didn't notice you downtown."

"I'm a master of disguise," Chase said, winking.

Caroline walked ahead and Chase half-jogged to catch up to her.

"Don't run off now. Sorry we pissed you off."

"You didn't."

"Travis…"

"He picks the worst times to put his foot down. I mean… I know he isn't like Zach, but he's defending a killer."

"Travis thinks different from you and I. His daddy was the sheriff of this town. That means something to him. This system works for him."

"It works for you. But you get it."

Chase shrugged.

"Fourteen hour shifts rarely give you time to think, but I talk to the guys on my smoke break. Old Town's always had two sides. A white side and a black side. We're closer to becoming one. I know that."

"I thought with Bud becoming mayor, that would end. Everything we went through didn't make a difference."

Caroline wanted to believe in Chase's vision of unity, but one side of Old Town refused that. There were still KKK members active in the town. Caroline stopped worrying about them when Buchanan left. But she'd been foolish to forget. Maybe if she hadn't forgotten, she would have worried more that Zach Owens came back to town. She could have done something. Chase pulled her out of her guilt and self-blame.

"That ain't true, Caroline."

Caroline wanted to believe him, but she couldn't help but think Chase only said this to make her feel better.

"What do you want, Chase? I'm not ready to come back. And I'm not ready to talk to Travis."

"You want the truth?"

"Yes."

"I want to walk with you. I don't want to be alone right now any more than you do. Caroline... I might kill my brother."

"What?! Chase... Don't you think that's extreme."

"Yes. But a life for a life. It's only fair. If he gets out of prison... I'll take his life. And I'll do my time. I'm not like other guys, Caroline. I know that I'm ready to lay my life on the line for what I believe."

Caroline stopped walking. Chase stopped too, and they faced each other. He stomped out his cigarette butt. Caroline squeezed her eyes shut.

"I can't believe I'm saying this but Chase Owens, promise me you won't kill your brother. Because if you leave me to go to prison, I will never forgive you. You aren't any use to anyone in prison."

Caroline waited for him to promise. She heard his boots against the gravel and then felt his hand on her cheek. And when she opened her eyes, Chase closed the distance between them and had both her cheeks in his hands, cupping her gently, like if squeezed too tight she'd fall apart.

"I promise," he murmured, "For you. Only for you."

He kissed her and spread her lips with his tongue instantly. And walked her off the path and against a tree with a large trunk. Caroline kissed him back, heat rising between them with each second that passed. She could taste tobacco on Chase's lips and smell his rough masculine musk. He took her hands and pinned them over her head.

"You make me crazy," he murmured.

Caroline giggled, but Chase ran his tongue along her neck.

"Chase," she whimpered, "What are you doing?"

"We're off the road," he whispered, "I can be quick."

Redneck Rebellion

Before Caroline could question him, he unbuckled his belt and hiked her back against the tree. Bark prickled Caroline's back through her shirt, but she didn't fight Chase. She wrapped her legs around his torso as he removed his hardness and stripped her pants down far enough to drive his dick inside her.

"Chase..." she gasped.

"I love you," he murmured, repeating it to her with each thrust. I love you. I love you. Caroline came. Fast. He was big. And urgent. He needed her and Caroline needed him too. She needed his broad, factory-hewn body to press against her and make her forget her hurt. She tangled her fingers in his brown hair, releasing a woody tobacco smell as he plunged into her deep.

"This is crazy," she gasped. Chase thrust between her legs harder and Caroline came again. Anyone could walk by, but by her third climax, she stopped worrying about the fact that they were only 20 feet off the dirt road.

Their bodies intertwined and Chase pressed his forehead to hers as his tongue played with her lips. He groaned as he erupted between her legs and Caroline squeezed her thighs around his torso as he removed his sloppy wet cock from her entrance and set her back on the ground.

"Dress," Chase commanded.

Caroline nodded. He'd fucked the good sense out of her, because she'd been about to wonder back onto the dirt road with her ass out.

"Anyone could have heard us," She whispered.

"They didn't," Chase promised, "We're alone. Trust me."

His fingers interlocked with hers.

"Home," Caroline whispered, "We'd better go home. And I'd better talk to Travis."

Chase nodded.

"We're protesting. He doesn't have to like it."

"I know. But I want him to support us. This matters. Ezra Mayfair mattered."

"I know that. Let's go home and talk. Travis loves you, Caroline. I don't want to say he loves you more than any of us, but what he feels is real. And Travis comes from an old Southern family. It's hard for him to watch this unfold."

"I know. I get that."

"Come here, little lady. Mind if I have another smoke?"

"You ought to quit," Caroline teased.

"I know. I know. But damn, it's hard not to have a smoke after a damn good fuck."

Caroline's cheeks warmed. Chase's bluntness appealed to her. And she felt safe with him. And after their wilderness romp and his loving touch, she was finally ready to go home.

5

A HORRIBLE INCIDENT

"Come. You have to see this."

Travis grabbed Caroline's arm as she walked through the door. Caroline slipped out of her shoes while Chase banged mud off his boots against the porch. Is this how Travis planned on talking about their disagreement? Bud was already in their TV room and he patted the seat next to him. Caroline sat. Travis jumped over the back of the couch and sat next to them.

Ezra Mayfair's picture flashed across the screen. Caroline's head swam. She wriggled uncomfortably.

"He'll come back on soon," Travis murmured.

It felt good to sit next to him again and remember that Travis loved her. For all his flaws, he cared. He had a strong sense of ethics and he wouldn't betray her. Caroline couldn't take her eyes off Ezra Mayfair's picture. His eyes. Large. Brown. And empty the way photographs usually are. A coiffed blonde reporter pursed her lips and rattled off information about Ezra from a teleprompter that was a sum of his life — but not the life Caroline knew.

"Ezra Mayfair, a young resident of a poor Southern Town was murdered by a police officer while walking home..."

Caroline's ears rang.

"... He attended Robert E. Lee High School in Virgil and lived with his sister. Our investigative reporters turned up some unfortunate evidence about Ezra's past that may have led to his death. John? Can you hear us?"

"What unfortunate evidence?" Caroline spat, her voice shakier than she expected. Bullshit. It was all bullshit. Ezra wasn't a perfect kid. He'd stolen flowers from their garden once when he was a boy, and Nikita Coulson had whooped him and sent him home to get another whooping from his mama. He fought at school sometimes and came home with a busted lip. He might have smoked cigarettes. But he wasn't a monster.

"He didn't deserve this!" Caroline yelled.

Travis grimaced and murmured, "I know. I know, Caroline."

She leaned into Travis.

"He's coming on," Bud grunted, tilting a beer back down his throat, his wide neck bobbing as he swallowed. Caroline couldn't read Bud's reaction. He didn't let much ruffle his feathers.

Chase stalked into the room and leaned over the couch, rubbing Caroline's shoulders briefly. A shiver ran down her spine from their public romp...

"Jesse Clark, Virgil resident and son of the county District Attorney, Jebediah Mason Clark, chose today to announce his run for Congress! Jesse gave his well attended public address outside of the District Attorney's office today. We'll show you some of that speech now..."

Bud's hand ran over her thighs now. He did that when he wanted to calm her. So whatever was coming would be bad. It would have to be to get Bud to react like this.

Jesse Clark appeared on the screen. Caroline didn't know him, but judging by Chase's offended grunt — he did. He was tall, around Bud's height, and lean, with a sharp clean jawline and curly blond hair that fell to his neck and hung around his head like a halo. Aquamarine eyes glinted in the sun, and Caroline thought he looked like a cat. He had a piercing stare, even on camera, and he made eye contact with each camera like he knew which one they'd choose for the evening news.

Like he'd been born for this. Jesse Clark was her opponent. A rich boy from Virgil whose dad raised him in politics. Caroline thought this was what her boys braced her for until Jesse spoke.

"My name is Jesse Clark. Today, I'm announcing my run for Congress..."

A cheer erupted in the crowd. Caroline's stomach flipped.

"... But I have a more important matter to discuss with you today. A matter that affects all the good and honest people in our country. A matter which represents the descent into dishonesty, criminal behavior and anarchy in this country."

He paused, and Caroline sucked in air. Each of the men had a hand on her now. Either they'd heard the speech before, or they knew Jesse Clark well enough to know what he'd say next.

Jesse continued, blue eyes matching the blue of his gingham button-down, tucked into his khakis.

"One of the good, upstanding citizens of Old Town, while performing his duties as a police officer fired at a young man, a criminal, no doubt, who threatened the safety of everybody in Old Town. This young man passed away, and the county currently holds the police officer in custody. I have a few words to say about this event..."

He'd said enough. Caroline felt sick. This was her opponent. And he didn't look like a monster. His polished words flowed smoothly. His face was Hollywood-attractive and when he smiled, even her chest flickered. She swallowed and leaned in, hanging onto his words, knowing each one would cut deep.

"Our county is a traditional county and always has been. We represent the good people of America. The honest, hard-working people who don't commit crimes, who don't do drugs, who don't lie and cheat and steal. Dishonest people, criminals and thugs, threaten our American values and they threaten everything the constitution of this great country stands for. When I win my Congressional seat, I will make sure Old Town and Virgil and every town in our county returns to these values. We need to stop seeing segregation as a bad thing. We need to stop this attack on our police officers. And more importantly, we need to destroy the roots of anarchy and disobedience in this town and return to law and order…"

Bud put the television off. Caroline buried her head in her hands.

"You have to whoop this guy," Travis blurted out, "I swear to God, if I could get in the same room as Jesse Clark, I'd punch his smug fucking face."

"You three know him then?" Caroline murmured.

She could barely hear her own words over her racing heart. Bud's large hand thumped on her back.

"Yeah. We know him. We stuffed his fucking ass into a locker once."

Chase scoffed.

"Bud, that was all you."

"He made fun of me 'cause I couldn't read. Well, who's laughing now!"

Caroline didn't have the heart to tell him that Jesse would probably have the last laugh. He was rich — he had to be, with daddy as the District Attorney. And he already spoke publicly. He had a foot in the door and Caroline was just... normal. An Old Town girl who wanted change but didn't have the teeth for this.

"I can't do this," Caroline whispered, "I'm going to lose. I can't beat him."

"Stop it," Chase snapped, "He represents a loud and vocal minority, but you represent the future. Change always wins. We can't avoid it."

Travis offered a more realistic perspective.

"We'll have to toughen up if he's who you're running against."

Caroline hadn't thought it possible to come up with a worse person as her opponent than Zach Owens. She wished he'd run for Congress. Not... Jesse Clark.

Bud finished his beer and grunted.

"Fuck Jesse Clark. I swear, I'll throw my entire weight as Mayor behind you, Caroline. I'll do whatever it takes."

"What are we going to do?"

Bud thumped her on the back again.

"We need to sleep on it. And tomorrow, we'll all discuss."

Caroline turned to face Travis. He leaned over and kissed her.

"I'm sorry," he murmured.

That would have to be enough. They'd been through hell together and they had more to go through. Jesse Clark might clean up good, but Caroline could tell he'd play dirty. Bud made supper. They showered and cleaned up nicely before heading to bed for the night together. Caroline curled up in Travis' arms while Bud and Chase passed out. Travis climbed on top of her, his hardness bursting through his flannel pajamas.

He didn't take it out or enter her. He grabbed her face and kissed her. He felt bad. Caroline kissed him back and his lips trailed down her neck.

"I'm sorry, Care."

"Don't," she whispered, "We're going to disagree sometimes. I get it."

"I love you," he whispered back.

"I love you too."

"I love you with them. I love you without them. I love you. Don't forget that."

"I won't."

Travis shuddered and rolled over, dragging Caroline close to him so she rested her head against his chest. He stroked her hair until he fell asleep. Caroline woke up alone in bed. She checked her phone. Shit. She'd slept in too late. She washed her face and wandered downstairs in one of Bud's giant red button-downs. He stood — naked — in front of the stove, frying eggs in a cast-iron pan.

"How can you cook with your dick so close to the fire," Caroline yawned.

Bud turned around and grinned.

"Sausage and eggs?"

"You're gross," Caroline muttered, "Where are the boys?"

"Travis went out for a run and Chase is with your brother at your family's place."

"Still planning the protest?"

"Yes, ma'am."

Caroline didn't expect Bud to be such a naked-person before they moved in together, but his thick meaty cock and tight athletic ass cheeks made a nice morning view. His butt cheeks looked good enough to eat. But not better than the eggs he fried up.

Bud slid the eggs onto a plate and poured Caroline an overflowing glass of orange juice. They ate in silence together until Bud slid his new phone across the table.

"I've been reading the Times every morning."

"Good. It's good to practice."

"Some words ain't easy."

Caroline nodded and glanced down at the article. It was about Ezra Mayfair. And despite all their digging, no journalist found anything in his past to drag to the surface, so they stuck to publishing unfounded speculations about possibilities.

"He was a good kid," Bud grunted.

Caroline nodded. Was. The 'was' hurt the most. The stopped potential. The future zapped away.

"Any word on Zach?"

"No. I made Chase promise not to go down to county."

"Good. Thanks. He's too… impulsive. We probably ought to stay out of trouble until election day."

"Yes, ma'am. Do we have a strategy yet?"

"If I did, I'd have to change it after what I saw last night."

"I fucking hate Jesse Clark."

Bud didn't hate anyone. Caroline found herself curious about why he hated Jesse so much. Everyone liked Bud, and he liked them back. He was one of the few people she'd ever met who was genuinely easy going.

"Why?"

Bud reached over on Caroline's plate to steal a bite of her eggs — he'd polished his off quickly — and shrugged.

"He ain't right in the head. Senior year, us fellas organized to go on a hunting trip. We took our guns and went out yonder. Jesse had the best guns. A new gun his daddy got him. Fancy ass semi-automatic Winchester shot gun. And he took the fucking gun, and he turned it on Jeremy Watts. And the kid. I mean… the kid fucking pissed himself. You grow up around guns, you never point a shotgun at a fucking human being. It doesn't matter if ain't loaded!"

"He didn't shoot him, right?"

"No. But the damn kid spent the entire day covered in his own piss while we shot the necks off turkeys."

Bud cleared their plates, and Caroline walked over to the sink to wash the dishes. Bud pressed his weight behind her. He was still naked. Very naked.

"What do you think you're doing, little miss?" he whispered.

"I think I'm cleaning up," Caroline teased.

"Daddy needs sex," Bud whispered, "Now turn around, let me hike your little ass on the counter."

"Bud..." Caroline protested. But there was no protesting Bud. Not while she wore his shirt. Not while he ate breakfast across from her with his dick hanging between his thighs.

He flipped her around and hiked her on the counter, running his hands over her thighs and feeling beneath her enormous shirt.

"No panties," Bud whispered, "Exactly the way I like my breakfast."

6

SLIDING TONGUES

BUD DROPPED TO HIS KNEES. He didn't work to spread Caroline's thighs. He couldn't have been clearer about what he wanted. Her wetness pressed against his face. His tongue driving deep between her legs. Bud growled as he spread her legs apart. Caroline's moisture dripped onto his tongue. Holding her thighs with broad, thick fingers allowed him to press his face between her legs, tickling her inner thighs and soft lips with warm breath before he kissed her outer mound.

Delicious. Was he supposed to want her this badly in the morning? She hadn't showered. There was only the authentic smell of pussy, the delectable warmth stewing between Caroline's thick thighs in the summer heat. His tongue darted from his mouth, coating her outer lips with wetness and spreading her lips apart so his tongue could slowly circle her covered little nub.

She moaned as he spread her with his first pointed lick. Bud's grip on her thighs tightened. The juicy soft patch between her legs called to him and made him stiff. He'd need to ease his stiffness between those thighs… soon. He'd need to caress her body, to see her naked, to watch her brown flesh respond to his touch, to watch his enormous, thick pink dick disappear into the tight sleeve between her legs.

But for now, tasting. That was the most important thing. Getting her flavor on his tongue. Diving into the smell of her. Grazing her thighs with his fingernails and watching her toes curl as he pushed his tongue and then fingers deeper. Bud spread her lower lips again with his, and his tongue circled her clit until she moaned. Caroline's moans shuddered and erupted from her chest, and her fingers gripped the edge of the counter until her palms turned white.

Bud ran his tongue along the outer edge of her lips again, flicking over her clit before he buried his tongue inside her. Deep. Bud had an insanely long tongue and Caroline couldn't stop herself from moaning as he plunged into her. Deep. His tongue was so deep and he wriggled and moved it around until she came. Hard. Bud slowly removed his tongue from her entrance and returned his tongue to massaging her clit. Her honeypot sopped with juices and he ran his fingers along the edge of her pussy lips and thighs, taking her juices onto his fingers before he pushed his index finger inside her.

Caroline moaned as the dextrous finger entered her love tunnel and massaged her inner walls. One finger plus Bud's tongue running over her clit pushed her over the edge again. She forgot about breakfast. She forgot about emotions. She dived into the sensations of Bud's tongue against her soft pussy, of his hands spreading her thighs and clutching them there with his raw masculine control. And his finger... God... his finger. He knew all the rights spots to touch and Caroline cried out again as she came.

Another orgasm meant another finger sliding into her soaked honeypot, pushing her juices and wetness from his lips into her tight entrance as he left no inch of her wetness untouched by his tongue. Two fingers easily massaged her to climax after climax as Bud's tongue roved around her clit.

Redneck Rebellion

When he pulled away, his eyes glinted with desire. He rose and kissed Caroline. He preferred kisses like this: wet and rough. He stuck his fingers through Caroline's thick curls and drove his tongue into her mouth.

She tasted herself on him, and Bud's lips always tasted sweet and soft. He was the largest of the three boys, and everything about him was super-sized. His hands clutched her hips like she had any chance of running away from him. Like she had any desire to run away from Bud. She'd let him use her however he wanted after he pleasured her like that. She'd become his. Bud was never the jealous sort.

Travis and Chase could come to blows over anything from football games to who deserved the last piece of chicken. But Bud had an easy-going temperament well-suited to soothing the animals on his family farm. And Caroline. She bucked her hips to the edge of the counter as he cupped her plump bottom in his enormous hands.

"I'm hard," he murmured, "I need you."

Urgency peppered his voice. He talked like he might die if he didn't slide inside her and rock her body against his. Bud's hands returned to her hips, and he kissed her again, their lips pressed so tightly that Caroline stopped breathing for almost too long until Bud pulled away and her chest opened, letting in a desperate breath of air.

"Touch me," he breathed, slow and easy.

Caroline's fingers ran down his chest, and he closed his eyes, sucking in air.

"I don't know what it is about today," Bud murmured, "But I need a memorable fuck."

Caroline smirked. He'd broadened his vocabulary in the past months and enjoyed showing off words like 'memorable' that wouldn't have been a big deal if anyone else used them, but for Bud represented months of practice, tracing his fingers over children's books, the newspaper and the Bible.

She let herself grow accustomed to his perpetual nudity. But when she took the time to notice the features of his body, Caroline could get drunk on the thousands of ways he was beautiful to her. Each of them stunned her differently. It wasn't exactly like loving different family members, but it was similar. She loved them all. Not one more than the others. And each had an idiosyncrasy in their personality and in their appearance that only made Caroline want them more.

Bud's broad shoulders carried a deep tan that turned his normally pink skin the color of a fall sunset. The muscles tightened around his back and narrowed around his abdomen. And his abdominal muscles flexed and tightened. They weren't lean, sculpted on purpose like Travis's muscles. Bud got his abs by accident, from lifting 300 lb bales of hay, chasing after runaway foals, fighting with his siblings and sex. Hard. Passionate. Deep. All night long sex.

Bud's hardness slid against Caroline's thighs, warmth pulsing up her spine. He hadn't entered her yet. The hot head of his pink, throbbing staff rubbed against her soaked thigh, teasing her like a snake ready to strike.

He pressed the head against the soaked apex of her thighs. Caroline whimpered and closed her eyes, but Bud grabbed her cheeks.

"No," he muttered gruffly, "You need to watch me."

She bit down on her lower lip as her thighs shuddered uncontrollably against her will. This part. This was the best part. And her body responded with a fervor of excitement mixed with fear. Bud's gaze gripped her with its intensity, with the certainty of his lust. He held her like prey in his grasp as he pushed the head inside her. Only the head. But fuck... the head of his cock was huge. Like an apple. And he stretched her as he moved his hips forward.

She cried out, mouth parting slightly as he ran his tongue over her parted lips, catching her moan in the back of his throat. His hips moved forward again and Caroline screamed. Big. He was too big. That was the problem with Bud. Getting him inside her proved difficult. He got her pussy soaked and fitting the head of his big fat cock inside her tight black pussy meant work.

Bud grunted and pushed another inch, coaxing Caroline with his firm hand on her back as she adjusted to the further intrusion.

"It hurts," she whispered.

He kissed her softly, so softly that she stopped shaking.

"It'll feel good soon," he murmured, "You can take it. You can take daddy's big fat cock."

Bud's slow, soothing speech helped her adjust and when he moved his hips faster and deeper to bury his entire length between her thighs, Caroline cried out so loud she swore she woke the neighbors. Bud's muscled tensed as her tight little sleeve wrapped around the immense staff hanging between his legs. The thick pole buried in her tightness sent waves of pleasure through every inch of her. He left none of her untouched, untaken by his monstrous cock.

Bud slid his hips back and Caroline braced herself on his broad chest as he pumped inside her. He was huge. So big he could break her in half. She moaned as he thrust. This thrust would be the one to break her in half. She could feel it beneath her belly button as he plunged into her. Tightness. Fullness. Pleasure.

Bud was right. The pain disappeared, and the pleasure left behind drove her properly mad. She dug her nails into his meaty shoulders as his hips moved in an S-shape, thrusting his cock into her so he hit her deeper and slower with each stroke.

He wanted to remember this. Her tightness. Her fullness. Her small body responding to the intrusion from his monster cock. He needed this to keep him sane throughout the day.

Caroline whimpered and came after a few strokes. Her nipples brushed against her shirt, erect and yearning for his tongue as his cock disappeared inside her again.

Bud moved his hips faster, edging closer to release as Caroline struggled to clamp her thighs around his thick torso. Her smallness compared to Bud's made her struggle to get her thighs around him properly. He was too thick for her to wrap her ankles around his body at this angle with his tensed back, his lusty hips plunging forward and cock driving wetness to drip from her entrance like a faucet.

She climaxed again and Bud drove his hips forward, pushing Caroline back against the counter so her legs stuck out and he entered her deeper. His dick pummeled her softness, teasing each sensitive spot between her legs to push her to another climax as he edged towards his.

He murmured her name, and she murmured his, sometimes calling him daddy. Her big daddy, Bud Landry. Mayor of Old Town. Her lover. Her friend. Caroline ran her fingers down his back and stopped right above his ass. Bud had an ass that looked delicious. An ass that made her think unspeakable things. An ass that looked like you could bite into it and you'd sink your teeth into fruit.

When she touched the top of his ass to draw him in deeper, Bud followed her lead and groaned as he buried his enormous cock to the hilt inside his tiny lover's pussy.

He ripped her clothes open and grabbed her breasts with his lips, squeezing the nipples between his teeth like ripe blueberries until Caroline howled and came again. This time as Caroline came, Bud let euphoria drag him over the edge. He grunted and groaned as he rutted inside her for a few last strokes. And when he came, the gush of hot cum coated the back of her pussy forcefully. She cried out, not expecting him to release so much and for his cum to paint the walls of her pussy with a blaze of heat.

They gasped as the kitchen fell silent, their moans fading into the Southern morning.

"Bud," Caroline whispered, using what she had left in her thigh's strength to pull him into her.

He removed his dick from her sopping entrance and kissed her.

"Little lady," he whispered back, grinning from ear to ear.

Caroline stroked his hair and his chin. After this, she wanted to touch him. She needed to touch him. Badly. He let her touch him all over. The tips of his ears. His cheekbones. His velvety shoulders. And when he pulled away, he winked at her.

"Breakfast?"

God, yes. She was hungry. Starving. And satisfied.

7
CREATING A PLAN

CALEB AND CHASE spread their protest signs over the dining table after noon. Caroline and Bud stumbled down to the kitchen after their third or fourth romp for the day.

"Where's Travis?" Bud asked.

"Fuck if I know," Chase muttered, "Protest tonight."

"You know I support you," Bud said, "But because of my office."

Chase nodded, sopping up beads of sweat from his forehead with a red kerchief.

"I know. I know."

Caroline leaned on her brother as he took a step back from his protest sign.

"Justice for Ezra Mayfair," she read.

Caleb snorted.

"Sorry, I'm not one for clever protest signs."

"Think it'll be okay?"

"Sure," Chase reassured her. He noticed the well-fucked look on Caroline's face and Bud's strawberry flush. Bud had done a good job of keeping her distracted today. Chase cleared his throat and touched Caroline's forearm.

"Hm?"

"You shouldn't come tonight."

"Are you serious?!"

Caleb cast a warning glance at Chase, but he ignored Caroline's brother.

"We've heard these protests get out of hand in other states. We don't want you caught up. If you get arrested..." Chase trailed off and adjusted his stance, popping his hip out and tapping his hands urgently on his thigh, "Look. You're running for Congress. Let me fight for you, Caroline. You fight for your seat in Congress. Black women in our country have fought so many fights. You don't have to throw yourself on the front lines. Not while I'm around."

Caroline's heart swelled. Bud rested an enormous hand on her shoulders. His touch reminded her instantly of the ache between her thighs from their insane morning.

"Fine," Caroline conceded, "But I'll worry sick about you. What about Travis? Will he stay home?"

Chase and Caleb cast worried glances at each other, and this time, Caroline noticed.

"What are you two hiding?"

"Nothing," Caleb said sharply.

Chase cast a pleading look in his direction. Caleb shrugged and muttered, "Your funeral."

"We got into another fight," Chase admitted, "I don't know where he went. His mama's house. Probably."

"What the hell did you two fight about?"

"This."

Caroline groaned.

"Seriously?"

"You can't expect me not to talk politics in this house. Bud's the mayor, you're running for Congress, I'm running my mouth. It comes up."

"You know how Travis gets," Caroline pleaded.

"He gets his way," Chase snorted, "Always."

"Don't. We shouldn't fight. We shouldn't let this stuff come between us."

Chase grabbed Caroline's cheeks and stared at her.

"I love you," Chase whispered, "I'll do whatever you want. But when it comes to what I believe... I won't let Montgomery push me around."

The invasive sound of a beer can opening distracted Caroline and Chase. Bud stared at his beer can guiltily.

"Want some?" he muttered.

Caroline sighed.

"I'll have one."

Chase nodded and grabbed two cans of Coors out of the fridge.

"If I'm not going to the protest, I'll help you with the signs."

Bud grinned.

"I'd offer to help, but I'd probably spell everything wrong."

"You can staple placards to wood," Chase offered, handing Bud the staple gun.

They worked for another hour before they had to leave. Bud handed Chase the keys to his truck.

"I swear," Bud said, "Get this thing caught up in a riot and I'll run you over with it."

Chase patted Bud on the back as Caleb and Caroline loaded the signs up in the back. Caroline watched them take off with Bud's arm around her shoulder. Bud groaned and let her go, running his finger over her shoulder.

"I should go to the office. In case shit goes South. I've got a shotgun there, don't worry."

That wasn't what Caroline worried about.

"How are you going to get around?"

"I'll walk to the farm first, get a horse."

"The mayor on a horse wielding a shotgun in the middle of a peaceful protest... that'll make us look good in the press."

Bud grinned.

"Don't worry. I'll only need the shotgun if folks make trouble."

"Chase and Caleb won't make trouble."

Bud's expression turned somber.

"I don't mean them. There are some folks in this town who are happy Ezra Mayfair got killed. They want it to happen again."

Caroline nodded. Bud wasn't stupid. He didn't speak much, and he'd learned to read as an adult, but he understood the way the world worked. He understood Old Town.

"Okay," Caroline murmured, "I'll stay here."

"Travis ought to be with you."

Caroline shrugged.

"No. He has his beliefs. We have to respect that."

Bud pursed his lips together. Unlike Chase, he didn't breathe a word against Travis or anyone. He listened, but he never spoke up against another. Bud. Sweet old Bud. Caroline returned to the house and locked the door.

Chase and Caleb arrived downtown outside the District Attorney's office, on Central Avenue, the first left turn off of Main Street.

Most of the shops on Main Street closed for the day. Their protest route would take them around the block. People filed in. Caleb and Chase didn't recognize most of them. People came from surrounding small towns and from big towns too.

Caleb met with one of the out-of-state organizers who promised to help them, and they discussed the details while Chase corralled people and broke up different group leaders. Caleb held the megaphone as they readied for the start of the protest.

Redneck Rebellion

The energy was thick and flammable. Light a match and they'd all burn up, Chase thought. His heart pumped as he distributed spare signs and spoke to people who knew he was the organizer. Mrs. Murray came with her teenagers, each holding signs with social media slogans that Chase wasn't very familiar with.

The Main Street business owners heard about the protest and sent their employees home early. Chase heard the Mayfair boy's name flying around the crowd, and then he saw Bianca. Women surrounded her and held her. And the pain on her face reminded Chase of Caroline. Everything that happened last year with Caleb nearly broke her. If this happened to her?

Chase had to fight for her. He had to do something. Some workers downtown joined the protest. Signs appeared in the window of the local deli and a shoe store. Justice for Ezra Mayfair.

Chase weaved through the growing crowd and thumped Caleb on the back.

"Ready for this, brother?"

Caleb shook his head.

"No. I still don't believe he's dead."

Chase nodded.

"We're going to get justice for him."

Caleb nodded and raised the megaphone to his lips. His words spread fire throughout the crowd. Chase felt the energy shift, and he led the march. One circle around the District Attorney's office and then a loop downtown. The police showed up after a few minutes. The energy shifted.

Here they were in jeans, boots, holding cardboard signs and men in riot gear came, ready to fuck them up or shoot them all. They could do it, Chase realized. One wrong move and they'd all die. That shifted the energy. People aren't the same when they're facing their death, when they're amped up.

The crowd changed around Chase. They weren't protestors. They were a different folk. They came dressed in denim on denim with yellow bandanas over their faces. They didn't have signs. One of them held up a flag with a snake curled in the middle and the words 'Don't Tread On Me' printed on the bottom. The man holding the flag stopped in front of Caleb, yanked the megaphone from his hand and pushed him to the ground. He raised his boot. Chase grabbed the man and threw him off, tossing him away from Caleb. He might have yelled, "RUN!"

Another man in a yellow bandana raised a pistol. Run. Everyone in the crowd ran. Or they tried to. An untamed herd of terrified people who never had a gun pointed their way in their lives. Teenagers. Kids. Chase wanted to throw himself in front of them, but he froze. No. This couldn't happen here. Not in Old Town. Who were these people? He recognized a brow beneath a yellow bandana. Loretta Calloway. Sonofabitch. And was that… Atticus Montgomery?

A scream. A gunshot. And then a large canister soared through the air from the police line. FUBAR.

"CALEB!" Chase screamed hoarsely, but that only made the burning worse. Oh God. The burning. More gunshots. The thick white smoke blinded him. It got everywhere. In his nose. In his eyes. In his lungs. Chase stumbled over to the side of the street. I'm bleeding, he thought, my eyes are fucking bleeding. He lost Chase. More gunfire. Fuck. I have to get up, Chase thought, I have to fight this.

A flash of yellow tore past him on foot, screaming the n-word. Chase grabbed the man's legs, and he swung. Screaming. Blind. Insane. Someone yanked his body back and cold metal clamped around his wrists as he tried to scream, but the tear gas only burned his throat more. He yowled and tried to fight, but the butt of a weapon slammed into his head. Another gunshot rang throughout the crowd. Women screamed.

This went wrong. This went so horribly wrong. There wasn't supposed to be fighting. Chase's eyes burned. Caleb. Where the fuck was Caleb.

"CALEB!" he yelled.

Another punch in his face.

"Kick the shit out of him," a guy grunted, "Fucking race traitor."

"Fucked over his own brother. We ought to kill his ass."

But they didn't. They hauled Chase off to the county jail and cleared the streets, leaving behind strewn signs, bandanas, and Caleb. He hit behind a trash can, a move that worked. Maybe they left him on the ground because they thought he was dead. He ran out of town, eyes red and swollen. He ran past the side street where they parked Bud's truck until he heard hooves on the street. Caleb froze. There was nowhere to run. Nowhere to hide. But then he saw the man on the horse, a hulking frame you couldn't miss.

"Bud," Caleb gasped.

A large hand reached down, and Caleb swung his weight up behind Bud Landry.

"Where the hell is Chase?"

"Jail."

Caleb's throat stung. Every word struggled to emerge from his throat. Bud rode his horse up the way, shotgun hanging from his left hand as he held the reins. Caleb clutched the large man's body, but he could barely get his hands all the way around Bud's enormous torso.

"What the hell happened?" Bud growled.

"I saw... Atticus," Caleb groaned.

He couldn't talk, and his heart hadn't stopped racing. He

could hardly breathe. He thought he'd suffocate grabbing onto Landry's back. The horse halted, hooves skidding against the payment. Landry cocked the gun and then lowered it.

"Travis."

"What the hell happened here?" Travis said, "I knew this would get out of hand."

"I got here too late," Bud said.

"Did you let Caroline wander into this shitshow!?" Travis yelled.

"She's home."

"And what about that idiot?"

"Arrested."

"Fuck! I knew this would be a big fucking mess, Landry. This ain't the way things are done. The deli's empty. Every fucking bit of furniture in there gone. The general store's ransacked. This is... fucking bullshit! This ain't a way to get justice."

"Travis, relax," Bud urged.

"Fuck! Relax? This town's destroyed! This happens when you give in to what they want. Do you think this will make things better?!"

"We don't know that they did this," Bud said calmly, "Chase Owens and Caleb Coulson wouldn't destroy Old Town. It's their home too."

"I'm waiting for any of you motherfuckers to give a shit about your home. Because this ain't the way to do it."

"Go to Caroline," Bud breathed with the voice he used to soothe horses. And her. She'd worry sick. By now the mess must have hit the news. She'd watch glued to the TV. She'd be there alone.

"I can't see Caroline," Travis muttered, "Y'all created this mess. Now Chase is behind bars and you're nowhere close to getting justice. I'm staying at my mama's place tonight."

Redneck Rebellion

8
FIGHTING

CAROLINE WOKE up with an acrid stomach. Nothing went right the night before. Chase sat in jail, Travis hadn't come home, and Bud tossed and turned the entire night. He spent half the night sprawled on top of Caroline in their bed, nearly suffocating her with his weight. Her brother slept on the couch downstairs. The mayor's house was safe territory, and he'd spent all night healing from his injuries when he wasn't pacing downstairs. Caroline heard heavy footsteps creaking the floorboards, but she couldn't bring herself to talk to him.

They weren't the ones who started the chaos. In the morning, Caroline snuck out before Bud woke up. She snuck past her brother on the couch and burst onto the porch. It seemed like a special cruelty that the morning was so bright. Travis didn't live far off from the old Buchanan house — Caroline still thought of their home that way once in a while — so she walked over. He was outside, jumping rope shirtless in the driveway, dripping in sweat while blond hair stuck to his head. He slowed his pace when she approached, enough to say hello.

"Hey," Caroline replied.

Travis switched to jumping rope with one leg.

"We need to talk about yesterday."

"I'm coming home," Travis asserted, switching to the other leg.

"I know," Caroline replied, "But Bud told me what happened yesterday and we have a lot to talk about."

"I can't change who any of you are."

"Do you want to?"

Travis stopped jumping rope and placed his hands on his hips as he gasped for breath. Caroline struggled not to stare at his chest, pink from his brief time in the sun and absolutely dripping in sweat. A bulge in his basketball shorts drew her attention as it flopped around to find a natural resting place between Travis's hips.

"No," Travis answered finally, "I don't. I'm an idiot."

Caroline hadn't expected that.

"Chase is in jail. He did nothing wrong."

"You weren't down there," Travis explained, "I shouldn't have said what I said but everything I grew up with… it's crumbling. Before us, before all this politics, I had a father who I was close to. I had a family. I believed in the law. I believed in this town. It's difficult to realize that everything you believe in only exists because it's built on the backs of someone else."

Caroline didn't know what to say. Travis didn't mind. He pushed hair out of his reddened face and sighed.

"There's still a right way to do things and a wrong way. But I watched the news. I talked to people. Caleb and Chase didn't start this fight. It's hard finding out that the people you grew up calling family are nothing but…"

He paused and licked sweat off his lower lip.

"Racists," Travis blurted out, "The people I grew up

calling family are racists. I heard what people are saying. My dad was in that crowd that started the fights. And there were others. Jesse Clark's brother and sister."

"My opponent?"

Travis scoffed.

"He kept his hands clean, but he has a vested interest in proving that any effort to get the truth out about Ezra Mayfair is nothing but anarchy and violence. He wants the entire county, including Old Town, segregated more than it's ever been."

"Don't," Caroline whispered.

Travis's hands fell away from his hips, and he folded them.

"I disagree with Chase and Caleb on many, many things. I still think the best way to fight these bastards is to play their game. And that means getting you to Congress. And I know you won't fight if Chase is in jail. So once I clean the sweat off, I'll go bail him out."

"Thank you."

"Not for his sake. He should have been smarter," Travis finished.

Caroline ran over and hugged him. She didn't care how sweaty he was, but Travis groaned and peeled her off him.

"Careful. I don't want to get you covered in sweat."

"Come home. Please."

"Come with me to the station. We'll get Chase Owens out and I owe the boys an apology. They're like brothers to me."

"I thought..."

Caroline stopped herself, but Travis put his hand to her cheek and she couldn't help being honest with him.

"What?" he murmured.

"I thought for a second you set the cops on Chase. To prove a point."

Travis shook his head.

"I know y'all think I'm not on your side. No one deserves what Ezra Mayfair suffered. But all cops ain't like Zach Owens or my daddy."

Caroline pursed her lips. She wanted Chase out of jail and she needed Travis back home. This wasn't the right time to point out that not all of them were like Zach or Atticus, but all of them protected Zach when he shot an innocent man. None of them spoke up. And from what she heard, no one arrested any of the agitators in the yellow bandanas. While her brother struggled for breath on the couch, and Chase suffered alone in jail, Atticus Montgomery walked free.

Travis showered while Caroline waited outside. She didn't enjoy entering the Montgomery house, and she didn't want Travis' mom to catch sight of her and think she was rude. When Travis walked out the front door, he smelled clean.

He wrapped his arms around Caroline's waist and kissed her.

"I wanted to do that the moment you came up the street," he whispered, clutching her hips like she would float away if he loosened his grip.

"Home," Caroline whispered, "Let's go home first."

Travis walked home with her. Bud's truck wasn't out front, and neither was the horse. Bud left a poorly scrawled note on the kitchen counter. He took Caleb home and then he'd have mayor business to attend to.

"Hungry?" Caroline asked Travis.

He nodded and Caroline made him a protein shake, which he guzzled like he hadn't had a bite since yesterday. Travis cleaned up the dishes and then grabbed Caroline's waist and set her on the counter suddenly.

"Travis! What are you doing?!"

He pressed his forehead to hers, eyes as blue as forget-me-nots boring into her.

Redneck Rebellion

"I love you," he murmured, "I don't want you to think I love you any less because of what's happening."

"I don't think that," Caroline whispered, drawing him in with her ankles.

Her hips ached from her last encounter with Bud. Travis wasn't as rough. He made every moment between them romantic. He ran his hand over one thigh and then another.

"Good," he whispered, running his lips over her neck. He grasped the nape of Caroline's neck and cradled her as he kissed her.

"I want you," he whispered, "I want you so bad it hurts. I know what we're doing is... sinful. But how? How can it be sinful? We love you. I love you. And you love us all back. How can it be wrong?"

His shorts tented as his stiffening member pushed out the fabric in an escape attempt. The heat emanated from the fabric on Caroline's thighs. The rush of blood to his swollen tip signaling Travis' desire provoked a warm gush between her thighs. She gasped as he adjusted her position on the counter.

"Bed," Travis whispered, "I ought to bring you to the bedroom."

"No," Caroline murmured, kissing him back, tasting his lips and getting drunk off the scent on his neck, "Here. I want you here."

He slid Caroline's dress up around her waist. Her lace panties buried themselves in her curves, and Travis' bare hands appreciated every uncovered part of her body. He moved her panties to the side and shuddered as his warm hand touched her dripping center.

"How the fuck are you so wet?"

With three eager studs constantly ready to please her, Caroline spent most of her day wet. Her body had magnificent muscle memory for all the signs that a well-hung man planned to enter her. She spread her legs for him wider.

"I want you," Caroline whispered.

Travis slipped his pants off.

"One day we're going to knock you up," he murmured.

Caroline giggled and dragged him closer with her heels. Travis eagerly positioned himself between her thighs and pushed the bulging head between her legs. The head entered her easily, a gush of pleasure surging through her body as more nectar seeped from her tightness. Travis groaned. Loud.

"Hot," he breathed.

Caroline didn't know if he meant the temperature of her honeypot or if he meant he found her attractive. He slid his length in with a long stroke, and Caroline moaned as he cradled her body against his. His sculpted, lean and muscular shoulders drew her in. She wrapped her arms around his neck as he eased inside her. Each slow, deep stroke made her want to lose herself in him.

He never stopped kissing her as he strokes. His lips marked every inch of her skin. Fuck. She was so tight and so hot. He drove into her deep, the animal desires for her mounting with each slow stroke. He wanted to take her faster. He wanted to make her scream. He wanted to fill her with his seed and watch her stomach grow with his child.

It was all instinct. The powerful instinct to mate with a beautiful woman. To change her. Travis's cheeks turned dark red and Caroline dug her nails into his back as he thrust into her. Harder. She wanted to beg, but Travis wouldn't listen. He fucked her to her first orgasm with slow, deep strokes, making the climaxes just as deep. Her screams echoed throughout their house as he made love to her on the kitchen counter.

"Cum for me," he murmured, his fiery breath tickling her

ear as he deep stroked her tightness. Her soaked thighs stuck to his torso with each stroke and he worked up a bigger sweat than when he jumped rope. Caroline came again, this time running her fingers through his hair and releasing the scent of his shampoo. Oh, God... She couldn't cum more than this. She was spent, but Travis gripped her thighs and kept his slow, steady stroke.

He could fuck for hours like this, watching her slowly unravel in his grasp as he buried his hardness into her slippery love tunnel, appreciating the softness and the firm grip around his long hardness.

"I'm gonna cum," Travis gasped after Caroline lost track of how much he made her cum.

"Cum inside me," she whispered, "Cum inside me, Travis."

She rendered him powerless. He bucked inside her, deep, so she screamed as his seed erupted from the head of his cock, painting the entire length of her wetness with a strong eruption that made her thighs tremble as his cock jerked and spurted ropes of cum into her. The hot cum soaked into the walls of her honeypot and Caroline's spread legs turned to jelly as Travis withdrew from her.

He couldn't take his hands off her. Her thighs, the color of burnt umber, drew him in. He pressed his palms to those thighs and watched her mound quiver and quake. He held back with her. He teased her. He tortured them both when they made love, making it slow and romantic so they could each reach a point of euphoria so strong they both vibrated within it.

Together, the four of them fucked. But alone, Travis made love to her. He'd loved her so long he couldn't remember a time when he didn't. He loved her so much; he had to share her with a selfless wish that others could experience the nirvana between her thighs.

The front door creaked open. Travis and Caroline muttered, "Shit!", at the same time. Caroline leaped off the counter, Travis' thick cum trickling down her thighs as he urged his cock into his pants.

"Chase," Travis breathed, "We ought to get Chase."

9

BAIL

TRAVIS HAD his buddy talk to the judge to get Chase out of jail. They got back to the house to find Bud sleeping on a couch, snoring. He woke suddenly and told them about Caleb leaving to check on Bianca Mayfair. She'd organized an Old Town clean up to repair the damage to downtown. Caroline wanted to join, but the look in the boys' eyes reminded her they had plenty of work to do at home. They hadn't worked out everything wrong yet. Caroline sighed. She hated fighting. Fighting with them hurt worse.

Caroline sat next to Bud, and he put a large arm over her shoulder, curving her back forward as she slipped under his weight.

"Hey, Bud," Caroline whispered, kissing his stubble. Bud chuckled.

"I need a beer."

Chase and Travis barely spoke on the ride home.

"We'll get beer," they said together, exchanging a glance, but no smile. Caroline worried about them, but they were both equally stubborn. You couldn't rush them into making up with each other. Bud rose and rubbed his palms against his jeans.

"I'll make those two sort their shit out."

Unless you were Bud. He could force the two of them to act right. He strode into the kitchen and a few short minutes of hushed voices later, the three of them came out with beer.

"Everything okay?" Caroline asked.

The three boys had their arms around each other and grinned like mischievous kids with something to hide.

"Yes. And we have a great idea about what might bond us together."

"A prayer circle?" Caroline teased.

She didn't know what they wanted, but considering what they always wanted, it didn't take much work to guess.

Bud grabbed Caroline and hoisted her over his shoulders. After lifting bales of hay, slinging Caroline Coulson out of her chair, even as she yelped, didn't take much effort. Bud carried her upstairs while she shrieked, "Put me down! I know how to walk! What did you guys say in there?!"

"Men folks' business," Travis answered, "It's between us."

"You three are crazy!" Caroline shrieked.

Bud lay her on the bed, knocking the wind out of her. Caroline wanted to believe he hadn't intended that effect. Before she could get her breath back, each of them grabbed an article of her clothing and wrestled it off her. Caroline gasped as they exposed each part of her body. Chase slid her thighs apart and pressed his body into hers, giving her a slow kiss. Chase didn't kiss slowly.

"You smell like jail," Caroline whispered, "This is filthy."

"You like it filthy," Chase muttered.

He didn't smell so bad. His slow kisses transformed into more Chase-like kisses. His fingers pressed against her temples and slipped through her hair as he urged her lips apart and drove his tongue down her throat. This close, Caroline saw how badly they'd messed him up. He had a black eye. His lower lip tasted of blood and she worked her lips carefully around the bruising while Chase contented himself to mash his face into hers like it didn't hurt.

But it must have hurt. She stroked the back of his head and there was a new bump.

Chase's hair fell in front of his neck, and Caroline ran her fingers over his shoulders. He winced.

"Take your shirt off," she whispered, wondering if Chase could hear how fast her heart thudded. She didn't want him to know how much she worried about him. Chase was the one she worried about. Travis was tough. Bud had an eerie calm. Chase threw himself at trouble every chance he got. Caroline pulled the unbuttoned shirt over his shoulder and sucked in air.

His neck had a dark red sunburn on it that Caroline suspected had become a permanent fixture of his skin tone. His shoulders were yellow and black with green around the edges. As she wrestled the shirt off him, she pushed back tears.

"What the hell did they do to you?"

Travis spoke up, "Nothing you need to worry about."

Right. Men folks' business. Caroline gently tugged Chase close to her, parting his lips gently with hers and tickling the tip of his tongue with hers. His hardness stretched his work pants and Caroline wondered how he could get aroused while bruises covered his shoulders and torso.

"I need you," Chase uttered hoarsely, "That's the quickest way for me to get better."

Caroline didn't have the energy to argue with him. She let him kiss her neck and chest and kiss every inch of flesh to her bare mound. He spread her open with his lips and slid his tongue along the length of her dampness. She moaned and her legs spread wider against her will. Travis and Bud both worked her wetness until she became sore. Chase's tongue licked at her swollen entrance, sending soothing surges of pleasure through her as he undid the hurt from their large members stretching her pelvis.

Chase flicked his tongue across her slippery pearl and as Caroline moaned, he flattened his tongue and circled her clit with his eager tongue. He kissed her like he meant it and didn't slow down until her first orgasm. When he pulled his face away, Caroline lifted her head anxiously. She didn't want this to end yet.

She saw immediately why Chase lifted his head.

"Juicy," he murmured with a grin and licked clear juices off his stubble covered upper lip before burying his head between her legs again, careful not to prick Caroline's sensitive mound with his stubble until his entire face was too wet for the rubbing stubble to hurt her. The ticklish pleasure of his tongue and facial hair drove her mad again, and she came harder.

Before Caroline recovered, Chase had his pants down his thighs and he slipped the head of his dick inside her. Chase didn't have Travis' patience. He buried himself to the hilt and groaned as he watched Caroline cry out. He held her face and made love to her roughly, nibbling her lower lip each time she came. Chase fucked hard and fast, but he made her cum so much she thought she'd pass out. When he finished, he groaned and removed his dick halfway, so he squirted his seed on Caroline's inner walls and painted her entrance like a toaster strudel as he removed himself and rolled onto his back.

Travis crawled along the foot of their custom-built mattress and slid his body like a warm, muscled snake over Caroline's. He kissed her slowly and pressed his weight into her. He didn't mind her mound dampening his underwear and watching her cum so many times already made him hard beyond belief. He wanted her. Bad.

Chase kissed her shoulders and neck as Travis slid into her slowly, letting her have him inch by inch. His eyes went from steel blue to black as his pupils dilated once he entered her. His skin flushed red, making his hair look silver in comparison. Caroline grabbed his taut, smooth buttocks and drew him deep into her. Travis shuddered as the tip of his cock met the base of Caroline's tightness.

This was everything, he thought. Her tightness. How hot her tightness became after another man made love to her. He would have thought Chase's dick would loosen her, but not even Bud made her more loose. They warmed her up, but they didn't ruin her. They made her sleeve hotter and tighter and wetter, and Travis struggled not to erupt from the first stroke.

She moaned as he moved his hips slowly between her legs. Travis didn't want to kiss her and have his eyes closed for a second. Their eyes connected and he used the gentle fluttering of her curled black lashes and the gasping rhythm of her nose and pert mouth to determine how deep and slow he'd take her. She'd never been hotter, and the firm grip on his hardness made withdrawing from her gorgeous pussy an impossible task.

Caroline lost herself in Travis' eyes. She didn't notice Bud's lips around her fingers, or his tongue flicking across her breasts. Travis had hypnotic eyes. She could disappear in his eyes the way she could disappear in Chase's words or in Bud's firm, animalistic grasp.

When Caroline came, Travis kept his hips moving deep and slow until she climaxed again. And again. When beads of sweat pooled on her brow, Travis buried his face in her neck and grabbed flesh on her neck between his lips as he erupted deep inside her. Caroline squirmed once his seed forcefully coated her depths and as Travis slowly withdrew, every instinct told her to keep him planted right there between her legs.

Travis got off the bed and leaned his forearm against the wall, facing away from Caroline as he caught his breath. Travis wandered sometimes after he came. He needed to breathe and get his heart rate down so his reddening skin could return it to its natural cream color.

Before Caroline could lose herself staring at Travis' perfect muscular ass, Bud growled and flipped her onto her stomach. Oh, God. Caroline forgot about Bud. Bigger, rougher, wilder Bud. On her stomach, Bud spread her legs apart.

A gush of warmth erupted from Caroline's wetness. Seed filled her sex. Bud always assured her that no matter how gross and messy sex got, it was nothing half as bad as what he saw on the farm. He wiped away a glob of her juices and cum with a bare hand and then pressed a thick finger inside Caroline. He wriggled his finger around her until she came. Caroline moaned loud as Bud found the right spot between her legs to stroke her to a mewling orgasm.

Bud pressed another finger inside her, and his two enormous fingers filled Caroline. He moved them in alternating strokes to massage Caroline's inner walls until she climaxed. Then he replaced his fingers with the colossal head of his dick. Caroline cried out as the first inch pressed inside her.

"I can't…" she whimpered.

Bud's firm hand on her back soothed her. Damn him. He knew how to work her perfectly. He didn't force more inches inside her until she relaxed. He pushed another inch between her legs and Caroline cried out loud. Travis came back into bed and whispered, "Shhh," as he kissed her.

Caroline whimpered and nodded. Travis's soft kisses helped. Bud eased more of his dick inside her and the pain began its change. Chase kissed her shoulders and Bud used his weight to slide the rest of his dick inside Caroline from behind.

"She can handle it," Chase murmured, his lips still on her shoulders.

"She's ours. We know she can," Travis murmured, kissing Caroline's lips again.

Bud groaned and thrust an initial powerful thrust between Caroline's legs. He was large. So large. And his cock felt amazing. He growled and pumped his hips between her legs until she came. It didn't take long. The three men brought her body to life. Each sensation heightened with them. Each climax more intense than the last.

If Caroline didn't know better, she'd think three men could get you addicted. That once you had three, you couldn't go down to two or even one. Bud grabbed her hips and drove into her after she came for the first time. As his enormous hands nearly encircled her hips, Caroline thrust her butt back into him.

She drove Bud mad with her body and he pumped into her fiercely. Bud grunted and rutted behind her until he finished with a shuddered gasp and pressed his enormous weight into her. His crotch nestled against her soft, curvy butt. He pulled hair out of her face and kissed her neck as his weight pinned her to the bed.

Caroline enjoyed the sensation of fear that he'd crush her to death mixed with the certainty that he wouldn't. He'd protect her. They all would. No matter how they fought, she was the one thing that brought them all together. She was the reason for their rebellion.

10

I WON'T HURT YOU

WITH OLD TOWN cleaned up and construction crews repairing the smashed windows downtown, the town was on its way to normalcy again. Caroline could walk downtown in pursuit of her favorite mug of coffee, or to sit on a park bench for a few minutes and think about her campaign.

Everyone knew she was running and interested people stopped and talked to her downtown. Chase and Caleb hadn't let the culminating insanity of their first protest deter them from changing Old Town. They wanted to make sure there wouldn't be any agitators. They wanted everything to stay peaceful. Caroline understood that, but every day, new journalists would question folks on the streets and their questions wedged a greater divide between Caleb and Chase's people and the rest of the town.

Caroline wondered if the journalists did it on purpose. No one was "against" Old Town. They wanted justice for the Mayfair boy. That couldn't be so wrong, could it?

Down at the factory, the workers wanted to stage another protest. There was so disagreement about how they'd get everyone to agree to another protest, but Caleb and Chase had a meeting planned with their arguments laid out. As they worked in the living room of the old Buchanan house, Caroline wandered downtown toward the cafe where Travis studied for the LSAT. Bud was at work still and Caroline finished her latest campaign strategy for the Old Town town hall meeting in a few weeks's time.

As she headed downtown, Caroline took a detour, passing by the Montgomery house and through the backyard of an empty lot to a park on the other side of Central Ave where she could cross over to Main Street. The Civil War memorial for Southern soldiers lost including General Buchanan and Colonel Owens caught Caroline's attention.

What would Colonel Owens think about his descendents? Caroline's fingers touched the metal memorial. Her ancestors might have died in the war too, but there weren't any memorials for the black folks. Mayor Buchanan said that if they wanted one on "their" side of town, they'd have to find the money on their own, which no one had.

"Good afternoon, Missus Coulson."

Caroline pivoted, taking a few seconds to place the enormous man towering behind her. He had to have been as big as Bud, nearly as big, at least, and Caroline only recognized him from the television. He smiled more in person and his eyes looked more black than green. But he stood a few feet away from her, hands stuffed into the pockets of his salmon colored pants.

"Jesse Clark," Caroline answered as she recognized him.

"Yes, ma'am."

He stuck his hand out to shake, and Caroline stared at it for a few seconds before realizing what he wanted. When she returned her hand, he squeezed it like he wanted to crush every bone in her palm. Caroline winced and pulled her hand away as soon as it was safely outside of her vice grip. Jesse didn't blink.

Redneck Rebellion

"I've wandered this town for forty-five minutes looking for you."

"Oh?"

"We have much to discuss given our pending Congressional race."

"Do we?"

Caroline couldn't stop her gut reaction from bubbling to the surface. She resented this man and everything he stood for. Despite his pleasant halo of blond curly hair and his disarming smile, Caroline saw through him. She glanced around, hoping they weren't in the park alone. Just her luck, they were. Jesse pointed to a park bench.

"Mind if we sit?"

"I'm meeting someone," Caroline responded. That was a half-truth. Travis knew she'd stop by in the afternoon, but they hadn't made definite plans to meet.

"I'm sure one of your boys could spare you for a few moments."

His tone unnerved Caroline, but she couldn't place why. Jesse sat and against her better judgment, Caroline followed him. On television, he'd projected a cold and calculating image, but he smiled so much Caroline couldn't imagine this was the same Jesse Clark. Once they sat, he leaned forward casually.

"Congress. I've worked toward it my entire life. I went to University and studied politics."

"It makes sense. Your dad's the District Attorney."

He shifted nervously when Caroline brought up his father. Jesse crossed his legs, resting his ankle on one of his thighs and exposing a pair of socks with a fraternity logo embroidered on them.

"Yes, my father is the District Attorney, and he has high hopes for his son. I want to make you an offer."

"Make one," Caroline said.

She didn't have much to say to Jesse Clark. She couldn't allow his overly friendly smile to give her too much cause to relax.

I have to remember he's dangerous, Caroline thought to herself. Jesse cracked his knuckles, then came right out with it.

"Miss Coulson, I'm politely requesting that on behalf of our county, you drop out of the Congressional race."

"Not going to happen," Caroline responded instantly.

She didn't give it a second thought. Jesse Clark might have convinced her to sit down, even to hear him out, but he wouldn't convince her to give up all she worked for. Caroline didn't have a proper job so she could focus on the election.

"Consider my offer, Miss Coulson. You and I both know that someone like you has no chance of winning. We could all sleep easier at night if I ran unopposed."

"I have to go."

Caroline eased her body forward to get up, but Jesse pushed down on her thighs to keep her seated. She scowled at him, readying herself to slap him for the overly familiar gesture, but his hand darted back to the other one like he knew he'd made an error and he cracked his knuckles again.

"Listen," Jesse insisted, "I have information which could prove harmful to you and your campaign. If you insist on running against me, I cannot promise to hold back my fire."

"I have nothing to hide."

"Nothing to hide, not no one."

"I don't know what you're referring to. I have to go."

"I have inside information onto the perverted company you keep. Miss Coulson, what one does in their bedroom is none of my business, but this is a town for families and traditional people. The town whore is hardly someone we need representing families in Congress."

"I don't know what you've heard, but I'm not the town

Redneck Rebellion

whore. I live with my friends and we've known each other all their lives."

Jesse chuckled.

"You sound convincing," he said, "If you denied it, maybe some folks would believe you. But my insider source has actual information. An interlude of public intercourse on the dirt road leading outside of town, an incident in young Mr. Montgomery's police car months ago, several incidents involving Mr. Travis Montgomery, Chase Owens, and your dear mayor, Mr. Landry. Do you know any woman who has sex with three men who isn't a whore?"

Caroline dry swallowed and tried to get up again. But Jesse yanked her back down and leaned over her, pinning her to the bench with two hands on her wrists. He stared at her, searching her face for an answer.

"It's true, isn't it," he whispered.

"Let me go."

"Don't worry," he answered, "I won't hurt you, Miss Coulson. We're in a public park and I will be a Congressman. I understand decorum."

"You're wrong about whatever you think you know. And I don't care what you say about me."

"I think you care," Jesse replied, tightening his grip, "But I think you enjoy being a whore. At some point, you must choose. Career aspirations or whoredom. I think we both know what choice you'll make."

He unleashed Caroline's wrists from his grip. She rose and faced him, even if she was shorter than him. And her heart pounded so hard in her chest she could feel it rising in her throat. She wouldn't give him the satisfaction of running from him and showing him her terror. How the hell did he find out?

"You have no proof for your slanderous accusations,"

Caroline said, rubbing her wrists unconsciously, "And if you lay your hands on me again —

"Careful," Jesse answered, taking a phone out of his pocket, "I'm recording."

"Sonofabitch."

Jesse grinned.

"If you insist on being stubborn, Miss Coulson, you'll learn that I'm not a man you want to mess with."

"We'll find out."

"Yes. We will. I can close my hands around your world and crumble it," he hissed.

"Try," Caroline snapped, "You don't scare me, Jesse. I took down the mayor of this town. Some spoiled preppy rich kid doesn't intimidate me. I'm running because of people. Not because of daddy's money. Now, excuse me."

Now that was an exit, Caroline thought. But she didn't stop shaking until she saw Travis waving to her through the cafe window. Caroline thought the coffees at this new shop were expensive, but she didn't complain when Travis ordered one and offered her a seat.

He had a half-finished practice test buried under a stack of flashcards and study guides.

"You okay?" he asked.

"Yes. I'm fine."

"You don't look fine."

Caroline could never hold back with them. She told Caroline everything, pursing her lips when Margie approached the table with her coffee. Once she finished, Travis shrugged.

"Speculation," Travis drawled, "That's all he has."

"I don't think so," Caroline mused, "I worked on the newspaper. He has a source."

"A source?"

"Someone who knows about us is feeding him information. I'd put money on it."

"Who might that be?"

Travis stretched his arm over the table, but Caroline jerked her forearm away, glancing around furtively.

"There's no one else in here."

"There's Mr. Wentworth."

Travis leaned in and whispered, "He's drunk. I'm certain he comes here to sleep off the hangover."

Caroline giggled, but didn't move her hands from her lap. Travis answered more seriously, "None of us would talk about it. We understand this might fly in Old Town, but Congress is a different story."

"Not just Congress but with everything going on…"

Travis nodded and Caroline sipped more coffee. Travis packed his belongings and offered Caroline to take her coffee to go. She agreed, but she kept her arms folded as she walked next to Travis. She'd never been afraid to touch them in public. Maybe she would never kiss one of the boys on the lips, but they'd known each other their entire lives. Not even Pastor Fielding could begrudge the innocent intimacy of touching someone's forearm or Caroline leaning her head on a broad-shouldered best friend.

She couldn't let herself go that far. Travis made a good point as they approached their street.

"The only reason he wouldn't want you to enter the race is he's scared you'll beat him."

"I'm nobody and he's the DA's son. I don't think that's it."

Travis scoffed.

"He might be the DA's son, but I can't think of a single person who genuinely likes Jesse Clark. Everyone has a story about him."

"Not even Bud likes him," Caroline agreed.

She and Travis said together, "And Bud likes everyone."

They both chuckled when Travis pointed to a figure coming their way on the path.

"Ain't that your brother?"

It was. Caroline waved to him, but Caleb didn't notice them.

"Caleb!" Caroline called. Caleb glanced up sharply, and they closed the distance between them.

"Were you just at the house?"

"Yes… I mean… no. I mean, I was there for a while, but I'm not coming from that direction. Precisely."

"Okay," Caroline answered, "This isn't an interrogation. We're only saying hi."

Caleb nodded nervously. Caroline noticed a pink stain on his collared shirt. Lipstick. Travis already started making conversation with Caleb, but Caroline couldn't stop staring at the stain on his shirt.

"Do you have a girlfriend you're not telling me about?"

Caleb's brow furrowed.

"I have to go."

Caleb shoved his hands in his pockets and hurried past them with uncharacteristic urgency.

"What's up with him?" Caroline muttered.

Travis shrugged, "Let's talk to Bud and Chase about Jesse."

He was right, Caroline thought. They had bigger problems to worry about than her brother acting funny. Jesse Clark touched her in the park. Not in a dirty way, only hands on her wrists. Caroline left that part of the story out talking to Travis. But she had to tell the others, even if it would drive the boys crazy.

11

PROTEST

IT TOOK CONVINCING to stop Bud from getting in his truck and driving to the District Attorney's office to beat the shit out of Jesse Clark. Caroline reminded him he was the mayor, and Bud came close to handing in his resignation. Bud Landry, the guy who got along with everyone, poured all the hate in his heart into one man. He hated the hell out of Jesse Clark. Chase changed the subject from Caroline's news, and Caroline was almost relieved.

"We're organizing a strike at the factory tomorrow to protest."

"What?"

"Most of the workers are from the black side of town. It makes sense that we protest."

"What about last time?" Caroline asked, frustrated. Couldn't they wait for tensions in Old Town to die down before diving headfirst into trouble again? Running a mostly independent campaign took a lot of work. The old Landry barn they'd converted to an office came in handy. Caroline stacked every surface to the brim with books, papers and all she needed for her Congressional run.

Since the Mayfair incident, she worked from home more often, sprawling out over the dining room table, or walking down to the town cafe. She worried about them — the boys and her brother both.

Caroline didn't want Chase or her brother getting into trouble again and distracting from the campaign. Plus, she didn't want anything to happen to them. With Jesse Clark prowling through their business, the future felt more precarious than normal.

Travis put his hand on Caroline's shoulder.

"I support you. But please... try not to let it get out of hand."

Chase tipped an imaginary hat, "Yessir."

Caroline relaxed a bit. Relations between them were mostly okay. Getting better daily. Travis supporting the protest had to mean some wounds were healing, if not better already.

"I'll look after Caroline. And help with the next steps of the campaign."

"I need to approve the lawn sign designs," Caroline said, "and get a distribution plan. There are a few places where we're allowed to put them up in the county, so we can go there during the strike. One site is near the factory."

Chase folded his arms and scowled.

"I don't want you getting involved. After last time," he cast a nervous glance at Travis before he continued, "we have to be ready for anything. We didn't start the fight last time."

Travis raised an eyebrow, but he didn't contradict Chase. Caroline nodded.

"We'll be careful."

"Good."

They had dinner together that night and the boys weighed in on the lawn sign designs and Caroline emailed the guy in town who printed them. He promised her a quick turnaround — 100 by tomorrow afternoon — and she could pick up the rest in two weeks. Quick enough, Caroline thought. After they cleaned up dinner, Bud brought out a bottle of whiskey.

Caroline could never keep up with their nightly whiskey drinking. They brought out a deck of cards and played a round of gin rummy which devolved into a series of screaming matches and then laughing fits and before Caroline knew it she was on her back in the middle of their living room. And Bud was on top of her, tasting like smoked lumber and whiskey with the faintest scent of pine on him. Caroline wanted him.

She wanted all of them. But she gasped, "Wait... Someone could be watching us."

Travis flicked off the light, leaving a lone pumpkin scented candle on the mantle, enough for Caroline to catch shapes and shadows, but not enough for her to see who touched and squeezed the different parts of her. That would have to be enough. Until they found out how much Jesse knew and who told him, these half-measures would do.

She ran her fingers over Bud's unmistakable back and groaned as he entered her. Their torrid love session didn't last long before Travis had her, flipping her onto all fours and running his hands over her back as he stroked her deep and slow. Chase was urgent and used his teeth on her neck and shoulders, stimulating Caroline to a loud climax as they finished together.

The four of them lay on the floor of the big Buchanan house. No, Caroline reminded herself, this is the Landry house. My house. And Jesse Clark doesn't scare me. Caroline wanted to believe the last part, but she couldn't help the effect Jesse Clark had on her. He terrified her.

She didn't want him to win. She couldn't let him, Caroline decided. Somehow, they made their way into bed in a tangled heap of half-naked bodies, washboard abs and Caroline's soft skin pressed between them. In the morning, Chase woke up first. He kissed Caroline's cheek, but she only grumbled and didn't wake up. He wanted to see her before leaving the house.

Caleb waited for Chase on the porch swing after Chase had a shave and a shower.

"Morning."

"The strike signs are at the barn," Caleb got right to business.

Chase eyed him carefully.

"You're here early."

"I wasn't far off."

"New girlfriend?" Chase inquired curiously. Caroline was one thing, but he didn't expect Caleb to have a woman on this side of town. Caleb made it clear how he felt about white folks.

"No," Caleb said, sounding short. Chase understood. They had a lot to handle today, and perhaps it wasn't the best time for small talk. They walked over to the Landry barn and picked up the signs, dragging them to the back of the factory. Their managers knew about the strike and stood angrily at the entrance of the factory. Chase and Caleb knew how this worked. Focus on those striking. Hope that nobody breaks picket lines.

Nobody did. Not even racist Joe, who grabbed a sign from Chase while shooting Caleb a glare. They started the morning slowly. Most people would show up late, happy to have a reason not to head into work at the crack of dawn for their shift. They chanted as drivers rode by. Anna-Mae's family drove by in their truck and honked their support. Chase's ma drove by — probably on her way to the grocer — and honked, but she didn't give Chase a direct look.

By mid-morning, Chase and Caleb broke for coffee. Bud donated the money for the coffee in secret and two of the employees from his office dragged the coffee over to fold out tables and set up a stand with styrofoam cups.

The owner of downtown's deli pulled up with coolers full of water, equally popular as the coffee, despite the time of year. They all brought their own lunch, but a few younger guys walked into town to pick up sandwiches for anyone who hadn't brought their own lunch.

With a PB&J dangling from his hand, Chase sauntered over to Caleb and grinned, taking an enormous bite from his sandwich.

"This is going well. Better than expected."

Caleb shook his head.

"Too well."

"Aw shucks," Chase grunted, "Don't be a pessimist, Caleb."

"I'm not," Caleb said, "It's just... we haven't seen a single cop. Not one."

"Maybe they've decided not to bring any trouble."

Caleb shrugged.

"Eat well. And pray you make it home to Caroline."

Chase grinned and reached for the back of his neck. Ouch. Caroline warned him about wearing sunscreen before spending all day in the sun. He thought the red handkerchief around his neck would be enough to protect him, but close to his hairline, he'd allowed the beginnings of a burn to form.

Shit. Chase walked past the factory, checking in on everyone who joined in the strike with protest signs of their own. He thought the police might not care because they weren't downtown and the factory business was factory business. Chase sniffed.

The air didn't smell right. He turned around, passing all the protestors until he got to Caleb. He sniffed again.

"You smell that, Coulson?"

"Burning."

"Think someone fired up the grill?"

The blast erupted ten times louder than Chase might have expected. The sound was so loud it left ringing in his ears before he turned his head to look. Flames erupted from the factory. No... There were still people inside. Managers. Top dogs. But there were people.

He started for the factory, but Caleb grabbed his arm and shook his head. He was saying something, but Chase couldn't make out the words. Everyone else ran. But they stood there, Chase firmly in Caleb's grasp. When the hell had Caroline's brother become so damn strong?

"We have to help!" Chase screamed, but he couldn't hear his own voice. Maybe the words came out an anguished howl or Caleb found himself just as deaf. He watched Caleb's lips. Run. Run. He was telling Chase to run, but he couldn't. The fires were already big enough he could feel their heat.

Not when there were people inside. He couldn't leave. The cops showed up. Fast. Less than 2 minutes after the explosion and the fire. People who were just returning from downtown must have heard the blast. They stopped and stared. Chase's hearing came back, worming its way into his head. Caleb hadn't left him there.

And now they had him. They bent him over a police car and Chase yelled, "Leave him alone!" as an officer put a knee in Caleb's back and dragged him into the back of the car.

"LEAVE HIM ALONE."

"Shut the hell up, Owens," another voice growled. Great. Someone else who knew Zach, Chase thought. They hit the middle of his back and he groaned before they shoved him into the car.

Travis and Caroline got out of the car once they heard the

explosion. Travis meant for them to watch from a distance, but Caroline took off screaming. They were too far off for her to run there, but she ran. Travis wondered if Caroline would really be the death of him one day as he tore after her. When the hell did she get this fast? Even with adrenaline pumping through her, she wasn't fast enough to outrun Travis and when he caught her; he grabbed her by the shoulders.

"Are you crazy? We heard an explosion. We don't know what happened!"

Cop cars zipped by and Caroline wrestled away from me.

"We have to find out!"

"It's dangerous."

"I know!"

She ran again, and Travis caught her much quicker.

"Stop. It's my job to keep you out of this. Chase and Caleb can dive headfirst into danger, but I won't let you."

"You can't stop me!"

"Think again."

Travis hoisted her over his shoulder. It was easy, even as she kicked and screamed.

"YOU MANIAC! PUT ME DOWN!"

He carried her down the street, ignoring the stares from window-watchers as he dragged Caroline into the car and locked the door. She pounded on the window.

"YOU ARE CRAZY! MY BROTHER IS OVER THERE!"

Caroline never got wild like this, but Travis never slung her over his shoulder so easily before. He must have spooked her. When he got back in the car, Caroline seethed. The cop cars flew past their parking space.

"They have someone in the back," Travis said, "We'll find out who it is."

"My brother could be dead," she snapped.

"He has a way of surviving," Travis responded calmly.

Tantrum or not, he'd kept her safe, hadn't he? She couldn't complain about that. She'd find a way, most likely.

When they pulled up outside of the station, Travis observed a bigger problem in his rearview mirror. Shit.

Jesse fucking Clark.

12

I'M NO RACIST

TRAVIS SLAMMED down on the car locks.

"Don't go over there making trouble with him."

Caroline shrugged.

"I wouldn't."

"Caroline, I'm serious. I'll go in look after your brother and Owens. You stay in the car."

"Fine."

It surprised Travis she didn't put up more of a fight. Caroline didn't normally listen to any of his requests. She couldn't help herself. But she folded her arms and leaned back. Travis figured it was safe enough. He left the car on and jogged into the police station. He heard the explosion but didn't think Caleb or Chase would be there facing arrest.

He pushed the door open and saw them. Officer Shields held both of them in processing. Travis leaned on the counter and flashed the officer his wide, Montgomery smile. Chase had better thank his lucky stars Travis still had friends on the police force, the way he appeared hell bent on worsening his situation.

Caroline kept her eye on Jesse as Travis jogged into the

station. He glanced over his shoulder and saw her. Shit. Caroline ducked. She didn't know why. Jesse didn't intimidate her — not with two out of her three boys right there in the police station — but she didn't like him. It wasn't just what he said to her or his crude politicking. Bud hated him. Bud didn't hate anyone. Bud hating Jesse was one of those red flags that Caroline couldn't bring herself to ignore.

Shit. Hiding didn't work either. He tapped on the window and when she kept ducking, he tapped harder.

"Miss Coulson? Are you okay?"

Caroline raised her head and rolled down the window.

"Hello, Mr. Clark. I'm fine."

She started rolling the window back up, but Jesse stuck his hand through the window and instinctively, Caroline stopped.

"Could you please remove your hand, Mr. Clark," she uttered through gritted teeth.

"Would you come out and have a conversation, Miss Coulson? I believe we ought to discuss the unfortunate incident at the factory."

"I don't know what happened at the factory."

"As my opponent, I'm offering you an olive branch so we may discuss it."

Caroline didn't know why she got out of the car. Probably because I'm clinically insane, Caroline thought to herself. She got out of the car and leaned against it.

"Nice ride. Is it your boyfriend's?"

"Travis isn't my boyfriend," Caroline responded.

She sounded calm, but her heart throbbed in her chest. Jesse was already searching for a rise out of her.

"I know he is. I don't have a problem with it. However, our constituents might."

"I'm getting back in the car."

Jesse grabbed her hand as she touched the door handle.

Caroline recoiled and turned to him, sneering, "Don't you dare touch me."

He took a step back, his eyes widening in alarm, like he didn't expect her to respond so fiercely. Was this spoiled rich boy so used to getting his own way that he thought he could treat anyone he stumbled across on the street like garbage and they'd accept it?

"My apologies, ma'am."

"What happened at the factory," Caroline snapped.

"While the strike went on, they think someone set off a pipe bomb. The factory's still burning right now."

Caroline noticed the faintest crisp smell in the air, but she assumed that the department already put out the fire.

"My brother had nothing to do with that."

Caroline didn't bother defending Chase. Jesse would probably take that and run with it.

"Perhaps your other boyfriend did. Or do you call them clients?"

"Mr. Clark, please get to the point. You didn't drag me out of my vehicle to rehash previous accusations."

"You're right. I wanted to look at you."

"That is inappropriate."

Caroline pursed her lips together and glared, like if she glared long enough the ground would open up and swallow Jesse right up.

"Maybe in your socialist version of America staring at a woman will become illegal, but right now we live in a free country."

"Mr. Clark, get to the point."

"I have a new offer to make you."

Caroline snorted. Was that because his last offer went so well?

"I want something from you. And I will drop out of the Congressional race."

"What could be more important than preventing America from descending into socialism," Caroline answered sarcastically.

He grinned, which wasn't exactly the response she expected from him.

"There are more important things."

"Like what? Racism?"

"I'm no racist, Miss Coulson."

"Agree to disagree..."

"I want to sleep with you."

"What?!" Caroline half-yelled, half-squeaked.

Had Jesse Clark lost his mind? She'd rather lose the election than sleep with him. She'd rather drink raw milk or slam her head against a brick wall. But Jesse was calm. He was joking, Caroline thought, testing her to see if he could use her response to prove his accusations against her true.

"I want to sleep with you," he repeated, "One night and we'll forget the entire election. You can have the county. Congress. Move to Washington with your band of hillbilly lovers. I don't care. I want you."

"Stop it," Caroline snapped, "I don't know what the hell you're playing at, but it won't work on me. I want nothing to do with you, understand?"

"I've offended you."

"Beyond offended me. Now, if you'll excuse me, Mr. Clark..."

"You already sleep with three men," he snapped, "What's one more?"

Caroline's cheeks grew hot. The difference was she loved Travis. And Chase. And Bud. And they loved her. They never accused her of being the town whore. They never treated her like garbage. Jesse Clark was a fucking maniac if he thought she would give up all her principles and sleep with him to win the election.

"How stupid do you think I am?" Caroline huffed, "Do you think all black women are this stupid?"

"I did not mean to offend you."

"I don't care what you meant. Propositioning the opponent for sex has to be a new low. If you'll excuse me, Mr. Clark. I'll sit in my car in peace."

"Any problems here?"

Travis. Caroline kept her back pressed against the car as Jesse whipped around to find red-faced Travis Montgomery jogging back toward the car.

"No problems, Trav."

"Back away from my vehicle, Jesse."

Caroline noticed he hadn't emerged with Chase, which didn't bode well. He was also spitting mad, and Jesse didn't move. Caroline rarely saw Travis get this angry. His ears turned red.

"I'll ask you one more time to back the fuck away from Caroline and back the fuck away from my car."

"Mister Montgomery, as a friend of your family, I see no reason for this hostility. I'd happily include you in this conversation."

He winked at Caroline, sending an unsettled, twisted knot through her esophagus. What the hell did Jesse want? Was this a mind game? A threat? She didn't know him. Travis ignored Jesse and turned to Caroline.

"What did he say to you?"

Caroline's tongue lolled heavily in her mouth.

"What did he say," Travis snapped. So Caroline told him. And as Jesse stared at Travis with a shit-eating grin plastered on his face, she watched Travis' hand fly toward Jesse's face.

"NO!" Caroline shrieked.

They were right outside the police station and two people she cared about would already spend the night behind bars.

The last thing she wanted was for Travis to end up right there with them.

"Travis, stop!"

He hit Jesse in the face, then grabbed him by his pink collared shirt and slammed him against the car. Caroline screamed and jumped back, nearly tripping on the curb as she leaped onto the sidewalk.

"TRAVIS!"

He punched Jesse in the face. Jesse was huge. Bud huge. And once he got over the initial surprise, he pushed Travis' head against the car and kicked. Travis had rage on his side and he overpowered Jesse and threw another punch at Jesse's stomach and another at his face when Jesse doubled over.

"Travis!" Caroline screamed.

Travis didn't listen. He shoved his foot into Jesse's stomach and pushed him over so he sat on his ass on the sidewalk.

"Fuck you, Clark," Travis snarled, spitting on the ground next to Jesse, "Get in the fucking car, Caroline."

Caroline flinched, even if she knew Travis didn't mean to direct his anger at her, she hadn't seem him wig out like this. Jesse wheezed and gasped for breath on the ground. But he was smiling. It was like their response to him gave him an answer to a question he hadn't explicitly asked. Caroline's stomach twisted in knots.

He knew. Now he did. Travis wouldn't have punched the living shit out of him if he weren't jealous. This had all been a setup. Travis pulled away from the curb and slammed his hands against the steering wheel. Caroline flinched.

"Sorry," Travis muttered, "I shouldn't have lost my cool."

Caroline bit her lower lip.

"Chase and Caleb?"

"They're in for the night. The cops suspect they set the fire."

"Jesse said there was a bomb."

"Jesse is a fucking idiot."

"I know."

"But he's right," Travis continued, raking his fingers through his hair to calm himself down, "There was a small pipe bomb. Nothing they would have been able to build without us noticing."

"Caleb and Chase wouldn't build a bomb. They want a place to work. It doesn't make sense."

"Good luck getting the cops to believe that. They're officially troublemakers. This is exactly what I wanted to avoid."

"They wouldn't do this. It has to be someone else."

"Fuck, Caroline, I know we disagree, but I had a point. Like it or not, the cops run this town. And now they have Chase and Caleb for the night."

"I know."

"And Jesse… I shouldn't have hit him. He'll get mad and then he'll want to get even."

"You didn't have to hit him."

"I did. I'm Southern. We don't play by our women."

Caroline smiled. She didn't want to encourage Travis to punch every guy who came at her sideways, but Jesse deserved it. And it was nice to know Travis protect her.

"Did you call Bud yet?"

"Yep," Travis answered, "He's at the factory."

"Is it really gone?"

Travis nodded.

"Bud told me to take you home. We'll talk about what happens next when we get there."

"What are they going to do for work?"

"I don't know. But everyone's blaming the protests regardless of the truth. Jesse Clark has his teeth sunk deep in the county media. Bastard."

"I have to beat him, Travis," Caroline asserted, "We've

worked hard on this campaign, but we don't have a choice anymore. If he set that pipe bomb or if he knows who did, that's a big deal. I put so much work into getting Mayor Buchanan out of office, and this Congressional race feels so far out of reach. I wonder if I'm screwing things up."

"You aren't," Travis said, "But you're right. It's time for all of us to dial up the heat."

They got home, and Caroline sat at her computer. She hadn't put up the signs like they'd meant to. Travis followed her into the dining room and sat next to her.

"We need to put up your signs. Then I think it's time for us to handle things the old-fashioned way."

"You don't mean punching anyone in the face this time?"

"Nope. But it's time we up the ante. We ought to go door to door."

"You want me to go door to door on this side of town?"

"Caroline. I'll come with you."

"What about studying for the LSAT?"

"We can listen to vocab in the car while we drive to different areas and I'll study at night. Nothing matters to me more than helping you win this race. I love you."

"I love you too."

Travis leaned over and kissed her. His kiss was soft and yearning.

"Mayor Landry will be home soon. What do you say I warm up his dinner in the bedroom?"

13

HEALING

"This is useless," Caroline moaned, "Jesse has signs everywhere. He even talked the factory owner into throwing in his support. We won't win this going door to door."

Chase spent two days in jail. Since then, he'd been tired and sore. He lay on the couch, hat tipped over his eyes, and groaned.

"Someone ought to torch his house…"

Bud registered his disapproval on his face, but didn't retort. Travis paced the room, stroking the two-day-old beard that sprung over his face.

"Shut the hell up, Chase. You're in enough trouble as it is."

Chase threw his hat to the ground and sat up.

"I told you, I didn't do it. How fucking stupid do you think I am to burn down the place where I work? The last thing I want is felony charges. Or to go on goddamn unemployment."

Caroline rubbed her temples. She didn't want them starting another fight.

"We need to get everyone together in one place. If we

can't go door to door to every person in this town, but if we got them all together..."

"We could have an event," Bud said, "Like what y'all organized when I campaigned. A healing event for the two sides of this town to air their grievances."

Caroline raised a skeptical eyebrow.

"What grievances do the white folks in this town have exactly?"

Bud sighed and turned red the way he did when he struggled with his words. Caroline waited patiently.

"Look, if I learned anything in politics, it's that you have to listen to everybody. You don't have to change your mind. You don't have to state your opinion. You just listen. Even if they don't make a lick of sense."

Caroline considered his statement. Bud understood people. He sure understood politics. He'd won the last mayor election, and he had that streetwise understanding of people down pat.

"You have a point."

"Perfect. We'll throw the event then. At the mayor's house."

"Here?!"

"Yes. We'll lock the bedrooms, but the house is enormous. We have all this space and never entertain."

Caroline suppressed the urge to point out the reason they didn't entertain was because of their private four-way relationship that no one in Old Town would understand. What were they anyway? A quad? A foursome? Caroline hated to put a label on it. And that lack of a label wouldn't exactly fly in a town that had barely moved past segregation.

"I think it's a good idea," Travis said, "You can speak at the event. We can get it catered."

Caroline glanced nervously at Chase. He was the most

likely one to oppose the idea, but he was the one she was most likely to agree with too.

"It's smart," Chase said, groaning as he adjusted his position and clutching his ribs.

Caroline was sure he had a fracture from his last arrest. She worried about him and the way he always landed into trouble right along with her brother. At least the two of them got along better now.

"It's settled then. We'll have a healing event at the house."

In the fortnight leading up to the event, Caroline worked on her campaign signs, her online campaign, courting donors and updating her campaign website. She'd almost forgotten about Jesse Clark, which was perfect. She'd helped Bud with his campaign, and she knew it didn't help to worry too much about the opponent. That was for everyone else but her. They'd bring her the important news.

Chase arranged with his mother and Mrs. Montgomery to have them cater the event together. Caroline was nervous around both mothers, but they agreed to help at a discount and they set a formidable menu. Chase had to drive out to a farm in Virgil to get the giant pig the mothers would roast. Travis promoted the event in his free time using word of mouth and the internet. He stood outside the cafe between LSAT study sessions, talking the ear off of anyone who would listen.

Caroline worried about what they'd all wear.

"I'll wear my jeans without mud on them," Chase suggested.

Bud had a proper tan suit, like the one Barack Obama wore on Easter that drove everyone wild. The controversy around the suit inspired Bud. He liked to stand out, and it wasn't hard considering he was bigger than damn near everyone he met. And louder. Travis picked out a suit without

Caroline's help, but she found his tastes perfect. The suit was dark blue, nearly the same color as his old police uniform, and he got a light blue tie that matched his eyes.

Bud and Caroline dragged Chase kicking and screaming to get a suit, but Caroline would have settled for anything that wasn't made of denim. Thankfully, she had Bud to help her get her way. Chase complained about nearly everything she picked out, but eventually settled on a black suit with a red bowtie.

"It's almost like a handkerchief."

Caroline disagreed, but she wasn't in the mood to pick a fight with him over this. She was barely getting her way as it was. Bianca Mayfair agreed to attend the event, and she asked Caroline to come dress shopping with her. Bianca Mayfair was a light tan color, with a few freckles splattered across her shoulders but none on her face, which she kept out of the sun to avoid getting "too dark".

Caroline bit her lip to avoid pointing out that she was several shades darker than Bianca could ever get sitting in the sun and that there was no such thing as "too dark". At least Bianca had wonderful tastes. She ended up getting Caroline an emerald colored silk dress that fell just below her knees.

"Silk knows all the right places on the body to sit," Bianca said as Caroline spun around before a mirror. Bianca was right, so Caroline got the dress. She didn't want to show the boys until the big night. They even agreed on their story in case anyone was nosy enough to ask: they were all roommates. Just roommates. Nothing improper or un-Christian about that.

On the big night, Caroline tried to calm her nerves. The boys swore they'd handle everything, and all she had to do was work the room and give a damn excellent speech. She'd also have an informal Q&A session towards the end. Bud planned the entire thing out.

And people showed up. At first, Caroline was nervous to talk to everyone, but the excitement got to her. It was hard to avoid. Everyone wanted to talk about the factory fire and everyone wanted to compliment her dress. From across the room, she saw the three boys murmuring to each other and when Bud caught her looking at them he winked. They were talking about the dress too. Caroline worked the room as planned and announced her Congressional run in person to several people who wondered if she were a different Caroline Coulson.

As she checked on Mrs. Montgomery and Mrs. Owens in the kitchen, they poured Caroline another lemonade — spiked with whiskey — and sent her back out.

"I wish I could say you'd have my vote."

Caroline froze as she exited to the foyer. There weren't many people around since the food came out.

"Mr. Clark. Thank you for attending."

"You have quite the mix of folks around here."

"Yes. We do. Now, if you'll excuse me."

Jesse wriggled his eyebrows and pointed upstairs.

"We could finish this. I promise I won't last long."

"I'd rather drop dead."

Jesse chuckled.

"You have a chance to make sure tonight ends well. Why won't you take it? Are you really that stubborn?"

"Tonight will end well. And it will have nothing to do with you and your repeated lewd requests."

Caroline stomped past him, only to land in Bud's grasp.

"Where were you? It's time for your speech."

"Already?"

"I have everyone gathered on the lawn. They're polishing off what's left of the pork and they're ready to hear you."

Caroline stepped outside. Jesse Clark stood in the front of the crowd. She avoided looking him in the eye. Screw Jesse

Clark. Caroline spoke earnestly. She'd written her speech from the heart, so she meant every word. She wanted to bring their towns together. She wanted to stop the division and create a world where Ezra wouldn't have died, where the factory wouldn't have burned to the ground and where people on Main Street hadn't had their businesses destroyed.

"... we don't want to change this town because we hate it. We want to change this town because we love it here. This is our home. From the scent of magnolias, to the dirt between our toes, we love our town and our county and our country. And we want to make this a place where everyone can live together. White folks and black folks, I love you all. If you want to see this place blossom and grow, vote for me in the upcoming election."

They clapped and then cheered, and when that died down, Caroline heard chanting from the back of the crowd. It wasn't anyone at the party, but people on the streets. She stood on the stairs, clutching her microphone and looking around for Bud or Travis to hand it off to.

She didn't see any of them. The chants got louder.

"NO NIGGERS IN OFFICE! NO NIGGERS IN OFFICE!"

Caroline tapped the microphone.

"It appears we have some folks protesting on the sidewalk... Mayor Landry?"

But the crowd had moved their attention to the screaming protestors. Caroline saw guns. Huge guns and trucks on the street. She grabbed the door handle to return inside. Maybe the boys snuck in toward the end of her speech, but as she jostled it, a hand touched hers. She glanced up at Jesse Clark, grinning like a Cheshire Cat.

"I told you to pick the easy way," he hissed.

Before Caroline could reply, someone yanked him back and punched him. Hard.

"Chase!"

The protest on the lawn already devolved. The men who infiltrated the party picked up party-goers and there were fist-fights and people running to safety. Bianca Mayfair ran for the house and Caroline let her in, staying outside and trying to get Chase off Jesse.

If someone called the cops again, this would be bad. Chase might not get out of jail so quickly this time. But Caroline was in heels, so she couldn't exactly jump into the fight and scrap. She took off one of her heels and threw it at Jesse's head. He let go of Chase, who didn't have the sense to run. He threw another punch at Jesse and used the opportunity to get a leg up on the much larger man.

Most people fled. Mrs. Montgomery and Mrs. Owens grabbed Caroline by the arm and pulled her into the house.

"Go upstairs," Mrs. Owens said solemnly, "Tell me where my boy keeps his gun."

There were guns stashed all over the house. Caroline tried to think.

"Kitchen. On top of the tall cupboard."

Mrs. Owens nodded at Mrs. Montgomery, and they grabbed shotguns and rushed out onto the porch. Caroline lingered inside until she heard one warning shot. And then another. All hell broke loose.

"Y'all get the fuck off my property…"

Caroline peered through the window. Bud had a pistol, and he waved it at one of the "protestors" who had Travis in a chokehold. Caroline couldn't let them handle this alone. She searched their private living room — not the one they'd entertained in — and grabbed a rifle from underneath the couch before running outside to defend her home.

14

HE'LL RUIN EVERYTHING

Cops stood by and watched the mess. They didn't bother arresting anyone. They let "protestors" beat up party guests. Bud got everyone off the property, but the entire event had been... a disaster. Caroline searched the crowd for Jesse Clark. He'd been trespassing. She could put her rifle up and give him two to the back of the head and end this whole Congressional mess. Wasn't that how the old boys settled things in this town? Gun fights?

Jesse had long vanished by the time Caroline armed herself and Bud dragged Chase and Travis into the house by their collars. Red-faced, he sputtered and gasped at Mrs. Owens and Mrs. Montgomery that they'd better leave before they got into any trouble unsuitable for women. They left their guns on the counter and snuck out the back.

Bud tossed Chase and Travis onto the couch. Caroline at first thought he'd been red in the face from exertion, but as he paced in front of Chase and Travis, she realized they upset him.

"What the hell were you two thinking?!"

"Thinking? I'm defending my goddamn home. I'm defending my goddamn woman!" Chase yelled.

Caroline pressed her back to the wall behind them. She didn't get in the middle of their arguments. And arguments involving her...? She'd never heard any of them argue about her before.

"Your woman?" Bud growled, "We share her. We've always shared her. She doesn't belong to you."

"I never said she did. But I'm the only one willing to punch a motherfucker's teeth in for disrespect."

"That's not fair," Travis grunted.

"Not fair? You're ready to sell her out to the damn police yourself."

"I would never do that," Travis growled.

"Watch your mouth, Owens," Bud snarled, "We ought to protect her. And fighting and carrying on like animals isn't protecting her."

"She's safe, isn't she? Caroline can handle her damned self," Chase said.

Caroline appreciated that sentiment. She'd gotten her own gun, hadn't she? It wasn't completely untrue. She could handle herself fine, given the chance. And with Jesse Clark, she would have more than handled herself if he'd stayed around for her to aim her gun at him.

She bit her lip to stop herself from mentioning that.

"When you play politics, you have to play," Bud explained, in a low, serious voice, "We can't afford to have any more of this. It's bad enough you might have blown up the goddamn factory."

Chase exploded, "How many goddamn times do I have to tell y'all I didn't blow up the fucking factory? I'm tired of listening to both of you. I love Caroline, don't you ever fucking question that, but I don't love you two assholes playing alpha male in my fucking house."

Redneck Rebellion

Chase stormed toward the door.

"Where the hell are you going?"

"I'm getting out of here!"

Chase slammed the door, and the house rattled. Caroline slunk forward, leaning over the couch.

"He's mad."

Bud scowled, but his expression softened when he laid eyes on Caroline.

"I know."

"Bud... Chase might be a little... mercurial... but he didn't hurt me. He wasn't trying to hurt me."

"He ought to be careful. He's too reckless."

"Agreed," Travis said, a little too loudly.

Bud folded his arms.

"You... You're not innocent here."

"What the hell did I do!?"

"The cops stand by while so-called protestors beat the shit out of our party guests. You know these people, Travis. You defend them. That don't help Caroline either."

"How the hell am I to change what the cops do? I'm not an officer anymore. And I tried to work from the inside but everyone in this damn house has a problem with that."

Bud put his hands on his hips.

"What would you have done if you went out that night with Zach Owens? You think you would've stopped him?"

"I don't know."

"I do."

"I don't need to hear this from you, Landry! You're supposed to be on my side, not some crazy ass radical like Chase."

"I'm no radical. I'm the mayor. It's my job to make sure both sides of this town get together. That's what tonight ought to have been about."

"This isn't my fault."

"I never said it was."

"Screw you, Landry."

Travis got up and stormed outside after Chase. Caroline sighed as she sat on the couch's arm.

"That went well…"

Bud scratched the back of his head.

"Those two…"

"You're all different. That's why I love you."

Bud raised an eyebrow.

"They're stubborn."

"So are you."

"Hm."

"They'll come back," Caroline sighed, "We ought to give them time to cool down."

Bud scoffed and sat next to Caroline. Sweat soaked through his shirt. He'd taken off his suit jacket and lost his tie in the scuffle. Bud groaned and tossed his head back.

"I ask myself every damn day why I took this job."

"You took this job because you're good at it," Caroline whispered, running her hand along Bud's huge thigh. He groaned.

"Oh, that feels good," he murmured.

"Thanks for standing up for me."

"Hm."

"You all care… in your own way."

Bud tilted his head to gaze at Caroline and bit his lower lip.

"Did I tell you that you look hot in that dress? And you looked hotter holding my gun."

"You saw that?"

"Hm."

He curved his finger, urging Caroline to lean over and kiss him. She ran her fingers along Bud's beard and gave him a soft peck. Bud opened her lips with his and kissed Caroline deeper. He groaned as he pulled away from her.

"That dress does things to a man."

"Like what?"

"It hugs your curves in all the right places."

Caroline giggled.

"We ought to clean up the mess outside before making a mess in here."

"The mess will be there in the morning," Bud murmured, shifting his position so he kneeled on the couch and grabbed Caroline's hips. The effects of Bud's grasp were highly predictable. He squeezed her hips and Caroline took a sharp inhalation of breath as his beard tickled her neck and his lips drew her flesh between them roughly.

Bud chuckled and whispered, "You are so dang sensitive."

Caroline wanted to retort that Bud was inexplicably and constantly horny, but he kissed her again, stopping her words before they could escape. She ran her fingers over his beard and through his hair as he adjusted his position on top of her.

"Did I buy you that dress?"

"I may have pinched $20 to help me along from your wallet."

"That is not a $20 dress."

"You're right. But it sure helped."

Bud peeled one skinny strap over her shoulder and kissed it.

"All I wanted to do as Mayor is spoil my girl."

"Consider me spoiled."

"Lift that dress, woman. I can't wait any longer."

Caroline hiked her dress up as Bud's enormous thumbs pulled her thong over her hips and ass. He forced his finger between her lips and rubbed her mound. Caroline mound and Bud pulled his wet fingers away, slipping them sloppily into his mouth and moaning as he sucked her juices off.

"Damn it, woman. I could get drunk off this..."

He lowered his face between her legs, his large tongue parting her lower lips as he slid between her legs with them, holding her knees high and apart so he could access every inch of her honeypot and thighs. He licked her hardened pearl and then planted kisses over her thighs and ran his tongue from her pearl to her ass. Caroline whimpered as Bud's tongue found her tender, puckered hole.

Holy shit... He never hesitated as his tongue roved around the hole and he licked furiously around her backdoor before his tongue returned to her lower lips and he nibbled her thighs as he kissed her lower lips until she came. When Caroline came, she moaned and shuddered, her legs thrashing as Bud firmly held her down. He never stopped kissing her mound until her orgasm soaked to the couch cushions. He moved his face away from her and lowered his dress pants, removing his hardness and pressing the enormous helmet against Caroline's entrance.

This was the worst part and the best part. That first piercing thrust sent a shiver of pain through Caroline. But Bud knew it hurt, and he soothed her as he thrust his enormous hardness into her. He kissed her this time as he moved his hips between her thighs, guiding the head into her cushioned tightness.

"I love you," he murmured, plunging the head between her legs.

Caroline wrapped her arms around his neck and moaned as the first thrust took her deep. He eased the rest into her as she moaned and her hips unconsciously bucked forward, urging Bud to have her and conquer her deeper. He nestled himself inside her, burying himself to the hilt and keeping her firmly pressed beneath his weight.

Redneck Rebellion

Her body was so small beneath his. Bud stroked her hips, carefully coaxing her to calm as he spread her with his cock. She whimpered and gazed at him with pleading eyes. She needed him the way he needed her. He'd always needed Caroline. Even when he'd been too shy to talk to her, an enormous hulking brute of a man who couldn't work up the courage to talk to the smart black girl he found himself and his best friends all attracted to.

"Caroline," Bud murmured before kissing her and thrusting into her deep and slow. He loved the way her name tasted on his tongue. He loved licking up the salt on her neck and teasing her earlobes and then the deep thrusting. She moaned with each thrust, a genuine uncontrollable moan that changed pitch and length according to how he plunged into her. Her breasts bounced with each thrust and every part of her responded to him perfectly, her nipples poking through the green silk that still covered her chest.

Bud replaced his tongue to her neck as he entered her deep, nestling his dick deep inside the perfect tightness that gripped him and grasped him as if her entrance possessed its own thirst and will. She moaned and begged him to plunge into her harder and faster. Bud obliged, pumping into her until she climaxed. And as he thrust, her climax never ended. He moved between her legs and groaned with each deep thrust, pulling his pants further down.

Anyone coming upon the scene would have seen Bud's thick muscular ass pumping between Caroline's splayed brown legs on the couch. Bud groaned and kissed her as he made love to her. She came again and Bud couldn't hold back. He erupted between her legs, taking her deep and pulling her close as thick pumps of his seed coated her walls and Caroline drew him to nestle on top of her with her heels.

"Bud…" she whispered, "Fuck… Bud…"

Applause. Slow, sarcastic applause filled the room. Caroline froze. Bud was still inside her. But there was someone else inside the house. As Bud scrambled off her and Caroline scrambled to lower her dress, she heard him speak, but she didn't have to hear his voice to know who witnessed their entanglement.

"That was a spectacular performance."

Bud rose, his hands clenched into fists and his pants around his ankles. Bud was a naked guy by nature and apparently unperturbed by the idea of getting into a fistfight with his elephant dick hanging out. Caroline clasped a hand over her mouth and covered herself with her dress, pulling a throw blanket over herself as if she could hide from Jesse Clark.

"I finally understand. Mayor Landry... a purveyor of the finest whore in Old Town."

"Call her a whore one more time and I'll knock every fucking tooth out of your mouth."

"Careful, Landry. I have this..."

He shook a cellphone and laughed, "Proof. Proof of the Whore Congresswoman. That has a ring to it, doesn't it? It is rather unfortunate that no one in this town would elect a whore to Congress."

He couldn't continue his speech because Bud punched him so hard that Caroline screamed. Blood splattered from Jesse's face and he hollered. Bud broke his nose.

"Get the fuck out of my house. I have a gun in every room of this house and I'm not afraid to use it."

"I plan to leave this house alive, Mayor Landry. Don't worry."

"Caroline?" Jesse asked, tilting his head as he clutched his bloody nose, "Now's a good chance to take me up on my offer. You've already been used once."

"What the hell is he talking about?"

Caroline bit her lip.

"Sex. I want to use your... woman."

"Take one more step and I'll break more than your nose."

"We'll discuss later, Landry."

Bud grabbed Jesse by the collar as he strode past, yanking him back.

"Give me the fucking phone."

Jesse, inspired by a sense of self preservation, and possibly blood loss, handed it over. Too easy. He wouldn't have handed it over so easily unless he knew it didn't matter.

"Talk about what you witnessed, and I'll shoot you myself, Jesse. I've waited a good long time for a chance."

He threw Jesse towards the door. Jesse called back, "If you were going to kill me, I'd be dead!"

Bud strode back to the door with his pistol, but Jesse fled, disappearing into the night.

"Smartest thing that motherfucker ever did," Bud growled, twirling the pistol before slamming the door behind them. He hurried back over to the couch, where Caroline wrapped herself in the blanket.

"Caroline..."

"He's going to ruin everything," she whispered, "We can't stop him now."

15

SECRET ENCOUNTERS

BUD'S PHONE RANG. Neither of us expected it, and it took him a while to figure out where he'd lost the phone between the couch cushions. Bud stomped in a circle as he listened to the person on the other end of the line.

"You can't be serious," he growled.

...

"You promised me this wouldn't happen."

...

"Dammit! Clark's a bastard. I'm coming down there. Now."

...

"No, Abernathy, I won't bring a damn gun."

Bud ended the call and threw the phone at the couch.

"Is everything okay?" Caroline asked.

"No."

"What happened?"

"They released Zach Owens. The press is around the courthouse and there's a shit show at the Mayor's Office. Caroline. This is bad. I had it on good authority that Owens wasn't going anywhere."

Caroline heard nothing else Bud said for a while. Her ears rang. Zach Owens shot Ezra Mayfair in cold blood and now he was getting out.

"How?" she whispered.

Bud grabbed her hands and squeezed them in his enormous hands.

"Listen," he murmured, "I need to go."

"I'm coming with you."

"Caroline!"

"I can't stay in this big old house all on my own."

"Yes, you can. You're safe here."

"Bud... Please. I have to be there."

"Fine. Get in the truck. But if shit goes south, I want you to take this car and get the hell away from there."

"What's going on?"

"He'll be walking out of the courthouse by the time we get down there. Come on."

Caroline's heart pounded. Zach Owens might have looked like his brother but he had a cold, heavy gaze barely concealing cruelty. His upper lip curled up in a perpetually cruel smirk. A shiver traveled down Caroline's back as she thought about him. He wouldn't smile as he left the courthouse, she thought, he'd grin.

Bud drove them down to the courthouse, pulling his car around the crowd and parking in the back. Bud pressed his hand to Caroline's thigh.

"No matter what happens, I'm doing my best."

"You wanted him behind bars."

"Yes. But it's more than that, Caroline. Come on."

"Releasing him doesn't mean there won't be justice," Caroline considered, "There will still be a trial."

"I'm going in there to hand in my resignation as mayor."

The words hung heavy between them. Caroline rested her hand on Bud's arm.

"You can't do that. You can't!"

Caroline knew she'd have to come up with a better argument than that, but those were the last words she expected.

"I have to, Caroline. If shit goes south, I know where I plan to be and it ain't in no mayor's office."

"The town needs a mayor!"

"I'll appoint Travis as acting mayor in my stead. He can handle things until we have another election. He doesn't want to get his hands dirty anyway."

"Bud... you can't."

"Why not? Tell me why I ought to stand back and let people hurt you. Chase is right about one thing. It's our job to protect you... no matter what."

Caroline leaned over and planted a fat, wet kiss on Bud's cheek. He turned red, like he was still an awkward giant of a teenager who didn't know the first thing about women. Caroline giggled and wiped away the wet spot with her thumb.

"I love you, Mayor Landry. But you love being Mayor Landry. I can't let you give that up."

"I can't let this town's shit fall all over you."

"I need you in the mayor's office. So please... let's go in there. No resigning. Nothing like that. We'll figure out what to do once we figure out why they're letting Zach go."

They entered the courthouse. Cops out front kept the media back, and they were about to release Zach Owens onto the street. Bud strode into the county office while Caroline sat in the waiting room, a flush of nerves overcoming her once Bud disappeared behind the scenes. She could feel the woman behind the counter watching her, and it all reminded her of Augusta Abernathy and the women she'd worked with in Mayor Buchanan's office before her unceremonious departure.

They looked at her like she was small and disgusting just for showing up in their space. This one eyed Bud Landry with equal suspicion, as if his association with Caroline were proof enough that you couldn't trust him as Mayor. Caroline texted Chase, but he didn't respond. She considered texting Travis, but she couldn't bear it if they both failed to respond to her.

Bud's raised voice echoed from behind the door.

"NO CHARGES?!"

Caroline flinched as she heard a slam and the clattering of file cabinets and a desk.

"I OUGHT TO GO OVER THERE AND PUNCH CLARK IN HIS FUCKING FACE..."

Whoever stood behind the door with Bud calmed him. But when he yanked the door open and stormed out, the door came off its hinges. He put his Stetson on and growled.

"Caroline. Come. We're going out back. This will get real messy in here."

He squeezed Caroline's hand as she joined him. She winced and must have felt the shiver running through her because he loosened his grasp. Once they returned to the truck, Bud slammed his hands on the steering wheel.

"DAMMIT."

"Bud," She whispered, "What did they say?"

"They dropped the charges."

"What?!"

"No manslaughter. No first or second degree murder. They're calling it an accident."

"But... Ezra did nothing wrong."

"We all know that. But the DA dropped the charges. He's suggesting Zach Owens do 40 hours of community service."

Caroline's blood boiled to a rage.

"That's not fair! It's not right!"

"Dammit, Caroline, I know! And the only reason I didn't resign and get my gun and handle this myself is... well... Fuck. Chase Owens is out there. When he finds out..."

Bud kicked the truck to a start and pulled off the street, driving past their house and toward the old Landry barn they'd converted to an office. They hadn't spoken in several minutes when Caroline whispered, "Where are we going?"

"I need you with me, Caroline."

She touched his thigh, and his shoulders relaxed the moment she touched him.

"I'm here."

"Chase and Travis are at the bar. I told them to meet us at my family stables."

"The stables?!"

Caroline's cheeks flushed as she remembered the last things to happen when all three men had her in the stables. But she couldn't imagine getting naked again with any of them when they hadn't discussed what happened with Jesse Clark. Maybe Bud wanted them to talk in private. That made sense.

It was late now — nearly two in the morning — and Caroline dozed off before they arrived at the stables until Bud lifted her out of the truck and she instinctively wrapped her arms and legs around him before waking up. He pressed her against the truck and kissed her, setting her down slowly as she awakened.

"We're here."

"Yeah. I fell asleep."

"Travis and Chase are out back. And they're armed."

"Do they know Jesse... saw us..."

Caroline could feel Bud turning red even if it was too dark to see him outside of the truck.

"Don't you worry about that."

Not worrying was tough. Jesse had what he wanted for blackmail and he had Zach Owens bailed out. Not just bailed out — charges dropped. Bud would have to give Chase the news and chances are all hell would break loose at the courthouse, anyway. The outrage had grown bigger than all of them. The faint light of a lit cigarette alerted Caroline to Chase's presence. He spoke to Travis in a hushed voice, but they quieted as Bud and Caroline drew close.

Chase took Caroline's arm and pulled her into a tight hug, drawing her in through a cloud of cigarette smoke that singed the insides of her nostrils. He smelled like tobacco and whiskey. And he still wore most of his suit. He'd ripped the jacket in the brawl on their front porch.

Chase put his lips to her ear and whispered, "I'm sorry."

Caroline didn't want him to let go. But Travis eased behind them both and put his hands on Caroline's waist to draw her away from Chase and into his own grasp. He smelled like tequila. Travis and tequila were a deadly combination. She'd seen him do crazy things while tequila drunks, crazy things that could make her forget that Travis was the most straight-laced of the group.

He ran his tongue over her earlobe without hesitation, but didn't kiss her. Or apologize. He just... tasted her. And held her. Until Bud put his hand on Travis' shoulder and cleared his throat.

"We need to talk."

Travis and Chase lowered themselves to the ground, sitting with their backs against the stable wall. Caroline sat between Travis and Bud. Horses whinnied inside the stables, hearing people and expecting licks of sugar or bites of carrots, or at least expecting someone to take them out for a nice long ride.

Caroline explained the Jesse Clark situation. Chase pulled a clump of grass out of the ground and threw it.

"Let me get this straight... y'all fucked? Without us?"

Caroline bit her lower lip. They'd never talked about "rules" for having sex separately. They just... did. Bud had her when he wanted to. Chase did too.

"I didn't know there were rules," Caroline muttered.

"There aren't," Travis asserted, guiltily.

"How many times have you... with us... this week?"

Caroline bit her lower lip. Would it sound bad to say she'd lost count.

"A lot."

"Jesus, Caroline!"

"You boys have enormous appetites."

Bud chuckled.

"None as big as yours."

"That's not the point," Caroline huffed, "Because I love the three of you doesn't mean I want to sleep with Jesse Clark."

Their backs all stiffened reflexively upon mentioning his name.

"None of us would suggest that," Travis replied.

"Right," Bud said.

"I'm only surprised Bud didn't knock him out."

"He tried," Caroline admitted.

"Fuck Jesse Clark. It doesn't matter what he saw or what proof he has. He might fuck with Bud, but he can't win against the three of us, no matter what he does."

"Y'all heard about Zach?" Bud steered them back along the uncomfortable line of conversation Caroline knew he desperately wished to avoid too.

"What about him?" Travis muttered bitterly while Chase fished his pants pocket for another cigarette.

"They dropped the charges."

Chase dropped his unlit cigarette and muttered, "Sonofabitch."

"He's going home tonight."

"I can see why you waited to tell me," Chase said.

"Do nothing, Owens. We ought to wait to see how this plays out."

"We ought to finish this the old-fashioned way. When our ancestors came to this town, we settled matters of honor with a gunfight."

"My first ancestor to Old Town died of cholera," Bud said, grinning from ear to ear, "And his wife, Mamie Landry was the town whore before becoming a schoolteacher."

Caroline struggled to see the relevance, but Bud had pride in his family history. Chase shrugged.

"I'll wait. One day. But only because I hate fighting with my best friends."

Travis snickered.

"You can be so sensitive."

"That's what we love about him," Bud added.

Caroline assumed they'd gotten over their anger at the party. Nothing like bad news to bring them all together. Only this time, they didn't know what they'd do next. Chase lit his cigarette and slammed his head back against the stable walls.

"This is all fucked up beyond all recognition."

"There's a way out," Travis said, "There always is."

"Even if we have to use our guns," Bud added solemnly.

16

THE FIGHT IN HIM

RETURNING to Bud's barn reignited feelings Caroline thought had faded into the background. Even when you're in a relationship with three strapping, muscular men, what used to be new and exciting can become normal. You stop noticing things. And maybe you don't just stop noticing things, but you stop doing them too. Caroline sensed the boys felt what she did. Everything felt new again when they leaned against the barn, when they moved on together from a festering hurt.

No more arguing. No more letting the election, the protests, Zach Owens or Jesse Clark get between them. Bud laced his fingers with hers on one side, and Chase did on the other. Travis strolled a few feet ahead. When they got to the door of their house. They stopped and gazed down at Caroline. They wanted her. Urgently. And if Jesse Clark hadn't rudely interrupted her and Bud, they might have had her right on the porch because they could.

"Caroline," Bud whispered hoarsely, "We'll need you to get upstairs."

"Now," Travis urged. His voice came across raspy and needy, unlike the Travis she was used to.

He felt it. The newness.

Chase pushed the door open and held it open for Caroline. Three southern gentlemen. All eager. All hungry. All needing her.

She scampered upstairs. They didn't bother running after her. They followed up the stairs, slowly shedding clothes as they marched in single file towards the bedroom. Travis shed his shirt and as Chase stepped over it, he lost his belt. Bud came up the rear and hung his hat on the railing. Once Caroline got to the bedroom, she flopped back on the sheets. They smelled cleaner than she remembered. Fresh with the scent of her three boys' sweat intermingling in the sheets. By the time Travis entered their bedroom, his cornflower blue boxers were the only article of clothing left covering his body. His pants tented as his hardness urgently thrust forward. He needed her. Oh, God. He needed her more than he could have ever imagined.

"Caroline," He murmured.

Travis climbed into bed on top of her and kissed her. His kiss was furious and deep, unlike typical Travis kisses. He kissed her like Chase now. Like he'd found the fire inside himself and, even better, found the bravery to unleash it. He grasped her arms and pinned them over her head. She allowed him to control her, to manipulate her body, so she lay powerless beneath him where he could tear her clothes off with his teeth, graze his tongue over every inch of her bare flesh and bury himself in her. She wanted all of it. She wanted all of him.

Travis pulled his lips away from her and released a shuddering exhale. His kiss felt new. His touch refreshed her. And his firm grasp on her hands made Caroline wonder what would come next. He ran his hands over her dress and murmured, "It's taking everything in my power not to rip that dress off of you."

Ripping clothes off was a Bud thing. He struggled against his animal urges, especially in the bedroom where Bud Landry was 100% animal. 100% raw. Travis fought his more animal instincts to peel the strap over Caroline's shoulder and kiss her there.

As she relented to his kisses, his grasp on her wrists tightened. Travis never held her in bed as forcefully as he held her now. Like he didn't mean to let go of her. Caroline squirmed as Travis' tongue found her neck again and he sucked hard on her flesh. As he took her into his mouth, she cried out and he returned his lips to her mouth.

Caroline couldn't see what Chase and Bud were up to. She heard their footsteps around the room. Bud had a heavy gait. Chase walked lightly and quickly. But they didn't speak, nor did they climb into bed and give Caroline some clue of what to expect. As Travis thrust his tongue into her throat, the lights went out. She gasped sharply before she heard Travis whisper, "shhh…"

She couldn't see a thing, but she could feel his warmth. His firm, lean ab muscles pressed into her and Caroline ran her heel down the back of his thighs and shins. She couldn't move, she couldn't grab him. All she could do was relent to their overpowering desire.

When Travis moved his hands away from her wrists, Caroline at first thought she was free. But they snatched away both her wrists from her. Bud held one and Chase held the other and they pulled her arms apart while she struggled to adjust to the dark light. Now Travis wasn't on the bed anymore, and she squealed as Bud and Chase dragged her to the top of the bed and silk fabric wrapped around her wrists.

"What are you three doing?" Caroline half-giggled.

She trusted them. There was nothing to worry about. But not knowing what came next made her heart throb until it felt like a frog trying to leap out of her throat. She gasped as

Travis stripped her dress off her, sliding it quickly off her hips so the sudden nakedness sent a sharp chill running through her.

"Travis…" she gasped.

But the next set of lips to touch hers left Caroline uncertain that Travis was the one kissing her or that he was even in the bed. They'd bound her hands, leaving her at their mercy. She heard a voice in her ear and she couldn't tell if it was the man on top of her or someone else.

"Who are you kissing right now?"

She let the man on top of her kiss her. He was painstakingly slow, too cautious. But she'd recognize those lips anywhere, even as he tried to fool her.

"Bud…"

He was heavier than the other two. That gave him away. But he tasted like Bud and smelled like Bud. His large hand touched her mound, and she whimpered.

"Wet," Bud said.

And Caroline shrieked as he ripped her panties off. She'd lost many panties to Bud's animalistic need. He hiked her thighs up and before she could protest again, he slid his tongue between her legs. When Bud ate between her thighs, he was sloppy. Juices dripped everywhere. They sprayed from her entrance and his tongue soaked every part of her thighs and pussy. Bud's relentless tongue poked her backdoor as he ate her until Caroline erupted in a climax more intense than any she'd had before.

Before she could protest, the bulging head of a man's member slid against her entrance. Not Bud's. She cried out as Travis thrust inside her, hard and deep. Bud made her nice and wet, but Travis was the first to have her and he took her deep. He grunted with each urgent thrust and pressed his lips to Caroline's as she came all over his dick. He ran his tongue over her breasts as he continued making love to her and when Caroline came again, he finished inside her, pumping her deep with his cum.

Caroline half expected Chase to take her next. But Bud thrust his enormous member into her next. She screamed. She couldn't grab onto him, or slow him down with her hands pulled away from her so she had to let Bud decide how much to hurt her and how much to please her. He was rough at first, sliding between her legs with desperate depth until her screams sounded too pained and he made love in a way she didn't know Bud could.

He was slow. And something about that monster cock hitting her slow and deep made Caroline cum harder than before. She wanted to grab onto him and feel his large ass tense as he plunged into her. But all she could do was moan. Bud grabbed her hips at their smallest point and enjoyed teasing her with the enormous dick stretching out her pussy. She came again. And again.

Bud groaned and erupted between her legs. That cum-filled feeling brought a hot flush to Caroline's face. Most other men (and women) would judge her for enjoying this. But it was hard not to feel a rush after two men spread her legs and came inside her. The cooler sticky liquid mixed with Bud's hot load between her legs and the dripping down her thighs and over her ass crack only ignited Caroline's cravings for more.

She used to hate how badly she wanted more. Tonight, wanting more felt new again. There was a flush of guilt. There were the shame-filled thoughts. And then there was Chase. And fuck, he kissed her like he meant it. He ran his fingers through her hair and grabbed her face and kissed her so long her lips swelled and she didn't think he'd end up making love to her until the swollen tip of his prick teased her entrance and his face collapsed against hers in another desperate kiss as he slid the entire thing between her legs.

Bud and Travis decorated her body with kisses as Chase made love to her. He'd never kissed her so hard or so much while they made love, but Caroline let his lips tease hers open and his tongue thrust into her as his dick mimicked the yearning between her thighs.

Caroline came and Chase groaned as the wetness between her thighs eagerly grasped his invading member, milking him and drawing him in deeper to her. She came again and her legs dragged him in deeper.

"Cum inside me," she whispered, "Please... cum inside me..."

When Chase finished, he held her body against his. They were both sweaty. Every inch of Caroline's body dripped — not only in sweat. She whimpered and struggled to break free from her binds. Caroline found herself grateful for the darkness. She didn't want to look at herself like this. She didn't want to be the woman naked and covered in sweat, succumbing to the animalistic desires of three grown country boys who loved as hard as they fucked.

But the lights would have to come on. And she'd lie in bed, exposed before them.

They were merciful. Bud undid her binds and rubbed her wrists, kissing her as Chase flicked the lights on. Chase carried her out of bed the way you'd carry a bride over the entrance to a new home. And he took her to their shower, closing the door behind him so it was just the two of them. Chase gazed at her like the sight of her aroused him and delighted him. Caroline looked away.

"You okay?" he asked.

She nodded. Why did she suddenly feel so ashamed? Chase came up to her and wrapped his arms around her waist. He leaned forward and whispered into her ear, "You... you are beautiful."

Caroline glanced up at him and he nodded.

"Beautiful, you hear that?"

"You don't think…" Caroline sucked in air.

Chase stroked her cheek. It hurt too much to ask the question. It hurt too much to think about it.

"Think what?"

He was sweet. Chase, despite the fight in him, could be gentle when necessary.

"You don't think I'm a slut, do you?"

Chase smiled and shook his head.

"I'm serious," Caroline pleaded. She didn't know what she wanted him to say. He'd given her the right answer, hadn't he?

"I love you. There's nothing wrong with what we're doing here. Nothing."

He hugged her and buried his nose in her neck. And his closeness reassured her more than a thousand affirmations ever would.

17

AFTERSHOCKS

AN EERIE CALM settled after an explosion. The factory fire, the failed racial unity mixer, and the unexpected visit from Jesse Clark had all blown up in one megalithic explosion that shattered all of them. Three mornings later and they were as close to normal as Caroline could expect.

She'd sent out another press release, put up signs around the neighborhood, and she'd gone door to door talking about campaign issues until her voice was hoarse and her shoes blackened with asphalt. The campaign didn't feel like it would ever end, and Caroline didn't know what would happen. The boys tried to get her to stop worrying about Jesse. Caroline didn't get how that was possible. Chase being out of work didn't help her worries much. Working and organizing workers had always been a part of Chase's life. Without it, Caroline didn't enjoy thinking of what trouble he'd get into.

Chase woke up late. Now he didn't have to organize his life around shifts, he didn't keep much of a schedule. Bud left for the office earlier, and Travis was studying for the LSAT at Caroline's office in the Landry barn. Chase stumbled downstairs in a pair of grey sweatpants with no shirt on. Caroline heard him shuffling upstairs and started frying eggs and bacon for him in the kitchen.

"Hey," Chase croaked.

"Hey."

"Cigarette."

Caroline opened the drawer next to the stove and tossed the pack to Chase. He caught it deftly with two fingers and pulled one out. His eyes were bloodshot, and he groaned as he lit up and sucked in the first relieving breath of tobacco.

"Hungry?"

"Desperately."

Chase sat and tapped his cigarette in the ashtray.

"Where is everyone?"

"It's 10. I shouldn't even be here."

"Hm. I hope you aren't here on my account."

Caroline faced him, the heat from the stove billowing behind her. He was the only reason she'd stayed home. Caroline worried about leaving Chase alone for long with everything going on. It wasn't good for him — so it wasn't good for any of them.

"I am."

"Oh."

"We're getting ready and we're going to the office. Travis is over there, studying for the LSAT."

"I don't... I don't want to do anything."

Caroline served his plate up and sat across the table, tapping away at a couple important emails on her phone.

"This isn't like you, Chase."

"I know. It's just... I'm not a guy who doesn't work. I've worked my entire life. When I wasn't working, I organized workers. And now... I have nothing. I'll run out of money and... I can't provide anything for you."

"That's not true."

"Travis is working towards law school. Bud's the mayor. And I... I've fucked up everything."

"Chase..."

He finished his cigarette and stuck another in his mouth. Caroline pulled it out.

"No. No more smoking. Eat proper food and then get dressed. I hate seeing you like this."

"I hate feeling like this. I need to make a change, Caroline. That's all I've ever wanted — to change society for the better. How the hell do we do that without giving up?"

"We keep fighting. We have to dig deep within ourselves to find the will to do it. We fight because we don't know how to do anything else."

"Do we ever have a chance at changing a town like this?"

"I don't know. It's why I'm running for Congress."

"I guess the best thing I can do is make sure you win."

"Not if Jesse Clark has his way."

"He won't have his way," Chase assured her. Caroline wanted desperately to believe him.

After breakfast and a quick shower, Chase had mostly pulled himself from his depressive funk. They arrived at the Landry barn to hear Travis hollering inside.

"WOOOO! YES! Damn right, motherfucker!"

Caroline swung the doors open while Chase stamped out a cigarette.

"Something exciting happen?"

Travis rushed Caroline and scooped her up, twirling her around as she squealed.

"Hell fucking yeah."

"What?!"

"I just got a perfect score on a practice test for the first time."

Caroline and Chase congratulated him.

"But I have more news... news that can't wait."

"What?"

"I know a guy on the force who can help us with something."

Caroline and Chase both visibly stiffened. Travis sighed.

"Look, I keep trying to tell you guys that not everyone on the force is a piece of shit. This guy wanted the DA to indict Zach — no offense, Chase — and he's against what Jesse Clark is doing in the county. I think he holds a grudge."

It appeared to Caroline that everyone who knew Jesse Clark well held a grudge against him. He was the sort of guy who you grew to hate if you got too close.

"How is this guy going to help us?" Chase steered Travis back to the subject at hand.

"Every weekend, Jesse takes a trip to a town three hours South of here. Every weekend for the past six years. He's hiding something. And this fella's going to find out. If Jesse Clark wants to blackmail us, we'll have something on him. Leverage."

Caroline couldn't stop herself from feeling gleeful. Blackmail and subterfuge weren't how she wanted to win the election. But she wouldn't use any information they found out against Jesse to win. She'd only use it to keep him off her back.

"Good," Chase said, "I'd better get some of your to-do list taken care of."

He kissed Caroline on the cheek and began work. Caroline hugged Travis tighter.

"All your news is amazing, but... I don't want the whole Jesse Clark mess to be more important than the LSAT."

"I'm going to kill it, Caroline. Harvard Law, here I come."

Caroline smiled, but she couldn't help but feel a pang of sadness. If Travis went to law school far away, they wouldn't see each other regularly anymore. Change could be fantastic for all of them, but if the four each went their separate ways, they couldn't all be together anymore. They couldn't share the weird magical bond they all had hundreds of miles apart.

Travis kissed Caroline and returned to work. His kiss landed on her lips so softly that it distracted her from feeling depressed. When she returned to Chase's desk to check on him, his cheeks were red and he slammed the work laptop shut.

"What?"

"Caroline. Did you know the county paper was running a poll?"

"Um. Yeah. The results come out next week."

"Right..."

Chase turned tomato red.

"Chase... Let me see that laptop."

He thumped his hand over it.

"Travis!" Caroline called, "Chase won't let me see the poll results."

Travis called from across the room.

"Poll results come out next week!"

"Shit," Chase muttered under his breath as Travis strode over to his side of the room. He might have been able to overpower Caroline, but he could counter both Travis and Caroline's willpower. Travis grabbed the laptop and opened it, slamming it shut immediately.

"Damn it, Owens."

"Told you."

"What are you two hiding from me! Let me see."

"No. Polls are stupid."

"They are not! Give me that laptop, Travis Montgomery."

Using his full name out loud distracted Travis long enough for Caroline to grab the laptop and open it. She slammed it shut.

"Fuck."

"Does Bud know about this yet?" Chase muttered.

"Fuck," Caroline rasped.

Travis wrapped his arm around her, but Caroline threw him off.

"Stop. I don't want your pity."

"It's not that bad," Chase said.

"Not you too? I'd expect Travis to coddle my feelings, but I didn't expect that from you."

"Caroline, we're trying to help," Travis whispered.

Caroline didn't want gentle. Not right now. She wanted to kick and scream and throw things. She wanted to blame them. If they hadn't been so damn distracting…

"I'm leaving."

"Caroline, wait!"

She stormed out of the office towards the stables next to the barn. She needed to breathe. She needed to get away from all of them. She yanked the stable doors open, hoping to be alone. But she found Bud, asleep on a bale of hay with his Stetson covering his face. Caroline didn't expect to see him there. He should have been in the office, not napping on a bale of hay. She yelped and roused Bud before she could stifle the little yell.

Bud's boots landed on the wood floor with a thud. Chase and Travis entered the stables after her, both of them equally surprised to see Bud Landry taking a mid-morning snooze.

"What the heck are you all doing in here?"

Caroline didn't know what else to do. She raced into the room and squeezed him. Bud… She needed to feel his body against hers. She needed his warmth. She buried her head in his chest as Bud wrapped his enormous arms around her.

"She's down in the polls by 15%," Travis said.

Bud said nothing. Maybe that's why Caroline wanted her arms around him so badly. Travis and Chase would say something to make her feel better. Bud would be quiet. He knew how to soothe animals, and he always figured people were

Redneck Rebellion

the same way. No words can say more than a good long hug. When Caroline pulled away, her face was wet.

"I've studied the election statistics for the past eight elections. No one has come back from a county poll gap that big."

Bud pulled her head close so she couldn't say anymore. He cupped her head in his giant palm and Caroline listened to his heart pumping slow and steady in his chest. The slow rhythm soothed her without him saying another word. Travis' phone buzzed. Travis ignored it, but the phone buzzed again.

"Sonofabitch."

"What?" Chase grunted.

Weren't there more important things than Travis' phone right now?

"Come see this, Owens."

Chase glanced at Travis' phone and whistled before exclaiming, "Holy shit."

"We've got what we need," Travis muttered.

Caroline pulled away from Bud and wiped her eyes. The disappointment had come as a surprise, but her plan wasn't to sit around and cry about it.

"What?"

"He got proof," Chase started, searching his pockets for a cigarette before giving up, "Jesse Clark has a child outside his marriage. And we believe not even his wife knows about this kid."

"What? No. You would all know if Jesse knocked someone up, wouldn't you? How the hell could he keep that a secret?"

"Contrary to popular belief, it's possible to keep a secret in a small town," Travis said. Caroline realized he had to be talking about their secret. And sure, they kept their secret in some respects, but Caroline was sure that most people figured out they weren't "roommates" and thought better not to ask.

Before they could celebrate, Travis' phone rang again. Caroline assumed it was the contact, but he handed the phone to Chase.

"It's your mom, Owens. She has to talk to you about something."

"She took Zach back into her home. I have nothing to say to my mama."

Caroline hadn't realized there was tension between them over Zach. She knew Mrs. Owens, and that she loved both her boys equally. She'd love them no matter what fucked up things they did, and Caroline couldn't hold it against the old woman. She hadn't realized that Chase took it all so... personally.

"You'll want to take this call, Owens."

Chase grabbed the phone. They talked for less than a minute. By the time Chase Owens hung up, his face lost all its color.

18

HE BETRAYED ME

CHASE HUNG up and staggered backward.

"What's wrong?"

"My mom. She didn't tell me. Fuck... Fuck, fuck, fuck."

"Chase," Travis urged, "talk to us, man. We're here to help."

"You can't help with this," Chase said hoarsely, "no one can. I can't even help with this. She... My mom has cancer."

"No," Caroline whispered.

"That's why she wanted Zach back. She was waiting for results from her biopsy... It can't be right. No. My ma... she's healthy. She's a healthy woman."

Caroline hurried over to him and she held him. Chase allowed her to hug him, but he was stiff, like giving into her hug would make his horrible news more real. Caroline ran her lips over the stubble on his face.

The last thing they needed right now was more bad news. And this hurt. They sat and talked together. But Chase couldn't sit around and talk. He had to do something.

"I'm going over there. I need to see her."

"Keep your hands off Zach Owens, no matter what he says to you," Bud said calmly.

Caroline would later recall thinking his addendum odd. With Chase gone, Travis leaned back in the chair, considering what they ought to do next. That was Travis. He hadn't met a problem that you couldn't solve — somehow.

"We have to do something."

"I am doing something," Bud answered, "But he won't like what it is."

"What are you talking about?"

"I need to get back to the office. Travis, you need to study. Caroline? Take some time. Don't let the poll results get you down. We'll nail Clark's ass to the wall. You have nothing to worry about."

"15% down. I don't know if I can recover from that."

"If there's one thing I've learned about you, it's that you pull off the unexpected."

Bud grabbed her cheeks and kissed her. Travis reluctantly returned to studying. He didn't have much time until the LSAT. Caroline researched, sent out email blasts asking for donations, and updated her campaign policy website. After that, she struck out downtown to talk to people about politics. Most people were friendly. Some weren't. That was the game of approaching strangers on the streets. They'd treat you downright nasty if they wanted nothing to do with you. They'd treat you worse if they were hardcore Jesse Clark supporters.

Chase didn't come back that night. Caroline understood. He wanted to be with his mother. He had to be with her right now. She still had so many questions. What kind of cancer did she have? Would she ever get better? How the hell would they pay for treatment? Bud worked late that night and Travis studied late for the LSAT, so Caroline had a rare night of falling asleep alone. It wasn't entirely terrible not to have hard dicks, stinky boys and giant arms pushing her around the bed. But it relieved her in the middle of the night when she stuck her butt back and it landed against Bud's chest. He dragged her close to him, like a caveman bringing in a hunk of meat from a hunt, and snuggled her close, burying his face in her hair and snoring like a growling tiger.

Caroline woke up earlier than all of them, made herself a bowl of oatmeal and walked to her parents' old house. She never surprised Caleb this early, but all the news about Chase and his mom... Caroline hastened, like she could get there and save her family members from pending medical doom. Getting sick made her nervous. Losing her family made her more nervous.

When was the last time she'd even called her parents since delving into this Congress thing? She texted them once in a while, but her parents weren't really "texting people".

Caroline knocked on the door. No answer. Weird. She called in through the cracked window on the porch.

"Caleb!" she yelled into the house, "Caleb! Are you in there?"

Caroline found the spare key and opened the house. Clothes. Everywhere. A pair of black heels. A black skirt. A white shirt. And a small magenta bra hanging on the staircase. She heard giggling upstairs and feet padding against the wood.

Caleb had a girl over. Shit. Caroline wandered into the kitchen. She'd write him a note if he had a girl over, and then she wouldn't have to bother him. She pulled a yellow notepad out of the kitchen drawer and searched the kitchen for a pen. Two pens were out of ink. She tossed them out and wandered into the dining room. Sometimes, Caleb would leave a working pen on the table. As Caroline found a silver pen with plenty of ink to leave a note, she heard footsteps coming downstairs. Fast.

Shit! She didn't mean to interrupt Caleb's date — or hook up. Caroline had every intention of sneaking off until she heard the voice. And she had to check if she was crazy. She turned the corner to the foot of the stairs and screamed. Caleb's date screamed too.

And then Caroline yelled, "LOTTIE FUCKING CALLOWAY?!"

Yelling was obviously the worst way to handle this. But she'd never sped up into a blind rage so quickly. Caleb struggled to throw his shirt on and stepped between Caroline and Lottie, like Caroline was an uncaged animal and Lottie was a damsel in need of protecting.

Lottie Calloway. She... Oh God... This couldn't be happening. Lottie Calloway hadn't just been involved in the drama surrounding Mayor Buchanan. She'd been a key player. A member of the town's undercover KKK chapter.

"ARE YOU FUCKING CRAZY!" Caroline yelled.

She picked up a vase off the dining table and hurled it at Caleb.

"THIS IS IT, ISN'T IT? THIS IS HOW JESSE FOUND OUT, YOU FUCKING IDIOT."

Caroline picked up a chair and threw it at her brother. Caleb caught the chair and Caroline's chest tightened as she expected him to throw it back. Instead, he turned to Lottie and brushed the blonde hair out of her face, kissing her lower lip and instructing her to return upstairs. Caroline wanted to push him down the stairs. She wanted to kill him. She'd never wanted to hurt someone that badly in her life.

Before Caleb could explain or say a single word she screamed, "Are you a fucking idiot, Caleb? Tell me. Because I need not remind you that woman is a RACIST."

"Stop it, Caroline. You're embarrassing yourself."

"I'm embarrassing myself? You're the one roleplaying as a SLAVE for a Klansman."

"Take that back."

"No! You're such a fucking idiot, Caleb. And the worst part of this is, I didn't see this coming. I... I need to go. I can't fucking deal with you right now."

"You're not perfect! Do you think everyone in this town hasn't figured it out yet? You're letting three white men run a train on you. So if anyone's acting like a slave, it's you."

Caroline couldn't help herself. She kicked Caleb. Hard. And then she pushed him. He fell over and Caroline kicked again.

"Caroline, stop it!"

"This is not the same thing!" Caroline huffed, kicking between each word.

Caleb probably could have stopped her from kicking him. He was larger and stronger than her. He eventually got up and yelled, "STOP."

Caroline froze. Only because she'd never heard Caleb raise his voice like that.

"What are you doing here?" he sneered, "This isn't any of your business."

"I came to check on you."

"Why?"

"I... You know she's the one who told Jesse about me and the boys, right? She's the only person..."

"You can't blame her."

"She's in the fucking KKK!"

"She changed!"

"I swear, Caleb. I thought you were the smart one. I thought... she goes against everything you stand for. Everything."

"Doesn't Travis go against everything you stand for? He was a cop."

"Unbelievable. You can't compare being a cop to being in a hate group."

"The klan didn't kill Ezra. Cops did."

"I don't know what this woman did to you, but you're fucked up in the head, Caleb. You realize you're defending the fucking KKK? The people who nearly…"

Caroline swallowed. She couldn't stand thinking about losing Caleb. What happened to him before had terrified her. Worry about losing him was what brought her here.

"I can handle myself, Caroline. Lottie and I have a good thing going. Well, we had. I'd better talk to her."

"I can't believe this is happening."

"Believe it. I let you have your personal life. You need to let me have mine."

Caroline left. She couldn't stand going around in circles with him over this again. She slammed the door — hard. How the fuck could Caleb sleep with Lottie Calloway, of all people? Had this town run out of people when she wasn't looking? And how dare he attack Travis?! Unlike Lottie, Travis was a good person. He cared about people. He might have been traditional, a little conservative, but he cared. That made all the difference.

Caroline stormed back towards the old Buchanan house. She'd never been so angry in her life. She hated the way it creeped around her neck and chest. She hated the way anger settled in her stomach. The only person who could share her anger would be Chase. He'd get it. But as Caroline approached her house, she heard the boys yelling. All of them.

She could hear them from the street which meant they must have all been pretty dang mad. She paused at the large willow tree with leaves that hung over the porch and she steeled herself for leaving one fight only to enter another.

"I'm going to shoot you in the fucking chest for this!"

"Put the damn gun down, Chase! You're drunk! And I won't let you kill your best friend."

That was Travis. The voice of reason. What the hell could Bud have done that would make Chase mad enough to shoot him. Travis' words hit Caroline. Chase had a gun. And he was pointing it at Bud. She had to get in there. They'd locked the door, so Caroline banged on it.

"LET ME IN!"

Chase opened the door, holding a pistol.

"Get inside."

"Not until you put the gun down."

"I'm not putting the gun down."

"Yes, you are."

"Really? Wait until you hear what Bud's done."

"Bud couldn't have done anything that would make it worth shooting him," Caroline tried to reason with him. Chase's face was so red, she didn't think she could make him see reason. She'd been that mad herself moments earlier. If she'd had a gun, Caroline hated to think what would have happened.

"He gave my brother a promotion. Zach Owens is officially the sheriff of Old Town."

Caroline paused for a moment. And then she said, calmly, "Chase. I'm going to need you to give me the gun."

"What?"

He hadn't expected that answer.

"I'm going to handle this."

Caroline looked serious. So serious that it scared the crap out of Chase.

"I'm not giving you the gun, Caroline."

"Why not?"

"Because... I can't."

Chase knew it was a shitty answer. Caroline lunged for the gun and he held it back, clicking the safety on as he held the gun behind his back.

"Give me the gun, right now."

Their argument went on too long. Bud grabbed the gun out of Chase's hand while he was distracted and unloaded the clip, letting the gun's guts fall to the ground.

"How about no one in this fucking house threaten to shoot me?"

Caroline pushed past them. Travis was pacing anxiously.

"Can we have a conversation without a fucking firearm?" Travis complained, "All of you know better."

Without Travis, they'd all fall apart, Caroline thought. His obsession with being rational could be painfully irritating, but at least he stopped them from all murdering each other.

"Why the hell did you give Zach a job?" Caroline snapped at Bud.

Fine, she wouldn't shoot him if they wouldn't let her, but she didn't have to be happy. Because this was bullshit. Total bullshit.

"I'm the mayor. And I don't need to explain myself."

"You'd better explain yourself," Caroline snapped, "Or I'll find one of the other scores of guns in here and finish this conversation the Southern way."

Bud raised an eyebrow.

"What the hell happened to you? I thought you went for a morning walk. You're madder than a wet hen."

"Caleb's nailing Lottie Calloway."

"What?!" the three boys yelled at once.

19

GET OFF MY PORCH

With Lottie Calloway, they could all end up on the same page. Chase broke their initial silence.

"Has your brother lost his fucking mind?"

"You tell me. He says she's changed."

Bud shook his head.

"I wish we could catch a fucking break."

"You caused half our problems giving Zach fucking Owens a job."

Bud's hand clenched into a fist.

"Damn it, Chase! I thought you'd be happy considering you're unemployed right now."

Travis' eyes got so wide, Caroline thought they'd spill out of his head. Chase stared at Bud like he wanted to kill him. Thankfully, this time, Bud had the gun.

"You watch your mouth," Chase snapped.

"What? I'm using my power to help your ungrateful ass considering you burned down your place of work."

"That's it. Caroline, get me the shotgun."

"No!" Caroline gasped. Now that she'd passed over her initial rage, she realized that killing Bud would be a bad idea.

She wondered whether it was such a good idea that they had an arsenal stashed in their house and joined Travis on his side of the room. He gave her a look that said, "Thank goodness you've seen reason."

"I gave your brother that job because your mother has cancer. And I know you want to bury that inside, but it's reality. I know what cancer can do to a family. I've lost two uncles to prostate cancer and an aunt to lung cancer. It's expensive. And I can't worry about petty problems. I'm the mayor of this town and I owe it to you to make sure that no matter what, your mother gets through this."

Chase's shoulders slumped. He might not have wanted to kill Bud anymore, but that didn't make it better.

"My mother doesn't need blood money to cure her cancer."

"Zach and I have an arrangement. He'll take care of her, or I'll break every bone in his body. Jesus. I never realized how little you three trust me. You think I'm the big hulking jock idiot Bud Landry, don't you?"

Caroline bit her lip. She didn't think Bud was stupid. Maybe he'd spent too much time on the football field, but what she'd always loved about him was the way he understood people. He'd become Mayor of the town. He'd learned quickly how to read, and even if he still made grammatical errors here and there, he could write riveting speeches too.

"Do you all think I'm stupid?" Bud repeated.

Caroline glanced at Travis and Chase, who glanced at their feet nervously.

"We do not!" Caroline asserted, glaring at them, "We know you aren't stupid, Bud. I'm sorry we didn't trust you."

Bud's fists unclenched.

"I don't want us to fight. Nothing gets better when we're fighting. Nothing will ever get better in this town if we don't stop fighting."

"I don't want to spend the rest of my life indebted to Zach when he represents everything I'm against."

"You'll find a way out," Travis said, thumping Chase on the back. Chase cracked a half-hearted smile. They were all desperate to see the good in this.

"There's too much going wrong," Caroline muttered, "We need a win."

Bud grinned.

"What?" Travis asked, smirking. Bud had one of those contagious smiles that could probably make you laugh out loud at a funeral.

"Whiskey. Dominoes. And... her."

Caroline touched her chest.

"Me?!"

"Yes. You make everything better. Everything."

"Let's start with whiskey," Chase said.

"I'm having a bottle. Glasses for you two?"

Caroline smacked Chase's forearm.

"You can't drink an entire bottle of whiskey."

"Oh, yes, I can. It's that kind of day."

"Don't we have too many problems to solve to sit around getting drunk and... playing dominoes?"

"That's exactly why we need to drink."

Caroline looked to Travis to see if she'd have one voice of reason on her side. He shrugged.

"Fuck it. They're right. When you're staring down a barrel of a gun, that's all you can say. Fuck it."

Chase returned to the room with two bottles of whiskey and three tumblers pinched between his fingers, dangling precariously as he jumped and clicked his heels together.

"Let's get this party started."

"It's not a party. It's a little drink and dominoes."

Bud grabbed one glass and opened the whiskey so furiously, Caroline thought he'd snap the bottle's neck. He tilted the bottle into his mouth before shakily poured glasses for Travis and Caroline. Like Chase, he opted to drink straight from the bottle, his Adam's apple bobbing furiously as he chugged whiskey like it was water.

"Woo!"

Bud cheered, "To Caroline! For bringing us all together."

Chase added, "To Bud! For looking out for me."

"To Travis," Caroline added, "For reminding me to let loose once in a while."

Travis grinned and hugged Chase with an enormous bear hug.

"To Chase. For bringing the fire to our family."

Caroline's stomach flipped. Family. They might not have a traditional relationship, but they were family. Bud pulled out the dominoes, and they crowded around their coffee table. Caroline struggled to maintain a reasonable drinking pace once she drank with the boys. Not only were they bigger than her, but they grew up on moonshine the way some kids grew up on Oatmeal or Cheerios.

Caroline's phone rang after Chase won the first and then the second round of dominoes.

"I don't recognize the number."

Travis picked the phone up.

"Could be about the campaign."

He answered the phone, "Hello, Caroline Coulson's campaign manager."

The rest of their tipsy bunch struggled to suppress their laughter.

"I see. I see. Well... Caroline is more than up to the challenge."

Now Caroline wondered what the hell Travis was talking about. He continued.

"Use the email address you have. Any place, any time. She'll be ready."

He hung up.

"Who the hell were you talking to?"

"Jesse Clark's campaign manager. He's challenging you to a public town hall debate."

"What?!"

Caroline tried to stand up quickly, but she was too drunk and she flopped back down, falling straight into Bud's lap. His arms immediately wrapped around hers and he held her close to keep her from falling over — or from reaching across the table and punching Travis in the face.

"You're not in a one-down position anymore," Travis pointed out calmly, "We have dirt on him. And if he tries to play dirty, we'll let the bastard know that we can play dirty too."

"I don't want to drag a child into this," Caroline warned.

"We won't," Travis reassured her.

Chase and Bud noticeably left out their reassurances. Bud pushed Caroline's hair off her neck and ran his tongue over her flesh. She giggled and leaned back into his enormous, firm chest. They'd never make it to a third round of dominoes, would they? Caroline turned around and scrambled around Bud, her legs stretching wide as she straddled him. He was almost too much bigger than her for her to straddle properly. Bud grasped the smallest part of her waist, squeezing Caroline close to him and pressing her body against his.

Bud enjoyed that soft feeling of her chest pressing into his and the way her body teased his awake with the gentlest touching. He needed her body. Urgently.

Bud rolled her onto her back and stripped her naked. Caroline squealed and then moaned as his enormous member intruded into her wetness. She was soaked. Liquor had that effect on her. Liquor also made Bud impatient, and it made him fuck hard. Really hard. Caroline cried out as he buried himself inside her to the hilt.

He clutched her hips as he entered her, watching the gigantic head of his cock form a knot inside her mound as he withdrew. He was enormous, and each stroke brought Caroline close to an intense climax. She didn't have to wait long before she came.

Bud pulled out of her and flipped her onto his stomach, peeling his shirt off and then sliding into her from behind. His hips slammed into Caroline's ass and she moaned and gripped their carpet as Bud fucked her from behind, pressing his enormous weight into her as he took her hard and fast. Bud groaned when he came and Caroline grabbed his face, kissing him, not wanting him to let go. Bud didn't have much of a choice. The moment he pulled away from her. Chase and Travis lifted her onto the couch.

Her tummy pressed into the couch as Chase positioned his hardness behind her and Travis coaxed Caroline's mouth open with his engorged member. She closed her eyes and allowed him to slide into her mouth while Chase took her from behind. She lost herself in the smell of men and whiskey and the pleasure mounting between her legs. Travis gently thrust into her mouth while Chase pumped into Caroline hard.

Having two of her hot men filling her mouth and pussy drove Caroline wild. She came again. She couldn't stop herself from climaxing now. Each thrust Chase drove between her legs caused another climax.

"I love that tight pussy," Chase moaned in her ear, "You have the perfect fucking pussy for my cock. Do you like when I fuck you like this?"

"Oh, yes..." Caroline whimpered.

Travis moved away from her mouth as Chase came inside her. Travis flipped her onto her back and slid between her

Redneck Rebellion

legs unceremoniously. Chase crouched next to Caroline's ear and whispered, "How does Travis's cock feel? Do you like his big cock inside you?"

"Yes... Oh yes..."

Chase licked her earlobe. Bud had her toes in his mouth. And Travis made love to her deep and slow on the couch. Caroline lost track of her orgasms. They couldn't allow anyone to break them up. She couldn't lose this. Jesse Clark would never understand. And it didn't matter if he understood. When Travis finished, Caroline held him on top of her. She didn't want to let any of them go, but she needed to hold Travis. She wanted to feel his warmth. His sensitive touch.

"Don't you two fall asleep. We're heading upstairs for more."

Bud and Chase prodded them upstairs. Caroline wished she'd been exhausted after taking three attractive men between her legs, but they'd only warmed her up. It wasn't enough. She craved more. More... When Bud spread her thighs again, Caroline closed her eyes and let him have her again.

By the time they'd all had her again for the night, they were properly exhausted and properly stinking drunk. In the morning when Caroline awoke, sun spilling into their bedroom forced her to wonder whether God made the sun brighter as they slept. One step out of the room and all the previous night's liquor sloshed around in her stomach.

Caroline fumbled into the bathroom for some Advil and winced down each step as she prayed someone was cooking eggs in the kitchen. No one was home. How late was it? She grabbed a plate for the scrambled eggs the boys left in the pan and went outside with it to see if she could find Chase smoking on the porch.

She didn't. But there was someone sitting on her porch, and he was the last person Caroline wanted to see. If she hadn't been so nauseous, she would have thrown her plate of eggs at Jesse Clark.

"What are you doing here?" she groaned.

"I'm here to talk business. I stopped by your office, but you weren't there."

"So you came to my house? Get off my damn property, Jesse."

"I came to talk to you about the debate."

"What is there to talk about?"

"I want to raise the stakes."

"Aren't the stakes high enough?"

"Listen, Caroline. I have help that you might not expect."

"Your little informant, Lottie Calloway?"

Jesse grinned.

"Ah."

He didn't expect her to know, did he? Caroline forked some of her scrambled eggs into her mouth. At least if she threw up, she could aim it at Jesse.

"Lottie isn't the only help I have. But we had to cut her loose due to her... unsavory affiliations."

"I didn't think you were above letting a Klansman help you."

"You think so poorly of me, then?"

"Worse," Caroline snapped.

"I'm not as horrible as you think, Miss Coulson."

"Prove it. Get off my porch."

20

DEBATE

CAROLINE AND JESSE'S debate was the same night Travis was supposed to get his LSAT scores. He had the envelope by mid-morning, but refused to open it until the debate ended. The boys threatened to get rid of Jesse once they heard about his indecent proposal. But Caroline calmed them down.

She couldn't figure out what the hell Jesse's game was, but if he wanted to intimidate her, it wouldn't work. After helping Travis prepare for the LSAT, preparing for the debate had been next on Caroline's agenda. Bud tried to work his connections to find out who the debate moderator was. Chase spent a lot of time over at his mom's house, and when he came home, he was always pissed about his brother. They couldn't spend over ten minutes in a room with each other. Zach wasn't always the one to start fights, but if he saw an opportunity to push his brother, he would.

Chase couldn't make it the night of the debate. His mom struggled to recover from one of her rounds of radiation and needed both Zach and Chase. Caroline got ready with her campaign team at the Landry barn. Bud rehearsed her talking points with her. Travis gave more general advice.

"Don't let him talk over you. And don't let him win."

Studying for the LSAT had given him an edge with logical reasoning, and he shared tips for debating with Caroline. They were worrying, fretting like mother hens, and for once, it felt good to be the one worried about instead of the one doing all the worrying.

As they drove over to the town hall, Bud cleared his throat.

"I ought to tell you, I found out who's moderating the debate."

"Who?"

"It's Buchanan."

"What!?"

"He's the link between Lottie Calloway and Jesse Clark."

"You waited to tell me until now!?" Caroline hissed.

"I had to tell you when I knew you couldn't kill me."

Travis complained, "Don't you think this will get her off her game?"

"Nope. Because if there's one person Caroline hates in this town more than Jesse Clark, it's former mayor Tommy Lee Buchanan. And I kept Lottie working in my office for far too long. I'm putting an end to that. Tonight."

"Is this because of the Caleb thing?"

Caroline knew the answer to her question before she asked it.

"Yes. I'm done letting these motherfuckers run Old Town. I promised to bring change, and I've done my part. But it's not enough. Time to pull out all the stops. No more Mr. Nice Guy."

Caroline giggled. She didn't think Bud could stop being a giant teddy bear. But she appreciated his willingness to try. Buchanan would be here tonight, along with anyone from the town who cared about the Congressional district. Bud was right that she couldn't worry about Buchanan now. There were more important things to worry about.

Caleb sat in the reserved seats for the family, but Caroline didn't make eye contact with him when she entered. She'd been reeling over the Lottie Calloway incident and ignored over fifteen of her brother's phone calls. What right did he have to call her after everything? He'd fucked up. Caroline didn't want to hear about all the ways Lottie changed. She still helped Jesse. She still worked with Buchanan. And this was Caleb's fault.

Backstage, Caroline could also see Jesse Clark's family. His first family. Travis' revelation about Jesse's secret meant he'd cheated on the blond woman with coiffed hair. He had four kids too. Jeez. Caroline wondered when someone her age would have had time to have so many kids. She wanted kids, but could she really afford to have kids before making it to Congress?

She had dreams, and when a kid would come, a kid would come. But four kids? Caroline sensed Jesse behind her before he put his hand on her shoulder. Bud cleared his throat and scowled, and Jesse shrunk back.

"Miss Coulson. I wanted to wish you good luck in tonight's debate."

Caroline took his hand, intentionally shaking limply. Jesse cupped her hand with both hands.

"My offer still stands, Miss Coulson. You lose, you climb into my bed."

"And what do I get if I win?"

"I can make that 15% dip in your popularity disappear."

"Let's get one thing straight, Jesse. I'm not like you. I'll win this debate. And then I'll win this election. Fair and square."

He pulled away and grinned.

"Great. Maybe when you win... we can get off on a better foot."

Caroline was convinced this was some game he was playing. There was no getting off on a better foot for them. She wanted nothing to do with Jesse Clark now or after the race.

"I'm not interested. You have a wife and kids to take care of. After the election, I'd rather go back to never knowing about you."

"You know how to hurt a man's ego."

"I don't care about your ego. And Jesse? Make one more threat to me and my roommates, and I'll end you. Understood?"

"Loud and clear, Miss Coulson."

They entered the debate stage to applause. Caroline cast a glance at the moderator's table and looked at the man who nearly ruined her life for the first time in months. Tommy Lee Buchanan had gone white. His hair nearly matched the color of the stupid linen suit he constantly insisted on wearing. He smiled at Jesse, but the look he reserved for Caroline Coulson was one of pure evil.

He was still wildly popular in the town. And his help behind the scenes would have made Jesse win over the old-fashioned county voters. Buchanan stroked his chin as he considered her. Jesse flashed Caroline a smile, but she stared straight ahead. She didn't have to win over Jesse, and she didn't have to win over Buchanan. She had to win over the voters in their county. No distractions. No excuses.

Buchanan gave his introductory words. Caroline read her introductory speech, and Jesse read his. He was good. Too good. Caroline wondered if he'd written the speech himself. Buchanan posed his first question.

"To the candidate Miss Caroline Coulson, we have this submitted question. Why do you promote anti-white policies that divide this town and further oppress your people?"

Redneck Rebellion

Caroline prepared to play hardball, but she hadn't been prepared for Buchanan to play this rigged game. There was nothing like keeping the peace with the three boys to prepare her for the unexpected. Caroline cleared her throat and answered his question.

"First, Mister Buchanan. My policies are not anti-white. The purpose of seeking justice is not to foment racial divisions, but to eliminate the barriers that prevent us from seeing each other's humanity. I worked diligently on Mayor Landry's campaign and unless you all remember a different Mayor Landry, he looks white to me."

That drew a laugh from the crowd. Caroline gripped her podium and continued. I'll win this, she thought, I'll fucking win this because I want it more than Jesse does. Caroline finished her statement and Jesse offered a rebuttal. Caroline wondered if his rebuttal was intentionally weak. He barely attacked her policies. He just asked her for proof that her policies wouldn't harm the people of their congressional district, a question that wasn't difficult for Caroline to answer.

She grew livid when Buchanan posed a question to Jesse.

"Mr. Clark, the audience question for you tonight is a tough question. As our congressional representative, what color suits will you wear in the House of Representatives to uphold our towns' traditions of valor and Southern masculinity."

"Excuse me?" Caroline interrupted, "Does that question seem fair?"

"If you interrupt again, Caroline, we will have to dock points."

Caroline's mouth hung open, but she didn't say a word. Jesse smirked and responded. Unbelievable. This had been their plan all along, hadn't it? Jesse rigged the debate so there was no way in hell Caroline could win. She tried to form a rebuttal, but how the hell could she debate suit colors?

The questions went back and forth like that.

"Miss Coulson, why do you affiliate with known anti-white terrorists?"

"Mister Clark, do you remember the last big Virgil football game?"

"Miss Coulson, your proposal to raise minimum wage obscures a dangerous agenda. Explain that?"

"Mister Clark, where would you draw the lines to re-segregate the town into sections?"

Caroline wanted to scream into the mic, but as Tommy Lee Buchanan fixed to ask her another question, a loud buzzing noise distracted Caroline. A bee. How the hell did a bumblebee get in here?

"Could you repeat the question?"

Jesse Clark attempted to wave the bee off, but it landed in the tangle of blond curls on his head. Caroline stifled a laugh as Mayor Buchanan repeated his question.

"Miss Coulson, how do you plan on ensuring you look after more than a pro-black terrorist's agenda?"

"Moderator, are you calling me a terrorist?"

"JESUS FUCKING SHIT CHRIST FUCK!" Jesse yelled.

He turned red. His wife rushed up to the stage, scrambling up awkwardly with an epi-pen.

"STAB ME DON'T FUCK AROUND MATILDA!" he yelled as his face swelled.

Caroline clasped her hand to her mouth. She couldn't have asked for a better way out of the question. Mayor Buchanan rose and quickly tried to regain control of the situation, not an easy feat. The debate ended unceremoniously and with no official winner declared. Jesse sat on a chair waiting for his stings to die down. Caroline used the free time to talk to people face to face.

"He didn't treat you fair," A gruff man with a Duck Dynasty style beard and a cowboy hat said, "I can't stand these government pricks. We need genuine people in Washington. People who care."

"Thanks. What's your name, sir?"

"Sorry, that's my private business."

"Of course."

Caroline talked to a few more people. Bud and Travis spoke on her behalf too. She walked to the back of town hall to go to the bathroom. Talking on stage made her nervous, which made her want to go. Once she finished, Caroline opened the bathroom door and saw Jesse leaning against the wall.

"The swelling on your face went down," Caroline said, trying not to delight in his misery, but failing miserably.

"Yes."

"Good."

"Caroline, wait."

"What?"

"I didn't plan for Buchanan to go so hard on you."

"Sure you didn't."

"I looked like an idiot."

"You did. Thanks to that bee."

"I could have died," He protested, like Caroline had some reason to care.

"So?"

"Listen, I know I've been a jerk. I know you think the worst of me. But I'm not that bad."

"Really? You've called black people thugs. You're racist. You stand for segregationist policies. You're exactly as bad as I think."

"Didn't Travis tell you about what he found?" Jesse whispered.

"Yes. And that's the only reason you haven't fucked up my life."

"My other kids are black."

Kids?! Caroline knew about one. But she hadn't known about the others.

"What does that have to do with me?"

"I'm doing this for a reason, Coulson. I... I hope one day I can explain."

"I don't care if you do. Listen, I barely know you and what I know, I don't like."

"That's too bad. Because... you're exactly the woman I want to be with. I want to be with you."

"You have a wife," Caroline hissed, "And I'm spoken for."

"You're fucking three guys. What's one more?"

"You don't get it."

"No. I don't."

"Don't waste your time trying. The answer is no. It'll always be no."

"I could fall in love with you, Caroline."

Caroline's back stiffened. She wanted to slap him, but she couldn't bring herself to move.

A whimper at the end of the hall startled both of them. Shit. Holy shit. Jesse's wife heard everything.

21

TAKE CARE OF MOM

MRS. CLARK WASN'T the only one to overhear the confession. Travis and Bud stood behind Caroline, arms folded, ready to make trouble. Jesse turned white.

"You'd best be leaving," Bud warned, in a low voice like the one he'd used with the animals on the farm.

"I... I... oh, fuck."

He disappeared. Caroline didn't know what to make of it. Jesse was crazy, obviously. He couldn't love her. He didn't know her. He was racist. He was her opponent in the race. Travis put his hand on Caroline's shoulder.

"Come on. We'd better go."

"What the hell was he thinking?" she mumbled.

"He wasn't thinking," Travis said, "We ought to tell that wife of his what he's up to."

Bud glanced over at the pair, arguing on the other side of the town hall together and grunted.

"Looks like they're talking already."

"We'd better go home. Tonight was a disaster."

"Don't lose hope," Bud gestured.

Caroline appreciated his vote of confidence, but she

couldn't will herself not to worry given how poorly she'd done. She had the hardest questions, and Buchanan questioned Jesse like it was obvious he'd won the election. Caroline knew she was behind in the polls and how impossible that would be to come back from. Now there was Jesse's creepy confession to worry about. The hair on the back of her neck stood up when she thought about it. Why had he sounded so earnest?

Chase waited up for them on the porch. Zach ended his shift and would spend the night looking after their mother. She was sick and Chase smoked three cigarettes on the porch worrying about her. He rose when he saw the three walking home.

"Good news, I hope?"

"Ehh," Caroline answered non-committally. They didn't have good news or bad news. Chase dropped his cigarette into the ashtray and wrapped his arms around Caroline. Good news or bad news, she was home. Caroline let his tobacco soaked clothing engulf her, and she buried her nose in Chase's neck. He smelled incredible. Always. And he held her like he didn't want to let go. Sure, the debate had been important, but Chase was more important.

Chase clutched the back of her head. Bud swung the front door open.

"How was it tonight?" Caroline whispered to him.

"Awful. I hate seeing her like that. She don't deserve to be sick. And I fucking hate seeing my brother every goddamn day and knowing I could put a bullet in his head for what he's done."

"Don't say that," Caroline whispered, "If you kill him, you'll go to jail and I can't live without you here."

"You have Travis and Bud," Chase muttered.

"It wouldn't be the same. I love all three of you. Equally. I can't lose any of you."

Chase pulled away and laced his fingers with Caroline's. Travis followed them inside. Chase insisted everyone take their mind off cancer talk and talk about the debate. Caroline wasn't sure the debate would calm him down. Chase lived for politics. And without work, he'd been restless. Itching for a fight.

Which was why Caroline decided not to bring up the Jesse thing. Travis wisely kept it to himself. But Bud, after an enormous swig of whiskey, blurted out, "And then that stinking musk rat Jesse Clark done confessed his love to Caroline in front of everybody."

Chase snapped, "He did what!?"

"He told her, right in front of his wife and God, that he was in love with her. That man is dumber than a rooster."

"Why the hell would he say something like that?"

Chase glared at Caroline, like she knew, like she'd goaded him on. Caroline glared right back.

"Why are you looking at me like that?"

"I dunno. Did you encourage him?"

"Chase! Why the hell would you say something like that?!"

"Did you?"

"Chase!" Travis snapped, "She didn't encourage him. And she's had a hell of a night."

"What about Jesse? Did you two knock his teeth in?"

Chase glanced from Travis to Bud, and both of them averted their gaze. He groaned.

"If I'd been there, I would have knocked him the fuck out."

"You can't put a fist through everything you have a problem with," Travis said.

Chase punched him. And Travis hit back. And soon they were rough housing like they were teenagers again. Mostly,

Chase punched Travis while Travis pleaded for his safe release. Caroline stifled her laughter.

"Can you two knock it off?"

When it came to the boys and rough housing, she had to be the responsible one. Travis pushed Chase off him and they reached for whiskey glasses, clinking them together before giving up their fight.

"We ought to mess with him," Chase said, "I don't know how but... Caroline's taken. Got it?"

Again, he looked at her. Caroline balked.

"Why are you looking at me like I want Jesse Clark or considered his stupid offer even for a minute?"

"What offer?"

"Um..."

"Caroline?!"

"He said that if I lost the debate, I should sleep with him. He tried to make a bet."

Bud growled.

"I swear I hate that motherfucker..."

"I said no!"

Travis called her name sharply. Caroline shrugged.

"I didn't think it was a big deal."

"How many times has this animal come on to you?" Travis grumbled.

"A lot. I don't know. I thought it was some stupid tactic to throw me off my game or get me to admit to... you know... this."

"He's a fucking idiot," Bud growled.

"If he comes near her one more time..." Travis muttered.

"No," Chase said, "He doesn't get more chances."

"Can you three at least wait until after the election before unleashing some evil plan?"

Chase reached for a fresh cigarette. Travis looked up at the ceiling. Bud turned red.

"Hello?!" Caroline yelled, "I need some agreement here."

"Fine."

They all muttered the word at once and under their breaths in a way far from convincing. Their night ended like it usually did. A heated conversation turned into a heated kissing session. Caroline kissed Chase on the couch and he didn't bother waiting before pressing her onto her back and entering her.

Bud carried her upstairs. And they made love until all four of them suffered too much exhaustion to move another muscle. Travis snuggled in Caroline's arm, curling himself into a nice little spoon. Bud slept upside down so his enormous toes were far too close to Caroline's face. And Chase slept on the other side of her, wrapping his arms around her so he formed a snuggly Caroline sandwich with Travis.

In the morning, Caroline woke up first. She had to check the morning news reports of the town hall debate commentary. She snuck out of bed and made herself a bowl of oatmeal while checking the commentary on her phone. The local and county news sources split down the middle. Caroline wandered out onto the porch with a cup of black coffee when she noticed a familiar face approaching their house.

She tried to hurry back inside before he noticed her, but it was too late.

"Caroline, wait! Don't run."

Zachariah Owens jogged up to the porch. Caroline set her coffee down and folded her arms. Zach had a dark, piercing gaze and a heavy brow.

"What do you want?"

"Is my brother awake?"

"No. But if he was, he wouldn't want to talk to you."

"Can you get him for me? Please?"

"What are you doing here, Zach? Other people in this

town might be afraid to say it, but you're a monster. You shot a man in cold blood and got away with it."

Zach's face turned pale. He wasn't armed, but Caroline couldn't stop herself from shaking. Zach was the old Old Town. He represented hate and terror and he wanted that hate and terror dragged into the present. Zach licked his lips.

"I don't want to change how you think about me."

"Good. Because I won't."

"But my brother... He's my blood. And I need to talk to him."

The front door opened, and Caroline's trembling settled. Chase had a cigarette in his mouth and he glared at Zach.

"What the fuck are you doing at my house?"

"We need to talk. Alone."

"Whatever you say to me, you say in front of Caroline."

"This isn't any of her business," Zach protested.

"Caroline. Come on, let's go inside."

"Wait!"

Chase paused before the door and lit up.

"Tell me what you want from me, Zach. And make it quick."

"I want to make up for the wrong I've done you."

"Me? What about Bianca Mayfair? Have you made up with her for killing her brother?"

"She... I've... I've tried to talk to her."

"Big surprise she doesn't want to talk to a murderer."

"It's my fault," Zach muttered.

"Yes. It is."

"No," Zach said hoarsely, "It's my fault mom has cancer."

Caroline couldn't help but stare at him with her mouth hanging open. Zach was... crying. Tears spilled from his eyes and he turned red before letting out a hulking sob. Had it been anyone else, she might have felt sorry for him. But he was a killer. He killed Ezra Mayfair, and he'd get away with it.

How dare he act like Mrs. Owens' cancer had anything to do with evil that was his to carry? Chase shared Caroline's lack of sympathy.

"It's not your fault," Chase grumbled, "Luck of the draw."

"I know you don't believe me, but this... I'm not the same person I was. I'm going to make right by everyone I've hurt."

"Good fucking luck."

"Please, Chase... you're my brother. That means something to me."

"I wish it meant more to you before you killed a man."

"I'm taking mom out west. I got a job with a private security firm in Los Angeles, looking after celebrities, and they know about my background. The pay is ten times better and I'm going to put every cent into treating her cancer."

"You're moving her away from her friends? From everything she knows?" Chase yelled.

"Please... I need money. Mom needs care. She'll only be out west for a while until I get on my feet. Then I'll send her back here and keep sending her money. I wanted to tell you not to fret about work because I'll take care of her. I owe her that much and more."

"Damn right, you do."

"And I need to talk to you about the upcoming election."

Zach glanced nervously at Caroline. Chase reminded him, "Anything you say to me, you say to Caroline. She's my family."

Zach bristled, but he didn't exactly have the upper hand. He shoved his hands in his pockets and continued.

"I already did what I had to. I took care of Buchanan and Lottie Calloway. They won't look for trouble with you anymore. They're done helping Jesse Clark. Trust me. I've known both of them a long time, and I know both of them well. Consider them taken care of."

"What does that mean?" Caroline blurted out.

She'd attempted respectful silence, but she couldn't help herself anymore. How the hell had Zach managed to "take care of" the two largest influences on Jesse Clark's campaign — aside from his District Attorney father.

"Don't worry about that. And I don't expect you to like me. I just... I need to put things right in my life. And this is the only way I know how."

"When are you leaving with mom?"

"Next week. Before the election."

"Zach? I don't want to talk to you again. I can barely stand to see your face. But if you think it'll get you right with God, take care of our mother. And if I hear from her, you've faltered even a little, I'll do what I've wanted to for a long time."

The threat hung heavy in the air. Zach licked his lips and wiped away his tears. He knew what Chase meant, and he knew that his brother had the same heart that he did: a wild stallion's heart, with the capacity to kill if he had to.

"Goodbye, brother," Zach said.

"Take care of mom."

"I will. I promise."

22

WE REGRET TO INFORM YOU

Travis scored perfectly on his LSATs. All his studying paid off, and he sent his scores off with his law school applications. From that point forward, they'd play a waiting game. Everyone's nerves were frazzled before election night. Bud spent most of his time outside of work with the horses. He rode until he worked up a big sweat and came home late. Travis celebrated his LSAT scores, but now worried incessantly about law school. He'd applied to Harvard and Caroline knew it was his dream school, but she couldn't bear the thought of Travis living all the way in Boston.

How had he lived in Old Town, working as a cop, while she'd gone away to university? When she was younger, she could have imagined leaving them. But now, the thought of the four of them separating made Caroline ill. What was worse was the thought she might only have one of them left. If she won the Congressional seat, she'd have to move to Washington, D.C. Chase was the only one who could move.

With his mother and brother out west, Chase doubled

down his efforts to find a new job. The cops finished their investigation of the factory fire and determined the entire thing an accident. Caroline didn't believe in the accident story, but Chase and her brother were no longer on the hook. As for her brother...

Caroline hadn't seen Caleb since the Lottie Calloway incident. If Zach Owens had been honest, she wouldn't see much of Lottie Calloway at all. Caroline thought that would bring her peace, but it didn't contribute much to her state of mind.

There was still plenty to worry about. Jesse's stupid confession. Election night. Her relationship with her brother. And the future. Caroline sat on the porch drinking whiskey alone the Monday before election night. Chase had a job interview in Virgil. Travis was on the phone with his dad having an unusually calm conversation. Bud was out riding at the ranch. They all handled stress in their own ways and this time, Caroline chose whiskey. If Chase had been around, she might have cracked and asked him for one of his cigarettes. She could use anything to take the edge off.

Caroline winced as the whiskey burned down her throat. Tomorrow evening, they'd count the votes until midnight, and then she'd know if all her hard work had been for something. If she didn't win the election, she'd have to hit the pavement like Chase and find another job. Could she even successfully get a job around here?

All the tension from Ezra Mayfair's death hadn't evaporated. Parts of Old Town treated Zach Owens like a hero. They claimed that Ezra must have done something wrong and if he hadn't, Zach Owens couldn't be blamed because he had a tough job. Caroline heard people discussing it at the cafe sometimes. And she'd freeze, numbing over as her old neighbor's murder became the subject of a hypothetical discussion.

Redneck Rebellion

The latest informal poll slated Jesse Clark to win the election. Caroline closed the 15% gap by a few points. Now she only trailed him by 8% of the votes. Bud wanted her to celebrate the good news, but he knew the way she did that it would take a miracle to overcome those odds. The postman sauntered up the past of the old Buchanan house, waving and smiling as he saw Caroline nestled on the porch swing.

"Good afternoon, Jebediah. Anything for us, here?"

"Yes, ma'am."

Jebediah's red hair glinted auburn in the sun as he leaned forward.

"What you drinking?" he asked as he handed Caroline a stack of envelopes and a small parcel.

"Bud's moonshine whiskey. It's strong."

"Oh, Mr. Landry does a fine job of bottling whiskey. When we were young-uns his younger brother would skim some off the top and sell it at school."

"Better not tell Mrs. Landry, she still has it in her to whoop him something fierce."

Jebediah grinned.

"Yes, ma'am. I wanted to tell you before I go. This is the first time I'll be voting for Congress. And I'll be voting for you."

Caroline smiled and waved goodbye before sifting through the stack of envelopes. Harvard University. Caroline pulled out the envelope addressed to Travis with the Harvard insignia on it. She set it aside, energy coursing through her fingertips. They'd accept him. And then it would all be over. They wouldn't be a "foursome" anymore. Caroline kept sifting through the envelopes.

Mrs. Owens sent her son a postcard in loose, loopy script. Bills, bills, bills. Most of the bills came addressed to Bud, and Caroline set them aside. Then she saw another letter to

Travis. Yale University. She set the letter from Yale on top of the Harvard letter.

The last letter in the stack was in a magenta envelope with Caroline's name printed on it in all capital letters. She opened the letter.

STAY AWAY FROM MY HUSBAND, WHORE.

Caroline didn't need a signature, or an address to know who sent that one. Caroline folded the letter and placed it back in the envelope. Mrs. Clark had nothing to worry about — well, she married a maniac, but aside from that. She hadn't seen Jesse Clark since the debate night, and Caroline had no interest in seeing him again.

He'd win the election, have something smug and racist to say, and then reveal his true intentions for his bizarre confession. He thought she was that stupid and easy to trick. She didn't have any trouble understanding how Jesse had ignited even gentle Bud Landry's ire. He was worse than insufferable.

As Caroline crumpled the pink envelope in a tight fist, Travis emerged from the house holding onto his cell phone.

"Hey," he said, "What you got there?"

"A threatening letter. And mail for you."

She handed Travis the letters from Harvard and Yale, moving her stack of envelopes aside so Travis could sit next to her on the porch swing.

"I'd offer you whiskey, but I finished it."

"That's okay," Travis said, "I... I don't need it. I need to rip the band-aid off."

"They'll accept you. They have to. You got a perfect score."

"Law school is more than a perfect score," Travis said.

He could be so obnoxiously logical sometimes, Caroline thought.

"If you don't want to, I'll help," she offered.

Travis shook his head and slid his thumb beneath the envelope flap, sliding it along slowly as he opened it.

"Dear Mr. Montgomery, We regret to inform you..."

He read the Yale rejection letter. Caroline put his arm around his shoulder. Travis turned red, but he said nothing except, "Aw. Shucks."

"I'm sorry, Travis."

"It's okay. I didn't have a shot at getting into Yale."

"They're the ones who missed out."

Travis scoffed.

"Here goes nothing."

Caroline kissed his cheek.

"Not nothing," she whispered, "You poured your heart into this."

Travis peeled the second envelope open.

"Dear Mr. Montgomery, We regret to inform you..."

After the first letter, he didn't have to read the entire thing out loud.

"Fuck," Travis muttered, crumpling the letter in a tight fist. Yale might not have got to him, but the Harvard rejection did.

"Fuck," he breathed again.

Caroline kissed his shoulder.

"There are other schools."

"Harvard was my dream."

Caroline took his hand and Caroline let her squeeze it. Travis bit his lip, swallowing his disappointment as he ran his thumb over the back of Caroline's hand.

"I'm glad you were here. I'd better tell Chase and Bud."

"I'm sorry."

"Don't apologize. You weren't the one to reject me."

Caroline kept her head on Travis' shoulders for a few moments before he mumbled something about getting some whiskey. He wandered inside and returned to the porch with a bottle of Jack Daniels.

"I thought we were saving that for a special occasion."

"Here's the special occasion: I'm fucked."

"Travis!"

"I have two more options but if I don't get in…"

"Don't say that. You'll get in. How many people with perfect scores don't get into law school."

"Should we look it up?"

Caroline took Travis' hands and shook her head.

"No. We shouldn't. We should crack open this bottle of Jack Daniels and get filthy stinking drunk until Chase and Bud get home."

"That sounds like a horrible idea… I'm in."

"We'll need to stock up on liquor before tomorrow."

Caroline groaned.

"Election night… Are we still having the office party?"

"Bet your ass we are. Bud's clearing out the barn right now."

"That's what he's doing today?! He told me not to go over there because I'd done everything I could and he was only riding the horses."

"Wish you hadn't taught him how to read," Travis muttered, "He's become a much better liar with all that book learning."

"Book learning?" Caroline giggled.

Travis leaned over and kissed her. He didn't taste like whiskey yet, but she did. Travis loved the taste of anything on her lips. He would kiss her until she tasted like him. He would kiss her until her lips made him forget Harvard or Yale or the other schools he probably wouldn't get into. They kissed so much on the porch that Caroline forgot anyone walking by could see them.

Travis pressed his lips to her neck, drawing her sharp attention to the brazenness of their affectionate display.

"Inside," she whispered, "We ought to go inside."

"I won't make it far," Travis murmured.

He hadn't exaggerated. Once they were inside, Travis pressed Caroline up against the door and hoisted her body into his grasp. He had her clothes off and pounded into her until Caroline heard knocking from the other side of the door. Given their track record, she half-expected Jesse Clark to be on the other side of the door. Travis chased Caroline off with a blanket from their couch and opened the door. Chase and Bud entered and Caroline poked her head up bashfully from the couch.

"Were you two fucking?!"

Travis was only in his boxers and red in the face. Caught red-handed. There was no denying it. Travis muttered something under his breath. Chase grinned.

"There's no leaving any of us alone with her, is there?"

"Figured we'd try to forget about election night."

"And what about this?" Bud picked up the envelopes, "I'm no big reader but ain't these letters from Harvard and Yale?"

"I didn't get in."

"Fuck. Sorry, man."

"It's okay. I... found a way to work things out."

"Bet your ass, you did," Chase said, "I guess it's my turn to tell y'all. I got a job."

"What?!"

"Yup. I'll be trucking from Washington, D.C. down South. The company's based out of D.C."

"You're moving?"

Travis' face reddened.

"No offense to all of y'all, but I'm still stiff. Can I take her upstairs and we get to personal business after I'm done?"

Caroline's cheeks warmed. Travis never spoke about making love to her with such urgent need before. She got up from the couch and let her blanket fall.

"They don't mind if you take me right here."

Travis didn't need more encouragement. He crossed the room and fell onto the couch with Caroline. She curled her thighs around his torso and cried out as he entered her. She came fast. And Travis came after switching positions. Once he finished, Bud dragged her onto the carpet and grunted between her legs. By then, the room smelled of whiskey and man musk.

Chase pulled Caroline into the kitchen and sat her on top of the counter. Before sliding between her legs, he murmured, "Caroline. You'll win the election. I'm not moving to Washington, D.C. without you. I believe in you."

Before Caroline could respond in pleasure or protest, Chase buried himself inside her to the hilt. Caroline moaned as she took him between her legs. When Chase finished, they were all covered in sweat. Bud ran into the kitchen from the living room.

"Owens. Your phone has been ringing off the hook."

"Fuck."

"I think it's Zachariah."

"What?" Chase answered the phone with a growl.

His face lost its color.

"No. Not tonight! That shit can't happen tonight!"

Chase paced the room and slammed a fist into the wall.

"Tell mom I say hello."

He hung up.

"Zach gave me a tip. Lottie's real pissed over how things

went down. She's making one last effort to fuck over your campaign."

"It's too late for that!"

"It's your brother. She's accused him of raping her, and she's done a video interview about it. Unless we get down to the newspaper office, they'll send it to local news tonight."

23

BUD'S BIG IDEA

"I TOLD Caleb not to get involved with her."

"We have to go down there," Bud said, "I'll sort this shit out. I swear. The election is tomorrow. We can't have this coming out."

"Maybe we should let the story come out. I'll renounce him!"

"Caroline," Chase balked, "You can't be serious."

Caroline hadn't been serious. But she was still angry with her brother for bringing these problems to her doorstep. Lottie leaked information to Jesse Clark, and now this. Caleb wanted her to believe he had everything under control, but he didn't have a damned thing under control.

"I can't go down there," Caroline said, "I wish I could. I know she's lying, but if I have to look my idiot brother in the eye, I'll smack him."

"Maybe he deserves a smack," Chase admitted, "But he also deserves your support."

"For what? He slept with someone who isn't just a casual racist."

"Maybe he had his reasons," Bud offered.

He was always trying to be the peacemaker, but Caroline didn't want peace. She wanted her stupid brother to recognize the error of his ways. She wanted him to admit that his idiotic mistake might have cost her the entire election. Caroline already lagged behind Jesse. This wouldn't help. Jesse must have known that.

"I'll go down there with you, Bud. He is my brother."

Travis folded his arms and sighed.

"Not to play devil's advocate, but is there a chance in hell he raped her?"

"Seriously, Travis?!"

"Sorry! I only meant to ask, you know… just in case."

"He didn't. But if it's that easy to cast doubt in your mind, imagine how easy it would be to flip this stupid county against him."

Travis mumbled an apology. Bud got the truck started and Caroline hopped into the front seat with him. They got to the newspaper office in time. Bud pulled rank as mayor to get in front of the story. Augusta Abernathy's younger sister, Melinda Abernathy, worked at the paper. Caroline always thought she was sweet on Bud, and her pale cheeks turned dusky pink once he sat across from her.

"We have a video interview. I have specific instructions to turn it over to local news. Mister Landry, I'm uncertain what you want me to do."

"I could sue you for slander! Does that help?!" Caroline snapped.

Bud put a hand on her thigh and Caroline slumped back. She ought to trust Bud to handle this. She knew that. Bud grinned.

"Don't mind, Caroline. She's nervous. I'm sure you know this story could harm her campaign."

"We can't cover up a rape because of politics," Melinda said, narrowing her eyes, "There's such a thing as journalistic ethics. Now, I hate Jesse Clark as much as anyone in this town. But it doesn't matter if a progressive rapes someone or if a conservative rapes someone. What matters is Lottie Calloway's story."

"Lottie Calloway's story is a lie," Bud replied.

"Excuse me if I don't take your word for it," Melinda huffed.

"Listen, Mel... I understand you can't take my word for it but consider this. Caroline's a woman and she hasn't spoken to her brother in weeks because she caught him and Lottie consensually in bed together. Then, Zach Owens finds out Lottie and Tommy Lee Buchanan are interfering to install Jesse in our county's congressional seat. He takes action against them, and Lottie weaponized her connection with Caleb to sabotage Caroline's campaign. I don't think you ought to take my word for it, but there's more to this story than meets the eye. Caroline's the most principled woman I know. If there were any truth to these allegations, she'd be the first to let the story run."

Melinda analyzed them both with a shrewd stare. As a journalist, she ran into a fair number of kooks and liars. Bud Landry was no kook, she knew that much, and he didn't have the brains on him to be dishonest, the poor man. And Caroline... Melinda watched the town hall debate, and she'd seen how unfair it was. She could believe that the old guard wouldn't want Caroline in Congress.

"Caroline?" Melinda asked softly, "Can you tell me about finding your brother and Lottie together?"

"Is this off the record?"

"On the record. Please. Maybe we can push this story until after the election, so I have time to hear the other side."

Bud relaxed.

"Mel... I always thought you were the best of the Abernathy family."

Melinda tucked hair behind her ears.

"You're a flattered, Mayor Landry."

"Oh, hell no. I'm an honest man."

"That too."

Melinda beamed as Bud made pointed eye contact with her. Caroline struggled not to roll her eyes. Bud could lay on the flirtations thick when he wanted to. He wasn't as stupid as other people thought he was. He knew how to work people the way he knew how to work animals.

"I'll talk to you after election night," Bud said, "Maybe I can get you exclusive sources."

"That would be incredible."

As they sat in the truck, Bud paused before turning on the ignition.

"Bud, is everything okay?"

"No."

"What's wrong?"

"I don't want you to leave."

"I'm not going anywhere."

"I have a good sense of things, Caroline. You'll win this election. And when you do, you'll leave. I don't want that."

Caroline bit her lip.

"I don't want us to be apart either. But we're working toward something bigger than us."

Bud scoffed.

"Right. Making the world a better place. I only care about that because of you. Before you, all I cared about was beer, guns, horses and chicks. Not all chicks. Mostly you."

Caroline leaned over and kissed his cheek.

"Thanks for handling Mel in there."

"Piece of cake."

"Even if we're apart, this doesn't have to end. We can still… be together."

"You know as well as I do, it won't be the same if it ain't the four of us."

"Let's go home. We can't jump to conclusions, can we? Maybe we'll find a way."

"I have a way."

"You do?"

"I can quit as Mayor."

"Bud! You can't! You worked hard for this."

He glanced over at Caroline and then lunged, grabbing her cheeks and kissing her hard. When he pulled away, he didn't break eye contact.

"Damn it, woman," Bud murmured, "You don't know what the hell you do to me."

He drove them home. They'd shut down the story for the time being, but there was still the matter of Caleb sitting in jail. Once they were home, Bud called his lawyer to get Caleb out. He nearly told his lawyer to bring Caleb over to their house, but Caroline insisted otherwise. She was still too pissed at Caleb to see him. And tiring of cleaning up his messes.

Travis and Chase cracked into the whiskey while Bud and Caroline left. Travis still had plenty of steam to blow off from his law school rejection letters, and Chase had a damned good excuse to get drunk. They belted out Shania Twain songs lying on the floor together until Bud kicked his boots off and Caroline hurried over to the couch to join them.

"How did you two get so drunk!?"

"Caroline... join us..."

So Caroline joined them and their night ended like it usually did: with her legs behind her head and three strong Southern men between her legs. Caroline woke up with a pit in her stomach. She'd promised herself she wouldn't let nerves get the best of her, but now the day arrived and terror wracked her body. She didn't want to get out of bed, so she rolled over and nudged Bud's arms so she could feel his warm grasp on her.

Bud kissed her, and she wrinkled her nose. His lips were soft and perfect, but he stank to high heaven in the morning like pure man musk. The sharp tangy smell upset her at first, but then it was like the sweetest smell in the world to her and she wanted to bury herself in his musky cocktail.

Bud woke up and unwrapped Caroline from his tight grasp.

"Game day," he muttered.

"Yeah."

"Nervous?"

"Like hell."

"Party tonight," Bud murmured, "Nothing to worry about. We'll be here for you. No matter what."

"What happens if I lose, Bud? I'll need to get a job."

Bud shook his head.

"I'll knock you up," He murmured with a grin.

"Bud!"

Caroline playfully slapped his cheek. He chuckled.

"What?" he murmured, "you've never thought about it? I want to every time I touch you. I want to watch you grow with my baby."

"I hate to break it to you, but that baby would be just as likely to be Travis' or Chase's."

Bud shrugged.

"I don't care."

He clambered on top of Caroline and spread her legs open. Caroline let him kiss her lips and then her neck. She needed to forget her worries today and Bud's desire to make love to her was the perfect way.

"Where are the others?" Bud murmured.

"Downstairs."

"So we can make a baby, you and me?"

"How do you plan for us to do that? I'm on birth control."

"Hm… We need a plan then?"

"Yes."

"What if… I toss your birth control?"

"You can't be serious."

"I'll do it right now."

"It'll still work for a few days."

"Okay… So I fuck you every day. Sounds good to me."

Caroline didn't protest, so Bud stripped her and thrust into her to the hilt. Caroline moaned. Talking about babies and having Bud's lips nibbling every inch of her drove her wild. He found her entrance soaked and ready for him once he slid inside her. Bud fucked her hard until she came, and then he buried himself inside her and spilled his seed deep into her tightness.

They lay in bed together and Caroline sighed before she noticed how high the sun was in the sky.

"Bud? What are you doing here?"

"Taking the day off."

"You don't have a day off."

"If someone doesn't like it, they can come drag me out of bed."

Caroline rubbed his giant back, and he moaned.

"I love having your tiny paws all over me."

Caroline giggled and pulled his face in for another kiss. Bud got a stern, focused expression on his face.

"Now. It's time for me to destroy those pills."

"Are you sure? Shouldn't we talk to Travis and Chase about this?"

"It's your body, Caroline. Ain't it your choice?"

"I guess."

"Do you not want this?"

"I don't know what I want. Can a baby have three dads?"

Bud leaned back against the headboard.

"Tell you what sweetheart, when we have goats on the farm, sometimes we don't know the daddy and all the daddy goats and momma goats raise the kid together. I imagine it'll be something like that."

"Fine. Destroy them. Let's do this."

"Let's do what?"

Chase stood in the doorway, shirtless and grinning with a cigarette hanging out of his mouth as he observed Caroline's fresh-fucked facial expression. Caroline bit her lip but Bud blurted out, "We're making an election day baby."

"Oh."

"I told Bud we should talk to you," Caroline pleaded.

Chase shrugged.

"I ain't mad. But I'll have to finish this cigarette. Having a kid means I gotta quit."

"What?"

Caroline hadn't expected that response.

"Have y'all told Travis? I'm sure his swimmers will want to enter the race."

Caroline's cheeks warmed as Chase sat on the edge of the bed to finish his smoke. Bud called downstairs, "Yo, Travis!"

24

WHORE OF BABYLON

CAROLINE KNEW they'd kill her if she was late to her own election night party. The boys had all gone ahead at Caroline's request. She'd been reeling at Travis' news from midmorning. He'd received an acceptance letter in the mail — from Georgetown. Too much rode on the back of this election. If Caroline lost, she'd stay in Old Town, where at least she'd have Bud Landry, who offered her a job at the mayor's office if it came down to it. If she won, she'd move to Washington D.C. and when Chase wasn't on the road, she'd see him and when Travis wasn't busy as hell with law school, she'd see him too. But there would be no more sweet Bud Landry, and Caroline didn't know if she could handle that.

She refused to let him quit. He'd worked hard as Mayor, and he'd just started making changes. Plus, tonight, Caroline had to see Caleb and her parents. Caroline could handle Nikita and Kingsley Coulson. But she still didn't want to see Caleb. If it weren't for Bud, he could have messed everything up. For all she knew, by the time Lottie Calloway finished with him, he'd end up in prison, anyway. If she couldn't stay in Old Town to take care of him, would everything fall apart between them?

Election night had the grim misfortune of being rainy. The rain poured outside and mud coated the entire front of the house. Bud left his truck for Caroline to drive over to the barn, but she'd have to put her shoes on in the car and wear rain boots and a heavy jacket to avoid getting her hair soaked on her way to the car. A crack of thunder resounded outside. Caroline gasped in surprise. Thunder didn't scare her, but she was jumpy. They'd started counting the votes by now, and these precious moments were the only few where she wouldn't know what was coming. She didn't have to worry about winning or losing, just getting dressed and prettied up.

Caroline stuck her earrings on and admired her figure in the dress. The boys liked her nice and curvy, but Caroline didn't mind shedding a couple pounds, even if she'd done so from stress. Tonight she could feast like a queen and not have to worry about her dress splitting down the middle. Caroline's red dress hugged her bosom and butt, but her waist was now closer to an hourglass shape. She heard the door open downstairs. Travis probably came to check on her since she was… shit! Fifteen minutes late.

Caroline grabbed her heels and bounded down the stairs, shrieking when she saw who — and what — waited for her at the bottom.

"What are you doing here?!"

"Don't move a muscle girl, or I'll put a fucking bullet in your head."

"Mrs. Clark!" Caroline gasped, gripping the railing, "What are you doing in here? I… Why are you pointing a gun at me?!"

It was one of those stupid questions that comes to you at exactly the wrong time when your brain is trying its hardest to find time to think.

"You... you have a hold on my husband and we are going to have a conversation about him."

"There's no need for a gun then, if we're having a conversation."

"Oh, there's a need for a gun. Because I need a confession from you before I do it."

"What do you want me to confess to? Jesse came onto me. You saw that. But I turned him down."

She cocked the gun. Caroline's body stiffened. She had to play this next part carefully. One wrong move and Jesse's wife could put a bullet through her head. There wasn't a woman in Old Town who wasn't handy with a rifle. Matilda Clark rocked forward, and Caroline caught a whiff of the one clue that might lead to her advantage. She was drunk. Piss drunk. And she rocked forward again, nearly stumbling. Caroline only wished she'd take her finger off the trigger.

Stumble too hard and she'd shoot my accident. Mrs. Clark might fly halfway across the room, but Caroline would still be dead if anyone shot her this close.

"I will do and say whatever you want me to if you put down the gun."

"No!" she yelled, "I'm not putting down the gun. You... you whore of Babylon!"

"Where is Jesse?"

"At his victory party. Because for all your wiles, you can't use that against him. He'll win and we'll get out of this godforsaken town and go back to Washington."

"Mrs. Clark, I promise you that whatever you think happened, didn't. I... I have a boyfriend."

It didn't seem like a great time to bring up it was more like three boyfriends. She'd only think Caroline had more of a reason to add a fourth to this... harem? Can women have harems? Fuck! Caroline couldn't stop her mind racing over useless information. Maybe the boys were the clue. If she could distract Matilda Clark somehow, she could run like hell upstairs and grab a shotgun from under the bed.

Then what? Shoot her opponent's wife in the head?

"Jesse has a wife. That didn't stop him."

Shit.

"Is that your plan then? To kill me?"

"I can't kill you until you confess!"

Confess: die. Don't confess: die. Mrs. Clark didn't offer her much of a choice. The door to the porch swung open and slammed against the wall. Thunder roared. Matilda swung around to look behind her, and Caroline ran. By the time she heard the gunshots, she was out of range. She raced into the bedroom and grabbed a shotgun. Where the fuck was the ammunition?

After their big fight, the boys made it harder to get to so they could think twice before trying to put bullets in each other's stomachs. She heard footsteps coming up the stairs. Fuck. Her fingers found Bud's secret ammo stash, and she ran into their ensuite bathroom, loading the magazine. Great. The one gun she found would blast a fucking hole in their walls. Shaky fingers didn't help her get the gun loaded faster.

Mrs. Clark's footsteps were on the other side of the house now. If Caroline moved slowly, she could have the element of surprise. She tiptoed into the bedroom and shut the hallway and bedroom lights off. She knew this house like the back of her hand. She could make her way around blindfolded and handcuffed. Jesse's dick-crazed wife didn't have that advantage. Caroline hoisted the gun and heard her go down the second staircase. Mrs. Clark needed light. Either that or she was thinking like a drunk person. Not thinking at all. Caroline tiptoed behind Mrs. Clark. She knew Mrs. Clark could see her shadow if she got too close.

Caroline's finger hovered over the trigger. She wouldn't have to worry about getting shot if she shot first. Mrs. Clark broke in. She came in with a weapon. She was an obvious threat.

But Caroline couldn't shoot her with her back turned. Maybe it was stupid, maybe it was for the best. Caroline took one step forward and creaked on the floorboard. Shit. Matilda Clark turned around, flopping around wildly. She looked to her right and shot.

"JESUS FUCKING CHRIST, WOMAN!"

Jesse. She shot Jesse. Caroline aimed for the wall behind Mrs. Clark's head and fired. She screamed and shot again. Jesse howled. Caroline couldn't tell if he'd been shot twice or if he'd wet himself in terror.

"Put the gun down, Mrs. Clark."

"Fuck you for coming to save your whore!"

"PUT THE GUN DOWN OR I WILL BLOW YOUR FUCKING HEAD OFF."

She squealed and dropped the gun. It fired again and Jesse roared, "You fucking stupid woman! You can't drop a loaded gun!"

"Get back," Caroline snarled, ignoring Jesse until he raced out of the other room and she pointed the gun at him.

"Back off. There's plenty in this clip for both of you."

Jesse's hands shot up.

"Get your hands up," Caroline snarled.

Matilda obeyed. She didn't have much of a choice.

"Against the wall," Caroline snapped.

They pressed their backs against the wall, next to the front door. If they ran for it, Caroline decided she'd shoot at their heels, but she wouldn't shoot to kill. She had a party to get to. She couldn't exactly kick the loaded gun on the ground out of the way, but she slowly descended between the Clark couple and the weapon. Caroline had control, but now she had to figure out what to do with them.

"Why the hell are you in my house?" she barked at Jesse.

"I didn't want my wife to hurt you."

"Looking out for your mistress? That's sweet."

"I'm NOT his mistress."

Jesse hung his head shamefully.

"She isn't. I promise. I only cheated... once."

Caroline scoffed.

"You had a baby after only one time."

"A baby?" his wife gasped.

Shit. She'd found out about the cheating but somehow missed the kid. Matilda Clark slapped Jesse across the face. Caroline cocked the gun.

"Hey! I don't want any part in this marital discourse. I want you two out of my house."

"I'm not leaving without my gun," Matilda huffed.

"If you take one step toward that gun, I'll shoot him."

"Shoot him! I don't give a damn. This is the last night I'll ever be Mrs. Clark. He showed up here. That's the only confession I ever needed."

Mrs. Clark reached behind her back quickly. By the time Caroline's brain caught up to what was happening, she had the handgun aimed at Caroline's chest.

"NO!" Jesse yelled, and he jumped in front of Caroline as his wife pulled the trigger. The scream she let out echoed through the house and she dropped the gun, covering her mouth and shrieking. Jesse fell slowly. She'd grazed him with the bullet before, but this time, she'd aimed to kill Caroline and the bullet lodged in his chest.

In a few minutes, he'd be dead, Caroline thought.

"You shot him!"

"I... I... I meant to kill you!"

Was that her best defense?

"You'd better call a damned ambulance!"

Matilda ran down the driveway and didn't look back. She

shot the father of her kids and left him in Caroline's foyer to die. Shit… Caroline grabbed her phone and called 911. This didn't look good. If Jesse didn't make it, she'd have a hard time convincing the cops she hadn't shot her opponent. Rumors would spread as they analyzed ballistics, and by the time the cops learned the truth, everyone would think she killed Jesse Clark.

Caroline kneeled next to him and his eyes fluttered open.
"Caroline…" he murmured, "I'm dying…"
"You jumped in front of a woman holding a gun. Are you crazy?"
"I'm sorry…"

He'd saved her life. He'd also been the one to put it in danger, but he'd jumped in front of a bullet to save her. Caroline wanted to hate him, but there was so much adrenaline coursing through her system along with relief that she couldn't. She stroked Jesse's hair. Hell, if he was dying, what did it matter? He ought to go in comfort, even if he was a bastard.

"Stay with me, Jesse. They'll be here soon."
"I'm racist…" he choked out.
"You're delirious," Caroline said, but she reflected to herself that yes, he was also racist. But speaking ill of the dying had to be at least half as bad as speaking ill of the dead.

Cops and an ambulance showed up. If she hadn't been at Travis Montgomery's house, the cops might not have been so gentle with her. They took all the weapons as the EMTs carried Jesse out. Caroline pulled one of the EMTs aside.

"Is he going to make it?"
"You can never tell. But I've seen worse wounds. It missed his heart. Once we get him to the hospital, he should come out okay."

Caroline wasn't sure if she was disturbed or relieved. By

the time the cops left, Caroline realized she was late — extremely late — and she had around fifteen missed calls from the boys. It surprised her they hadn't come back to the house by now to drag her to the party. Fuck! Caroline texted their group chat and jumped into Bud's truck.

25

AN END TO THE FOURSOME

CAROLINE HURRIED out of the truck and flung the barn door open. Chase picked her up and spun her around.

"What's going on? Sorry I'm late."

"YOU WON! YOU FUCKING WON!"

"What?!"

Everyone threw papers in the air. Caroline half expected gunshots to go off. Bud grabbed her hand and spun her around before leading her in front of the crowd.

"Here she is, Caroline Coulson, our district representative!"

A cheer broke out. Travis hugged her and became the first person to notice something was wrong with her.

"What happened? Why were you so late?"

"It's a long story…"

Travis touched her cheek.

"Is that blood?"

Shit. Caroline wiped her face anxiously.

"We can talk about it after I get a drink. I can't believe it."

"Believe it, babe. We're going to Washington."

Yeah, all of us except Bud, Caroline thought. They celebrated until the sun came up. Caroline had done it. Once the party fizzled out, Caroline sat the boys down behind the barn with a bottle of whiskey and explained everything that happened with Matilda Clark and Jesse.

"I ought to go to the hospital and pull the plug on that sonofabitch."

"Don't," Caroline warned.

Travis handed Caroline the bottle.

"Did you see Caleb and your parents tonight?"

"Yes. I guess Lottie dropped her charges. I'm still pissed at him."

"Give it time," Chase said, "Caleb's a good guy. He's organizing people in this town again, and he'll keep working at it while I'm gone."

"So that's it, then? We're moving to Washington, D.C."

She glanced at Bud, who tilted his head back against the barn, letting his hat fall a few inches behind his neck.

"Except me."

"Right."

"Don't worry, Coulson. I'll only be... a 7 hour drive south."

"That isn't as comforting as you think it is."

"Hmph."

"We ought to go home," Travis said, "It's nearly sunrise."

"And I'm out of cigarettes," Chase added.

They walked home together. None of them had the right condition to drive, and they spent plenty of effort reminding Bud that he could get a DUI for riding his horse drunk and that might be normal for a mayor of Old Town, but might not be the best idea. Caroline had forgotten how much of a mess she'd left the house. Blood on the hardwood. Weapons strewn everywhere. A couple bullet holes in the wall.

"I didn't realize you required this much supervision," Bud teased.

Caroline's cheeks warmed. She'd won. She'd really won. And this house, which had terrified her at first, she loved. She'd have to leave her home for at least 2 years. That meant leaving Bud. Caroline didn't think she could stand it if it weren't for Travis and Chase. But wouldn't they miss their best friend too?

They had an intense night in bed. They were all drunk and made love slowly and passionately, but with an intense feeling that signified both an ending and a new beginning.

Travis left for Washington, D.C. first. He started law school in January and wanted to get settled. Bud spent nearly all his time working and traveling for work, which left Caroline and Chase at home, packing her things and getting ready for the big move. Chase used his free time to write a lot. He had a lot to say, and he wrote about his experiences as a Southern working class man and he wrote online about politics. He planned to write in between trucking jobs.

"Maybe one day, I'll write a book worth reading," he'd told Caroline. She saw no reason to discourage him. Chase had one of those sharp, restless minds, probably destined to do great things.

Chase drove Caroline to D.C. She never thought she'd cry so much as when she said goodbye to Bud Landry. This was it. The end of them. Chase waited for her in the car as she held him on the porch. Bud touched her lips and kissed her forehead.

"You're going to do great things, Coulson," he murmured.

"What about you? I can't bear to think of you in this great big house all alone."

"I'm the mayor of this town. I'll keep busy."

"You'll find another girl?" Caroline asked, her heart quickening.

She didn't feel she had the right to ask any of them to remain loyal to her and only her. She had three. And if Bud stayed here all alone, he'd have no one. She couldn't bear the thought of another woman keeping his enormous bed warm at night. She couldn't bear thinking of another woman in the kitchen while Bud strutted around the house naked.

"Never," Bud murmured, "I love you, Caroline. That won't change."

"It might."

"Not for me. You're my finish line. There's nothing after you. Nothing could compare."

"I can't," Caroline whispered as she grasped his brawny body, "I can't leave you alone."

"You have to. Because you're making the world a better place. And that's exactly what you've made me want to do."

"Bud..."

"I love you."

"I love you too."

"Now go... You don't want to keep Owens waiting."

Caroline bounded over to the truck, glancing over her shoulder to Bud leaning on the porch, a big smile on his face. She fought back tears. Goodbye for now wasn't goodbye forever. Chase pulled onto the highway and she let herself cry. Chase glanced over and put his hand on her thigh.

"Don't fret, Caroline."

"I'm sorry," she whispered, "I need to toughen up. I'm going to be sitting in Congress arguing with the worst of them."

"If you can handle Jesse Clark and his wife, you can handle those old geezers."

Caroline grimaced.

"Ugh. I don't understand what happened. But they need a divorce."

"They're getting one. Everyone's talking about it."

"Who is everyone? Where did you hear this?"

"Daddy got him a job. He's working for a law firm in Washington now. Maybe he'll go head to head against Travis some day."

"Ugh," Caroline groaned, "I never thought I'd have to see Jesse again. That was like one of the best things about leaving Old Town. I'd rather not have to shoot him."

"You can't, buttercup. We can't bring our guns to D.C."

"Maybe it's a good thing Bud isn't coming..."

Travis promised their new place would be amazing, but he hadn't warned Caroline how enormous it would be. It was dark by the time they arrived in the city, and Caroline's legs felt like they'd snap in half if she sat in the car any longer. Her tummy growled. Their last McDonalds stop had been hours ago and Travis texted to tell her he'd make a special welcome home dinner.

She gazed out the truck window as Chase arrived.

"Chase! What the hell is this? I thought we'd live in an apartment."

"Surprise..."

Chase parked the car, and Caroline leaped out, racing toward the door.

"It's a mansion! How the hell did you two pull this off?"

Chase stuck his key in the lock and pushed it open. Caroline yelled.

"BUD LANDRY?!"

"SURPRISE!" the three boys yelled.

"No! We left you on the porch..."

"I hauled ass to the airport and took a flight. I got in two hours ago."

"Bud!"

Caroline hugged him tightly and pulled away, a questioning expression on her face.

"Wait a minute. What about your job?"

"Well... I talked to city council. I'm resigning and get to appoint a mayor for the duration of my term. I'll be appointing Caleb Coulson and then I'll move here permanently. And I'll be running for senate in the next election, two years from now."

"What?! How long have you three kept this secret?!"

"Why don't you come inside," Travis called.

Caroline stepped in side. The smell of steak and potatoes made her stomach rumble even more.

"You sold the Buchanan house..."

"We always knew you'd win, Caroline. We've saved up for this place since you announced your run. We're renting out the Buchanan house for the time being. But this place is ours. If you're going to change the world, you need the right house to do it from."

"It's beautiful..."

Caroline ran her fingers along the walls.

"Dinner's ready."

They sat down and had a meal together, laughing and chatting and celebrating. Bud cleared his throat when they finished.

"I'd like to propose a toast to Congresswoman Coulson."

"Hear, hear!"

"Caroline, you inspire us to be better men every day. If it weren't for you, I wouldn't have learned to read. Travis wouldn't have gone to law school, and Chase might have never left the back-breaking work at the factory. Without you, us lowlife rednecks might have never rebelled against our prejudice and our upbringing. People in Old Town may gossip, but they don't understand what we've got here. We're a family. And nothing in this world could break this family apart."

"Thank you," Caroline whispered.

"Cheers!" Travis added, "To Caroline, for helping me

make it to Georgetown law school."

"Cheers!" Chase said, "To Caroline, for inspiring me to write a book that will hopefully change lives."

Caroline clinked her glasses with theirs.

"It's not fair," she sighed, "You all thank me, but what the hell am I supposed to do to thank you? There are three of you and... well, I'm only one woman."

Bud grinned and elbowed Travis and then Chase.

"We have some ideas about how you could do that."

"Like what?"

Chase sighed.

"We talked about it and we think it's time..."

"Time for what?"

"It's time we put our best efforts to what we all three do best together."

Bud blurted out, "It's time to put a bun in the oven!"

Caroline giggled, and they enjoyed the last of their champagne before Bud swept her off her feet and ushered Caroline upstairs. They had an identical bed here. Large and warm and perfect for four adults.

Bud unbuttoned his shirt as Caroline stripped her clothes off.

"Congresswoman, we're about to engage in some indecent behavior."

"Mayor Landry, I think we've earned the right."

"If we're going to knock her up, we have to get her ready."

Bud dropped to his knees.

"I'll warm her up," Bud agreed.

"And I'll get the handcuffs," Travis added.

Caroline moaned as Bud slid his tongue between her legs. She couldn't have asked for better men.

REDNECK RETRIBUTION

FREE Preview ahead...
smarturl.it/rednecksretribution

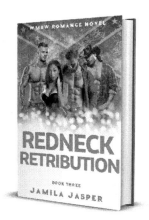

DESCRIPTION

The three friends loved Caroline since high school, but can they share her heart when there's a baby on the way?

Oops, Caroline's knocked up!
There's only one thing that the three beefy country boys who share her bed can do...
Take her back to their small town and fuss over her growing bump.
With a new mansion, new car and a new **gigantic 4-person bed** for the quad, what could go wrong?

A lot has changed since Caroline became a Congresswoman.
Their small town isn't the idyllic portrait of racial healing they left behind.

Not everyone approves of the multicultural love they share...
And racial tensions are <u>**10x worse than before.**</u>

Even with a baby on the way, Caroline wants to help.

The boys just want to keep her safe.
No matter who they have to hurt.
No matter what they have to do.

Protecting Caroline & the baby means everything to them.
It doesn't matter if the world falls apart.
As long as they can all be together.

1
THE CONGRESSWOMAN'S BOYFRIENDS

THE THREE WERE in bed when the letter came. Bud Landry lay naked on top the comforters with a Sharpie drawing of several hearts on his thick butt cheeks. Caroline lay next to him, spooning with Travis, who cupped her stomach with his firm palm and drew a freshly tattooed bicep across her, holding her close. Chase curled up at the end of the bed like a cat still dressed in a black t-shirt from yesterday.

Georgetown was quiet on Sundays and after a raucous Saturday night, no where was more quiet than Caroline Coulson's mansion. That is, until something broke the silence. A deafening crack echoed around the room and then...

Bfffffmmmmggggbbbbbbttttt...

The smell hit Caroline's nostrils first and she gagged, immediately launching herself upright and completely awake.

"Bud! You farted..."

Chase groaned, the toxic cloud of Bud's gas edging its way to his comfy spot at the foot of their gigantic bed. Travis woke up coughing shortly after. Bud appeared unbothered by their coughs, chokes and gasps for air. He let out another loud smelly fart.

"That's it..." Caroline muttered, grabbing her pillow and smacking Bud straight over the head. He groaned, but instead of waking up, he farted again.

Caroline snatched the pillow away from his head and pressed it to her nose.

"Who allowed him to go to that Mexican joint?!" Chase yelled, scrambling off the edge of the bed and flinging open their bedroom window, gasping desperately for air. Travis scowled, still too exhausted from a night of studying to answer.

"I'm afraid that may be my fault," Travis mumbled.

"Travis!" Caroline balked, turning on him with the pillow. Travis caught it deftly and set the pillow aside, gazing at his best friend's exposed rump like it was about to set off the next bedroom-sized nuclear attack.

"Wake up you big asshole," Travis snapped, smacking Bud across the ass with his flat palm. *Hard.* Bud opened a single curious eye and then grinned.

"G'morning."

"Your toxic farts woke us all up," Caroline snapped. "What have we told you about going to that food truck?"

"That food truck is *amazing...*" Bud said, smiling gleefully and wriggling his butt as if he was readying to let another one out.

"That food truck gives you *beans*, Bud. Your delicate European gut flora can't handle the damn beans and we can't handle your farting!" Caroline yelled, hitting him again with a pillow.

"Chase and Travis aren't complaining."

They cast sullen and weary glances in Bud's direction. He rolled over and sighed.

"Fine. I'll break up with my food truck. After I finish my leftovers."

"We should put him out," Travis grumbled, rubbing his eyes. "I have a lecture tonight at 7 and work all day. I need *sleep*, Landry."

Bud fondled his dick, uninterested in Travis' complaints about needing sleep and far more interested in Caroline, crouched nearby and scowling at him.

"Travis is right. He needs sleep. And I'm a recently resigned Congresswoman. Believe it or not, I need sleep too."

"You both need a vacation. And Chase…"

"I need to call my ma and brother."

Caroline threw him a sympathetic look. The cancer had gone into remission for a while. Chase and his brother had another falling out, but then the cancer came back and the news thrust them back together again, forcing Chase into a complicated situation.

"It's been a long time since I've been home," Caroline admitted. "But we're city people now. No one judges us here the way they would at home. I like my freedom."

"A vacation couldn't hurt," Travis added.

Chase leaned out the window, but added nothing. He'd grown his copper brown hair down to his shoulders and there was a slight curl to it now. He'd pulled the hair into a messy knot at the nape of his neck and the wisps blew around his face as he stared onto the streets of their new fancy neighborhood.

Home. What the hell would he do at home except remember all the ways their lives had been fucked up?

"Why bother going back to Old Town? We moved on. We did what everyone else wanted to do… we got out."

Chase had a point, Caroline thought. Old Town had been a hard place to live and harder because of their relationship. Three white men loved her and they were content to share her — best friends who shared everything found their way into her bed and the love they shared had been explosive. But not exactly accepted.

Bud's fingers made their way to Caroline's and she let him take her hand in his, suddenly wanting to forgive him for his disgusting farts. Bud was handsome. And big. He was mountain man enormous, with a broad smile and a deep sonorous voice. Caroline's heart fluttered as she recalled some of their special moments together — teaching Bud how to read, working on his Mayoral campaign and of course, their time in bed together. Bud was rough and animalistic when he took her. There was always something so pleasantly primal about his manhandling.

That morning, he had a similar animal look in his eye that neither Travis or Chase had noticed because of the sleep in their eyes. Caroline noticed. It was as plain as the cock rising to slow attention in the middle of the bed, practically beckoning her fixation. Chase pulled out a cigarette. He was down to one a day, but he savored every puff of tobacco from the window when he could.

Caroline leaned forward, edging toward Bud's exposed staff and Travis finally stopping thinking about his class and noticed the scene unfolding before him. He liked taking Caroline. The sensation of entering her felt phenomenal. She was tight. Eager. Yet watching another man take her turned Travis on just as much. He never thought about Bud's dick as something he might be interested in, but Travis got hard at just the idea of watching his best friend enter her soft body. It was Caroline that entranced him. He could watch her make love for hours. He could watch her do anything.

Caroline's body moved deftly on top Bud's. He hadn't impaled her yet but his rough fingers moved between her lower lips, readying her. Travis could feel himself getting hard and his responsibilities as a law student nearly fading from his mind. Pussy. That was all he could think about now. Not just anyone's but hers... Caroline.

He loved her and that pussy so much. She kissed Bud, losing herself in his roughness and letting his primal morning arousal flow into her until she couldn't imagine why she'd ever wanted to toss him out of bed only a few moments ago. Chase sat on the windowsill watching them kiss, smoking his cigarette slowly and watching. Chase didn't mind watching.

Caroline was sensitive and beautiful and built for this. Chase knew most in his family wouldn't approve — not just of the three of them but of her. She was the wrong color for a man like him according to his family. He'd heard rumors about girls like her and found all of them completely false. Caroline was smart. Beautiful. And wickedly sexy.

Bud slipped his finger into her lower lips and she moaned. Chase could feel himself stiffening in his pants and he moved his thighs to allow his cock to enjoy the sensation of rising and the teasing slowness of his action. Not until I finish my cigarette, he thought. I can't have her until I finish the damn cigarette.

Bud pushed her close to the edge. Caroline bucked her hips and he grunted before plunging into her deeper. Bud's fingers sank into her thighs and the urge to finish tightened in his groin. He clutched Caroline like she might try to escape and their bodies shuddered together until Bud erupted between her legs.

Damn. She had great legs. He grinned stupidly as Caroline leaned forward to kiss him. Her breasts draped on Bud's thick chest. His muscles were insane from hoisting bales of hay over his shoulders as soon as he could walk. He'd been the tallest boy in Old Town growing up and he'd never stopped being a giant.

Caroline ran her hands over his chest, taking him all in.

Once one had her, the others wouldn't leave her alone for long. That was the best part about all of them sharing her. She was never dissatisfied. Ever. Travis was the first to act as Caroline slid off Bud's shaft and rolled languidly onto the bed. He snaked her arms up over her head, kissing her sweetly.

"Bud got you nice and wet for me," Travis whispered.

They had all been doing this so long now that none of them was particularly shy about their favorite parts of the entire arrangement. Caroline spread beneath Travis' pale body as he allowed his finger to feel her wetness slowly before he caressed her clit to full attention.

Chase set his cigarette in the ash tray. *I can have the other half later.* He moved to the foot of the bed as Travis hiked Caroline's thighs up and she moaned as he entered her. Even after Bud, she was tight and *loud*. Travis grinned as the slow movement of his hips teasing her to the edge of a climax made Caroline moan… *loudly*.

They kissed again and Travis' hips instinctively moved deeper. *More. I need more of her.* He ground his hips into Caroline more forcefully. She arched her back upward, allowing her nipples to rub against Travis' stiff chest. Everything about him turned her on and his new tattoos made Caroline want him more.

She resisted his grasp and yanked her hands free, reaching behind her to cup Travis' ass and pull him into her deeper… and much slower.

"Careful officer," she whispered. "You wouldn't want to hurt your prisoner…"

He groaned and leaned forward to kiss her, grinning with delight. Travis left the force, but he liked Caroline's fingers grazing him and her delicate teasing voice was enough to make him erupt. Plus, he could feel what Bud had left inside

Redneck Retribution

her. It was warm. Sticky. And compelled him to leave something of his own behind.

Travis edged his hips forward and erupted alongside Caroline, the two climaxing together in near perfect harmony. Caroline shuddered and then twisted immediately in Travis' embrace. Hips still joined, they kissed and kissed until Chase thought he would burst just watching them.

My turn…

Travis cast a glance in his best friend's direction and winked at him, tossing Caroline onto her stomach. She landed with a surprised squeak and then felt a pair of rough, unmistakable hands spreading her thighs apart. Bud opened her as Chase dropped his clothing to the floor and eased into bed, lying on top of Caroline as he pressed the tip of his hardness into her pussy from behind.

Bliss.

Caroline cried out as he guided his hips forward in a swift motion, burying his dick in her to the hilt.

"Fuck…" Chase growled, losing his manners and all sense once he met Caroline's vice grip. The squishy softness surrounding her entrance made her easier to get into and tighter. Hotter. Chase could feel his cheeks turning red and burning as he moved his hips slowly teasing her open wider as he thrust into her.

"More…" Caroline whispered. Her insatiable moaning turned them all on. It hadn't been easy to get Caroline to open up like this. But she was open now. Chase lubricated his thumb with his tongue and teased at Caroline's back door as he worked her from behind. She allowed him to spread her slowly and press his thumb inside her. The sensation of his rigid thumb entering one of the most forbidden parts of her body with deliberate slowness made Caroline weak.

She shivered and allowed his body to press against hers as

his thumb slipped in deeper. Caroline moaned and Chase responded by planting the rest of his thumb in her back door.

"Like that?" He whispered, taking her lips into his and biting down as he pressed his thumb deeper into her ass. Caroline couldn't stop herself from moaning as Chase's thumb probed the tender, wrinkled skin of her sensitive back door. It would have been easier if it hurt, but instead the strange sensation only heightened her despite for him.

"Yes," she whispered. "Just like that."

With his dick in her pussy and his finger in her ass, pleasure hit Caroline like a freight train. Her body trembled as she pressed back against Chase's lean, muscular body, chiseled from years of hard work since he was a teenager. His copper hair dusted his shoulders now and as he leaned forward, thrusting deeply into Caroline, his hair brushed her cheek, tickling her and heightening the sensations between her thighs.

She moaned, her nipples pressing forward into the pillow as her thighs spread apart even more. Chase observed her subtle signals, holding her hips as he slid into her deeper. When Caroline moaned louder, he struggled to hold himself back. He had to have more of her. He had to.

He grunted and edged his hips forward ardently. Caroline moaned, an unexpectedly strong climax mounting within her as Chase grunted and thrust into her from behind.

"She likes it," Bud growled. "Fuck her hard…"

Caroline couldn't take it anymore. She loved when they acted like a pack of possessive animals crowded around their mate. Chase grabbed her hips and pulled her body closer to his.

"Cum for me," he murmured. "Cum for me, babe."

Caroline couldn't hold back any longer. Chase's command made it easy for her to cum hard and the deep throbbing in her core only felt better with Chase's finger pressed deep in her ass. As she came, he withdrew his finger painfully slowly and thrust deeper between her legs. He moved his hips faster and Caroline angled her hips up, knowing exactly what to expect.

Chase released inside her with a final grunt, thick ropes of his seed jettisoning from his dick and coating the walls of Caroline's squishy wetness with more Southern white boy seed. Three of them. She had *three* of them. Caroline squeezed her legs together, delivering an unexpected jolt of pleasure through both of them where they were still joined.

"Careful," Chase whispered. "I might have another load for you."

He palmed Caroline's gorgeous walnut-colored ass with a hard spank and she squealed as he withdrew his cock. Mornings with the boys were all like this.

But that morning was different, because the doorbell rang early in the morning, long before the mailman normally came.

2

TRAVIS

TRAVIS WALKED DOWNSTAIRS shirtless to answer the door. He'd just graduated law school and had plans for the summer. He was taking an extra class to learn the ropes for starting a private firm — just a small town law firm, nothing fancy, but something that could earn good money. He hadn't told Caroline about the plans yet but with her news... this plan made sense. He could make more money than he ever had as a cop. And ever since Mr. Emerson died, there was an opening in Old Town to practice family law.

He could hear Chase and Bud creaking on the floorboards upstairs. Travis smirked, imagining they'd probably pounced on Caroline for another session. Mornings had been *intense* amongst the four of them for a *long* time. When Travis opened the door, he scowled as his gaze fell on Jesse Clark. The last time he'd seen the man who ran against Caroline for Congress had been... years.

"What are you doing here?" Travis snapped.

Jesse and Travis were similar heights, both blond. But Jesse's hair was still long and curly.

"I stopped by to deliver this."

"Stopped by? How do you even know where I live?"

"Caroline."

Travis' cheeks darkened. Caroline? Since when had Caroline talked to Jesse Clark. It had been four long years since they'd left Old Town... four years since the election and four years since he'd seen Jesse in person. Clark looked older, but not wiser. Travis still thought he owed him a good punch in the throat.

"What do you mean Caroline?" Travis sneered.

"We've been talking. Don't tell me she hasn't told you."

As if she could smell him downstairs, Caroline emerged from the bedroom and Travis could hear her feet padding down the stairs.

"Jesse!" She shrieked, wrapping a robe around her semi-clothed body and cinching it shut. "What are you doing here?"

Travis turned to her and raised an eyebrow.

"He says you've been talking."

Caroline snapped, "We talked twice. He's my constituent. I have to talk to him."

"I personally enjoyed our conversations," Jesse said, smirking haughtily.

Travis glared, positioning his body between the two of them and flinching as Caroline came up behind him to wrap her arms around him.

"I'm sure you did," Travis snapped. "Now why are you here?"

"I already told you."

Jesse impatiently pulled a letter out of the breast pocket of his jacket. Caroline snatched it.

"Why did you have to hand deliver this?"

"Because... I was told to."

"By who?"

"I can't tell you. Will you just open the damned thing?"

"Want to come in for some lemonade?" Caroline offered, her Southern hospitality taking over her common sense. Travis' cheeks turned red and she bit down on her lower lip, expecting Travis to haul Jesse Clark's ass to the curb. Travis scowled but found politeness overtaking his desire to beat Jesse to a pulp. His Southern hospitality proved just as strong as Caroline's.

"Come on in," Travis said, smiling through gritted teeth. "But make any trouble and I'll have Landry stick his dick up your ass."

"Is that what the four of you get around to?" Jesse asked, grinning as if they were on friendly enough terms to make jokes.

Travis didn't respond with a smile or a hint of familiarity.

"Joke about us again Clark and you'll find out."

Jesse's back stiffened and he fell silent.

Caroline sat at the kitchen counter while Travis set about fixing Jesse a glass of lemonade. He tried not to bristle when Jesse took the bar stool next to Caroline. Travis' reactions were the mildest that Jesse had to worry about. Caroline heard the sound of a shotgun cocking before Bud's large foot stepped around the corner. He had the gun aimed straight at Jesse's head.

"I thought I smelled a rat."

Caroline barely flinched.

"Bud, relax. He's bringing me a letter, that's all."

"A love letter?" Bud's voice roared. Caroline didn't take the idea that he could be jealous at all very seriously. However their relationship had progressed, jealousy hadn't been part of the equation.

"No it's not a damned love letter," Caroline snapped. "Can you calm down."

Chase appeared around the corner next.

"Calm down?" He snarled. "We ought to eat that motherfucker for breakfast. Bud, shoot him."

Bud raised his gun again until Caroline screamed, "Enough!"

He lowered the gun and Caroline shoved her thumb beneath the seal of the letter to open it. All four men watched her. Travis handed Jesse the lemonade.

"We're feeding him now?" Bud roared.

"Bud!"

Caroline's eyes darted to the front of the letter.

"Who is this from?"

"I don't know."

Caroline read the letter, her face wrinkling.

"Say something," Chase said impatiently, snatching the letter. Travis stepped behind him. Caroline's chest fluttered seeing them together. They belonged to her as much as she belonged to them and just as they were protective of her, Caroline wanted to protect them in her own way.

Chase read the letter out loud.

Dear Miss Coulson,

There have been many changes in your beautiful town since your departure. Many more white families, nigger families and mixed race families now populate the streets of Old Town. Our organization has determined that a key cause for this unwanted miscegenation is government policy brought forth by former Congresswoman Coulson.

Unfortunately, we must take action. If you do not respond to this letter with swift arrival in Old Town, we will proceed with our plan to TAKE BACK OUR TOWN from the niggers, the spics, the race mixers and the race traitors. Every family with a race traitor will be under our watch including the Coulson family, the Montgomery family, the Owens family and the Landry family.

Already by the time you receive this letter, Ariana Landry will be raped and punished for her relationship with the new nigger in town, Kareem Baker.

Heed our warning. We are very powerful people with very powerful connections. There will be cleansing and then there will be war. Miss Coulson, you must return to Old Town and convince all the niggers, the spics, the race mixers and the race traitors to LEAVE OUR TOWN or we will TAKE BACK OUR TOWN by force.

You have 90 days to get every nigger off their porch.

— *The Committee*

Chase stopped reading. It was so quiet, you could hear a pin drop. Then Bud's phone rang. Travis grabbed Jesse by the shirt and snarled, "You move a muscle, I'll snap your fucking neck."

Bud picked his phone up, but they all knew who was calling and what it was about. Jesse Clark, as foolish and wicked as he was had seemed genuine in his handing off the letter. Caroline *had* been meeting with him and she'd noticed him acting strangely. But this... It was all too similar to what happened years ago. The year Bud ran for mayor. The year their relationship became more than a few friends fooling around. That was the summer Caroline had told them how she felt... *about all of them.*

Now the cold was settling in. She'd just resigned as Congresswoman and they'd had real plans to settle down for a while, stop worrying about money and just get ready. This would change everything. It would have to. Bud said a few soft words into the phone. His deep voice always sounded like he was soothing a wounded animal. But then he cracked and became the animal that needed saving. He hung up and broke down into tears that Caroline had never seen before.

The letter was true. Someone had raped Ariana Landry. Bud's younger sister had just turned 16. She'd joined the cheerleading team at Old Town high and she was always sending him Gen Z memes that Bud would ask Caroline to interpret for him. She'd just started dating a football player, but she hadn't told Bud his name yet. *Kareem Baker.*

Caroline threw her arms around him and held him close. Chase reached into a pocket for a cigarette with one hand and put another on his best friend's back.

"We're going home," Chase said, rolling the cigarette between his lips. "We're going to find who did this and whoever wrote this shit and we're going to fuck them up."

Travis snarled and pushed Jesse's head into the counter.

"I think we *know* who did this."

Jesse yelped as his head hit the granite. Caroline winced and shot Travis a glare.

"I didn't do anything! I swear. I got a fucking letter too with specific instructions and they threatened me, okay?! The last thing I wanted was to come up here and deal with you redneck mother—OW!"

Travis slammed his head into the counter again.

"Who the fuck you calling redneck rich boy?"

"Ow!" Jesse yelped again. "You're hurting me."

"Maybe we'd get better answers out of him if you stopped assaulting him for a minute," Caroline muttered. Travis took note and let go of Jesse's neck. He'd only busted his lip, Travis reasoned.

"How the hell did you get this and why are you here?" Caroline snapped. "And tell me the damn truth Clark or I'll watch Bud hunt you like a white-tailed deer and I'll laugh as you hit the ground."

Jesse blanched. Caroline could be ten times scarier than the boys when she wanted to be.

"Listen, they threatened someone I love. Someone I care about."

"Your wife?"

"Ex wife. And no. I'm dating someone else now. For her privacy, I'd prefer to keep that to myself."

"So they told you to bring this to me... via letter?"

"I don't know who it was, but I've heard rumors about this Committee. They have goals, aims, an agenda for Old Town. I don't want to be involved in politics anymore. I don't want any part of this. But whoever this is... it's serious. There have been an increase in strange attacks and... a couple boys have gone missing."

"What do you mean gone missing?" Caroline said. But she didn't have to wait for Jesse's answer to know what he meant. America's long and violent history against her people wasn't a mystery to her. Jesse's blue eyes flickered towards hers sympathetically.

"I'm sorry. I probably should have said all this in the meeting but the new Sheriff is working pretty hard to cover this up."

"Who's the new sheriff?" Chase asked.

Jesse gave him a disdainful look.

"Have you people already forgotten where you came from?"

"Spare me the act," Travis snarled. "Answer the fucking question."

"Zach Owens won the election eight weeks ago. Your brother's the sheriff."

Chase turned red and lit his cigarette. So much for quitting.

"We have to go," Caroline said.

"No," Bud snarled. "We aren't going anywhere. Not with your condition."

"My condition?!" Caroline balked.

3

CAROLINE

"You're pregnant," Travis said. "You aren't supposed to run around hunting down racists. You're supposed to knit onesies and get foot massages."

"I'm not some fragile female."

"Holy shit, you're pregnant?!" Jesse asked. "You don't look pregnant."

"Flirt with her again and I'll wring your neck," Bud said softly. "*Sir.*"

"Bud. Calm down," Caroline said. "We're selling the house, we wanted to go back anyway. Now we have a good reason. I'm not scared of anyone. I have the three of you. If we're down there, we'll be stronger and our families can stand up against this committee."

The boys glanced at each other skeptically and then back at Caroline.

"If I can stare down Mitch McConnell on the house floor and look directly into his tortoise eyes, we can survive a winter in Old Town hunting down racists."

Bud balanced the gun on the floor and leaned slightly.

"I miss hunting."

"After the city, I thought we could stay at a ranch," Caroline said. "Skip Mayor Landry's house and stay on a nice ranch with horses."

Caroline was already fantasizing about watching Bud handle the horses shirtless. He was always dripping in sweat when he fed them and stroked them. And the horses liked Bud's pleasant demeanor and booming voice.

"My cousin just moved to Idaho," Bud said. "He was asking me if I wanted to come down and manage the ranch for a while."

Travis scowled.

"We're supposed to be keeping her out of trouble, not encouraging her to rush into it. We agreed."

"Agreed to what?" Caroline snapped.

"You have a way of always getting your ass into trouble," Travis said. "We agreed."

Bud and Chase muttered and looked away from Caroline, leaving Travis to his own defense since he'd just mercilessly flung them under the bus.

"I get into trouble? Mister Montgomery, what kind of a statement is that?"

Jesse cleared his throat. Travis and Caroline ceased their fighting to glare at him.

"With all due respect, I would like to take my leave. As much as your couple's fight intrigues me, I have other business to attend to in Washington."

"I'll help your skinny ass find the door," Chase growled, pushing Jesse out. Bud's expression was somber.

"Even if I go alone, I have to go. It's Ariana. She needs me."

"We aren't letting you go alone," Caroline said firmly. "If he goes alone, I'll get a paternity test and I know none of you want that."

The boys weren't sure whether Caroline would make

good on her threats, but they didn't particularly want to find out.

"But... we had an agreement," Travis muttered, his cheeks turning red.

"Then you'll listen to me. We have to help our town. Plus, we all hate Washington, D.C. We just can't admit it to each other."

"No one likes my 'Big Butts And Lifted Trucks' T-shirt here," Bud complained.

"I find the women a bit... desperate?" Travis said. "I get propositioned daily."

Chase shrugged. "Cities are bullshit."

"So that's it. We head back to Old Town. We help Ariana and we stop this blackmail stuff from getting out of hand."

"And," Travis interrupted rudely. "You relax for a change and just let yourself be pregnant."

"I'm not disabled. It's just a baby."

"Or three babies with three different dads," Bud said hopefully.

"Bud," Caroline said, sighing desperately. "That's biologically impossible."

They argued about babies for a while longer before they planned their move back to Old Town. There was so much they'd left behind and all the troubles in the past seemed so far away that all they had left were their romantic notions of their small town. In Old Town, everyone knew everyone. Caroline could remember getting annoying with her brother Caleb for his involvement in her dating life. Looking back, it felt good to have him trying to protect her, even if he was way off about the boys.

She remembered hot hookups with Chase in the fields. He never cared about getting dirty and mucking around outdoors. If you did that in Washington D.C., you'd be in prison faster than you can say 'Capitol Insurrection'. She missed the grass. And she missed seeing Travis. Law school kept him busy and even if he wanted to provide for her, she wanted him home more than that.

Together the four of them were a family. A strange family, but a family that held Caroline down through everything. In the evening, Bud had his sister on the phone again. He explained that they were coming back and the plans were confirmed. They'd live on the Landry ranch, a little off the beaten path so they could keep out of trouble.

On the day they left Washington, Caroline expected to feel sad. She'd dreamed about Congress for so long, but the truth about it had been underwhelming. They spent so much time arguing with out of touch old men and so little time actually helping people. Pregnant or not, she might have been tempted to return to Old Town. At least there, they'd managed to make a difference.

It's all good to dream about the big city, but what about a little slice of home? What about a community where people smile at each other and know each other's names? Old Town hadn't been perfect, but they'd come close to healing some of the wounds of the past. According to Jesse Clark, that had all ended. Their hard work had been for nothing. Bud in the mayor's office and even Congress hadn't changed a thing.

Bud drove their new white Escalade back toward the countryside. Chase slept in shotgun while Travis held Caroline sprawled in the backseat. More than any of the others, his need to protect her had surged with news of the baby. He'd always dreamed of a family, making Caroline the mother of his children.

"How do you feel? Still nauseous?"

"I'm fine," Caroline groaned, sitting up and yawning. "Just wondering what kind of welcome we'll get."

"A Landry welcome!" Bud yelled. "The ranch is in good shape and Ariana's been cooking since morning."

"I can't wait to rest," Caroline said. "But I don't know if I can stay down for long."

"You'll be getting into trouble by Friday," Chase grumbled in the front seat, as if he wasn't just as much of a troublemaker. He kicked his feet up on the dashboard and turned up the Kitty Wells song Bud had been playing. The boys sang along and Caroline nuzzled on Travis' lap. Going home felt like the right thing to do.

Maybe this time, we can make a difference, Caroline thought. They weren't the young kids who didn't know anything anymore. They'd stuck it out in D.C. and saved money for years. Now, coming home, they were experienced. Smarter. But would that make a difference?

⚠️COCKY COWBOY FREE⚠️

Get This Book FREE! 👇

READ FREE HERE 👇: https://dl.bookfunnel.com/qm6r71bgzx

NEW SERIES...

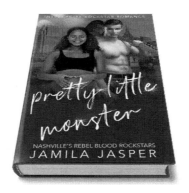

Flip the page to read a small sample...

PROLOGUE

5 years ago

Seb Jefferson
21-years-old

Angie Victor
18-years-old

"PLEASE DON'T HURT ME," she whispers, "I want to have sex with you but...I don't want it to hurt."

"It won't hurt if you do what I say," I snarl.

This girl is pretty. And she's dark. I like them dark. I like them even better when they're pretty. But that don't really matter for my purposes. She nods and then makes sure that I'll hold up my end of the deal.

"You'll leave him alone after this? You won't beat his ass no more or anything?" She says.

"Listen princess, I won you fair and square. Your shit head boyfriend will be fine. Now show me what I paid for."

"Seb Jefferson," she whispers her voice dripping with loathing, "People wouldn't believe what a monster you are."

Her hatred gets me hard. Really hard. But that might be the cocaine. I can hear the twang in her voice too. She probably worked for years to hide it, trying to make something of herself in L.A.

Tonight, that doesn't matter. Tonight, *she's mine*.

I push the pretty dark skinned girl against the wall and she grabs me, pulling me against her. Succumbing to me.

"I love doing this," I whisper, "I love destroying another man's property. Trust me, princess. If you were mine, I wouldn't share you. Not for all the money in the world."

I run my tongue over her neck and she trembles. I want to grab onto her hair and kiss her neck more, but I'm *high* and there's an even better prize waiting for me between her pretty chocolate legs.

She takes her clothes off and I drop to my knees. She's surprised, but she accepts my face between her thighs. She's perfect. They don't make girls like this back in my part of Tennessee.

Or if they do, they keep 'em locked up far away from redneck assholes like me. That's the best part about having money. I can fuck who I want. Eat who I want. White or black. No woman says no to Sebastian Jefferson. Not anymore.

I dip my tongue between her legs and come away with a muscle coated in her clear juices. When I gaze up at her, ready to mock her for her dripping tightness, she closes her eyes. I lick her lower lips until she moans. I make her scream.

Her fingers sink into my hair, which is my favorite part. Women always do that when they're about to cum hard on my face. My day isn't complete until I've had a shot of pussy juice and let's be honest... it's so much better when that pussy is black.

Not like any of my fans could ever know. I play the part well. Hell, I'll even wear the rebel flag once in a while to keep 'em guessing. Fuck fans. Fuck fame. I don't care what they think anymore. *I'm too high to give a fuck. It's not like anyone gives a fuck about me.*

All I care about is pussy — the pussy I have between my lips. The eighteen-year-old digs her fingers into my hair, uninhibited once my tongue spreads her open like a lotus. My cock yearns to get between her legs. I bought her for the night. That means I can do anything to her. *Anything.* But all I want to do is press my tongue between her thighs and bury my nose between her lower lips.

I love the way she smells...

Right before she cums, I pull away from her and kiss her inner thighs. She trembles, uncomfortable with the intimacy. Fuck, I could snort a fat line of coke off those thighs.

I suck on her inner thighs and she moans. She wants my tongue back between her legs but she knows how nasty I'll think she is if she begs for it.

"Spread them wider," I snarl, hoping she feels her absolute submission to me. It's what I demand from all my conquests, even the borrowed ones like Angie Victor. She obediently spreads her legs and I press two fingers inside her. They should have never sent my ass to Hollywood. She moans as I take her with my fingers and groan as I fill her.

"You like that?"

She moans as I plunge them deeper into her.

"I love black pussy, princess. I've had my eye on yours for a while."

I can tell she wants to punch me in the face, but I press my tongue between her thighs while I have two fingers buried inside her and she cums instead. She moans and cries out and I suck every drop of juice out of her black pussy as she bucks her hips against my mouth. Her body is *interest* on a loan.

That shit head Yannick Reynolds borrowed $75,000 for me and two broken toes and a black eye later, he still couldn't come up with the money.

Now I have what I really wanted... *her*. I remove my fingers from between her legs and force her lips apart, thrusting the fingers in. She obediently sucks her juices off them and swallows.

I chuckle and kiss her forehead before murmuring, "You good?"

"Sex," she whispers, "The job isn't done until we have sex."

"Good girl," I sneer, "it was that fucking easy to give your pussy up to another guy, huh? Any STDs princess?"

"You're one to talk," she snaps, "And trust me, it is *over* with Yannick. I'm only doing this to save him from himself."

"It couldn't be because your cunt's absolutely soaked."

"Watch your mouth, white boy."

I lunge for her and grab her arm. She screams and I press her against the wall. Fuck, she's scared. She really does think I'm a total monster. I glance down between her legs and snarl, "Listen. $75,000 gives me the right to cum in there."

"Are you crazy? What if I get pregnant? You're *famous*."

"I didn't pay for you to question everything I say," I snarl, "When I ask you to cum inside you again, you will ask me *which hole*. Do you understand?"

"You're sick," she snarls.

"I know," I whisper, "But you agreed to this, princess. Back out, and I'll break your boyfriend's back tonight."

She says nothing but I can tell I've nearly broken her.

"I want to cum inside you, princess."

"Which hole?" She asks, her voice cracking a little.

"I'm a Southern boy. I like me a taste of black pussy. So that's where I'll cum tonight. Get on the bed."

She lies back on the bed like a good girl, spreading her legs wide and exposing her soaked flower. I strip down faster than I ever have in my life. I haven't been so excited since I lost my damned virginity. I crawl between her legs and line my cock up with her perfect entrance. This girl is the blackest I've ever had, mind you. Such perfect skin I think I'll cum before I get my dick in her.

"Last chance at freedom, buttercup. Last chance before I breed you," I whisper, chuckling as a look of horror crosses her face.

She turns her gaze away from me. I grab her cheeks and force her to look at me. $75,000 was worth something, damn it. I don't just need her consent, although I definitely need that, I need her co-operation. She nods and I slide an inch inside her. She cries out. Fuck. I could pound her and empty myself inside her in ninety seconds flat. I don't have to care about her pleasure. I'm here for that final moment... coating the walls of her tight black pussy with *cum*.

"How the hell did he leave you a virgin?" I snarl, "Fuck... you're tight."

She cries out and pulled me deeper into her. Not so resistant now. Cock has that way with women. It makes them pliable little pets.

"You're tight, black girl. So tight."

I ram the rest of my length into her and she screams. I pump my hips between her legs, taking her hard. And deep. She moans and cries out to the heavens and screams in the most undignified manner as I thrust between her legs.

"Cum for me, baby. Cum all over that Southern white boy cock... I want that black pussy juice on my dick for the next week."

She cums. Hard. I plunge into her deeper. I can't wait to cum inside her. She is so perfect. So tight. So *wet*.

I pull out of her and groan.

"Turn around babe."

Angie turns around and gasps as I slide my tongue between her lower lips. *Nope. I won't give you what you want, babe. I won't let you forget the night you had Sebastian Jefferson between yours legs.* I spread her lower lips and drive my tongue deeper. Angie moans and wriggles, struggling to get away.

I pin her down and eat her until she cums again. As Angie catches her breath, I slide my cock deep into her. She moans again and I slide back and forth into her tightness until she cries out and soaks my cock in her juices. *Fuck.*

I drive into her one last time and I finish inside her, exhausting myself and spilling every drop of my cum between her perfect black thighs. I pull out of her and say, "Damn. I think you are the best I've ever had, princess."

I kiss her and she kisses me back.

"You have what you wanted," she says, her voice shaking with fear, "Now leave him alone."

I grab her arm as she rushes for her clothes. She looks back at me, terrified but defiant.

"You can't go back to that guy, understand?"

"You need to mind your business," she snarls at me.

"I'm serious, princess," I whisper, "Any guy who would sell you to a scumbag like me doesn't deserve you. You're fucking beautiful. And you were fucking great tonight. Best I ever had, I swear on my mama."

She puts her clothes on and rushes out of my room, slamming my door behind her.

Angie Victor. I don't think I'll ever see that chick again.

1
THE GUY

@Celebz_Leaked
#CANCEL Sebastian Jefferson
Hey Gossipers,
*I have some tea from y'all today. Y'all might not believe me but I have **SOURCES** and pictures from my exclusive sources. Sebastian Jefferson, like THE Sebastian Jefferson, SPAT on one of his fans. This shit is crazy.*

These nasty ass white boys are doing too much and their dusty fans keep supporting them. We are done. Remember last year when he refused to take a picture with a fan? Ew. Ew. Ew. Who the hell streams that shitty band's music anyway? 1 Billion views on their last video? 🙄

If y'all can get #CANCELSEBASTIAN trending tonight, that would make all the difference.
SPAM THEM! Let them know that we won't let these racist af crusty white boys get away with this shit anymore.
— Celebz Leaked

ANGELINE VICTOR

"Why are you showing this to me, Meg?" I snap, rolling my eyes at yet another stupid clickbait post about Seb Jefferson.

"That's the guy, isn't it," Meg says, "Your baby daddy is the insane but low-key fine white guy who spits on his fans."

"He's not the guy," I lie to her.

Meg has been my best friend too long not to see through my bullshit.

"Yes, it is. It's Callie's..."

"Stop it, Meg. We aren't doing this," I mutter, "Yes. Sebastian Jefferson is the guy. Their band *blew up*. It doesn't matter."

"Are you fucking crazy?" Meg hisses, "It matters. He's rich and you have his kid. You secured the bag. I think you should sue him."

Meg's a divorce lawyer now, and she thinks I should sue everyone. Don't like the music? Sue the radio station. Don't like the coffee? Sue Starbucks. She thinks in lawsuits. She wanted to sue a dating app for setting her up with too many losers. I talked her out of it... Barely.

Meg Nigel's long faux-locs hang away from her face with a yellow head-wrap that looks incredible against her brown skin. When I was younger, I used to want to be as light as Meg, who is still pretty dark. But she's not as dark as me.

She's still folding her arms and waiting for a response to her lawsuit suggestion that I am definitely *not* going to follow.

"I'm not suing him because I don't want him in Calypso's life," I snap, "I don't care if he's rich and famous. That was the worst night of my life. I'm not going back there."

"You said the sex wasn't bad."

"Sure," I snap. "The sex part was fine. But that doesn't change the fact that he's a monster. I was a complete idiot back then. Yannick *sold me* to him for a night. I don't want my daughter knowing that her father is a —

Calypso runs from the swings towards us.

"Mom! Mom, I found a bug!"

She's holding a large green insect with long antennae and I'm trying not to freak out as she turns around and runs toward another kid.

"Callie, no! Put it back! Callie! Don't put it in his shirt..."

Shit. I race for her and pull her away from the little boy she is about to torment with her weird playground bug. I scoop my daughter up and put her on my hips. She's getting big. Five years old is big. She has her own little personality that's so sassy and cute. Until it isn't.

Meg sticks her hands in her pockets and joins us.

"Next time, I'll hold your mom back so you can torture boys with bugs," Meg whispers to her. Callie laughs and wraps her arms around my neck.

"Mommy, can I have ice-cream."

"No, you can't. We need to get you home so you can get plenty of rest before your lesson tomorrow."

"What-ever, lady."

"Excuse me, ma'am?"

"Bye, Felicia."

"Callie?"

"I mean... yes, mommy."

I wonder if she gets that sassy attitude from me. Or from him. Sebastian Jefferson. He doesn't even know that he *has* a daughter. I don't want him to know. He gave me $50 for birth control that night. I pocketed the cash to hitchhike from Los Angeles.

I had enough of the so-called glitz and glamor after my

encounter with Seb. Los Angeles was a place that used women up and spat them back out. I was just lucky that my parents forgave me for running away at sixteen. Yannick was thirty-three when he convinced me what we had was love.

I'm not that stupid kid anymore. I don't believe in love.

I slept on Meg's floor for three months before I found a job. Three years of working nights and I started my bar. At least you don't get sexually harassed by your 55-year-old manager when you own your own place.

Back then, when I slept on Meg's floor, I didn't even *think* about my missing periods. I was too busy trying to get a roof over my head and stop Yannick from tracking me down. Six months of stalking me while I was pregnant. Meg went out and bought a gun. I'm more California that way and I couldn't sleep as long as she had it in the house.

At least she was trying to protect me. It worked, didn't it? Here I am with both of them and Meg's talking to Callie about bugs.

When Calypso finally came, my family was *furious*. I wouldn't tell them who her father was. I *couldn't*. I signed an NDA.

But... I was *human*, too. All humans struggle to keep secrets. We either have to tell someone or let the secret hold us hostage until it turns into something else. A heart attack. Cancer. *Secrets kill eventually.*

And Meg was my lawyer, so I could talk to her about the stupid NDA. Now that she's showing me stupid blog posts about him, I regret ever telling her about Sebastian Jefferson. A part of her probably thought I was lying and wanted to use the news story to get me to confess that I got knocked up by a bum or something. The only thing she knows for sure is that Calypso's daddy is white. I rarely go for white guys, but I didn't exactly "go for" Seb. He took me.

Callie's skin is the gentlest shade of brown, lighter than a walnut.

"I'll text you if I have plans, Angie," Meg says, drawing me back into the moment.

"Great. My mom said she could take Callie tonight if you think of something we can do."

Callie sits up straight. "Yay! I want to go to grandma's house. Her food doesn't taste yucky."

I scowl at Callie, who gives me a cheeky grin, and then kisses my cheek. My mom's Southern cooking might be delicious, but I think vegetables *don't* need sugar in them. Callie and my mom disagree.

Callie offers a sympathetic comfort, "It's okay, mommy. I know you try your best."

Kids can be so harsh. Damn. I wave goodbye to Meg and take Callie to the car. I'm a long way from the girl who had to sleep on Meg's floor. But not far enough. The bar is hard work, and it's even harder doing it all alone as a single mom. At least in Tennessee I have family. I didn't have anyone in Los Angeles.

Calypso's teacher wants to enroll her in a performing arts school and the bar isn't doing well enough for me to pay her tuition.

Callie's really talented. I wonder who she gets it from.

And her tuition? $7,000 a term, three terms a year. $21,000 is way than half my income after tax and bills. I have some money put away, but not enough to commit to a lifetime of tuition like that. If business at the bar picks up, *maybe*.

For Calypso, I'd do anything. I'd never buy new clothes again if it meant allowing her to pursue her dream. To *have* a dream.

My baby girl saved my life. But could I really sue Seb Jefferson for child support? I'd never given him a chance to meet her. He still doesn't know about her.

He's a creep, anyway. What kind of guy buys a girl for a night? A rock star. An asshole. A sin-soaked playboy without a care in the world. The thought of him makes me sick to my stomach. Unlike everyone else in America, I don't care about his sparkling blue eyes or the fact that Rolling Stone called him "the next Cash". Yeah, except Johnny Cash had a soul and Seb Jefferson's a monster.

I haven't needed Sebastian so far. I don't need him now. Once Calypso and I get home, I lead her through the door and straight to the bath. I need to search her pocket for bugs every time she plays outside. The worst week of my life was when I took her to a boy's birthday party and he had tarantulas the kids could pet. Callie begged for a tarantula for two weeks, much to my horror.

Nashville has more bugs than anywhere else, I swear. And Callie has a way of finding them. Spiders. Cicadas. Horrific centipedes. Yuck.

During bath time, I comb through Calypso's long curls and twist her hair into two cornrows down the side of her head. Her hair is longer than mine has ever been. It's so thick and curly. I should take better care of my hair, but I just wear wigs or braids now and spend my time worrying about Callie.

She always asks for complicated hairstyles that get attention from the kids at school. I'm a wallflower by nature, so this extroverted daughter of mine must be like this because of Seb.

"Okay mocha cookie," I tell her. My heart warms every time I look at Callie's smile. And after bath time, she smells amazing. I just want to cuddle her up. Now that she's getting more independent, I know I don't have too much longer to appreciate her like this — all small and innocent.

"What do you want for dinner? Chicken and salad orrrr do you want to see what grandma's cooking?"

"I like grandma's food," Callie says confidently.

"Cool. Let's get you ready then. I'm sure she'll be happy to see you tonight."

Callie nods, and then she sticks two of her fingers in her mouth, glancing at me nervously.

"Mommy. Are you a lesbian?" Callie asks.

"What?"

Where the hell did she learn that word? She's only five...

"At school Ronnie said if I don't have a daddy it's because I have two mommies and that mommies can be lesbians now."

"Listen, we'll talk about that another time, okay? Tell Ronnie that gossiping isn't nice."

"Oh-Kay."

I call my mom, who is more than happy to have us over. Our place in Nashville's only a few blocks from hers. Seb Jefferson's from Tennessee too, but he's a country boy. You can hear it in his voice. You can't fake that accent. He probably couldn't get rid of it if he tried. When I close my eyes, I can still hear his voice.

Thankfully, I'll never have to see him again. He's too big to come back to our city, too caught up in the Los Angeles grind.

He's probably paying for sex with someone's girlfriend right now. Ugh. Why did Meg have to make me think of him?

My mom takes Callie into her arms as I enter her front door, careful to make an awed gasp at the hydrangea bushes out front as I walk up the front steps.

"Hey mom."

"Hey," she answers, clutching Callie tightly in her arms, "Meg called."

"She did?"

"She said she was coming over to whisk you out of here so make sure I'm ready to shoo you out."

"Whisk me out *where*? I just want to watch Desperate

Housewives re-runs and chill. I need some white people mess to forget my problems today."

My mom raises an eyebrow and blurts out, "Meg says you need a man."

"She *told you that?*"

My cheeks gush warmth and I nervously fuss with my wig's middle part. Calypso pretends not to listen, but she's a kid. They're little sponges and my little sponge listens to everything.

"Grandma, can I show you my performance? I have a lesson tomorrow."

"Sure, mocha cookie. Let's go."

Mom leads Calypso to her living room. Since finalizing the divorce from dad, she's done a lot of work on the place. It's nice. Callie walks to the center of the room without a hint of shyness. That must be him, mustn't it?

I was so shy I barely spoke to anyone when I was a kid. Sebastian Jefferson is... her *dad*. He's performed on stages for millions of people. He must be fearless. Brave. Confident. Like Calypso.

The similarities make me uneasy. Callie clears her throat and taps her foot before giving her polished introduction.

"My song for the audition is called O Little Town of Bethlehem."

I haven't said yes to performing arts school yet, but Callie's voice teacher has been preparing her for the audition, anyway. Mom's helping me cover that expense, but I know it's a lot for her. Since the divorce, she's had to pinch her pennies while watching dad spend all his money on women fifteen years younger than her. I try not to get in the middle of their mess, but I know she loves watching Callie grow.

Callie clears her throat and does her whole bit. She sounds *so* good. I can't believe she's only five. I can't believe she's *already* five. I can remember the night with Sebastian like it was yesterday. I'll never forget it. Not even my mom knows about him. She doesn't care who Callie's dad is anymore, now that she has a grandkid to spoil and trash talk my cooking with.

Mom enjoys reminding me that decent Southern men like a woman who can cook. She cooked for my dad every day for 35 years and he still cheated on her with our neighbor while she had breast cancer. But I keep that thought to myself.

We sit down for dinner after Callie receives all the praise she can handle. Callie finishes eating quickly and hurries off to play with the little ukulele I bought her for her fifth birthday. She seems to have figured out some chords, but she doesn't have the hang of it yet. That doesn't stop her from making up little songs.

"Callie asked if I was a lesbian today," I whisper to my mom so Callie can't hear me over the music.

"Are you?"

"Mom! No. Callie has a *dad*."

"You could have fooled me. I don't know what white boy you let knock you up or why he abandoned his daughter, but he's scum. Lower than scum."

Sebastian *was* scummy, but not for the reasons my mom thought. If she knew Callie's dad was one of Nashville's greatest rock stars, she'd probably say exactly what Meg said. *Sue him.*

"Yeah. You're right," I mumble, hoping she doesn't press me about him.

Meg arrives half an hour later. She's close with my mom and doesn't even bother knocking before she rushes "Aunty Daveena" (my mom). Meg's outfit is *crazy* even for a night out. High go-go boots. Hot pants. A tiny little top.

"Meg, what the hell are you wearing?!"

"We're going to a concert, girl. I'm going to twerk on a white boy and secure the bag. Let's go!"

"I'm dressed like... a *soccer mom*."

"So? You look hot!"

"I'm *not* going to a concert dressed like this."

"I have a top you could wear!" my mom calls. I flash her a stern glare and she winks at Megan before running upstairs to get the top and shoving me into the powder room to change. I'm wearing normal jeans and Adidas sneakers. The top is a cute pink halter that I can't imagine my mom wearing to anything.

Once I exit the powder room, Meg grabs me with an unyielding grasp.

"Goodbye, Aunty Daveena!" Meg calls into the house.

Meg never dresses like a lawyer when she's not at work, but I don't think her hot pants and go-go boots will attract the type of successful guy she needs. I keep that part to myself. I'm mostly trying to convince her to slip out of the hot pants and underneath a weighted blanket so we can watch Diary of a Mad Black Woman for the seven hundredth time.

I don't think I can come up with a plan fast enough.

"Bye mommy!" Callie calls, barely looking up from her ukelele.

Meg shoves me into her car like I'm a captive.

"Where are we going?"

"A concert. I told you."

"I don't have tickets anywhere. It better not be country..."

"Angie? Shut the hell up," Meg says. "Get excited. It's a pop-up show, and you're going to love it."

I don't know what my crazy ass best friend has planned, but I don't think I can escape. I'm stuck here with her.

2

THE GIRL

SEBASTIAN JEFFERSON

"I DON'T CARE what some dumb chick gossip blog says about me. We get on that stage and give the best fucking show of our lives. You hear me?"

Mickey fingers his bass guitar and Earl beats out a drumroll. He's always a worse player when he's off his meds, but at least he brings the energy. Mickey's too drunk to do more than nod his head, put on that pink flush and strum. We're only here because I convinced our shit head manager to give us a damn break from the LA grind. We have to justify our stay in the sticks if we want to keep our heads down and out of LA — which all three of us want.

"It's a sick gig tonight. Small. Intimate. The type of gigs we always play in Nashville," I say, knowing it's my role to hype the guys up.

This is my damn hometown and you won't catch me turning down a night in the city for anything. I *hated* Los Angeles. I never want to leave the damned South again. Until our next album drops, we can stay here working and writing and "getting inspiration" as long as we do a few key shows and a few key press interviews.

I tell our manager it'll be easier to stay out of trouble in our hometown. Nashville's always been good to me and it'll be good for Mickey so he can stop his damn drinking and Earl, so he can stay out of trouble with the fucked up women he keeps entangling himself with.

I even got myself a second home in Nashville — somewhere that would have never let a redneck motherfucker like me through the front door ten years ago before I had the tattoos, the electric guitar and the platinum blond hair. Not to mention more money than any man alive ought to have.

Earl keeps tapping out a nervous beat with the tip of the drumstick. Kara fingers her guitar and nods her head. "Sweet crowd we got. We can handle it."

Kara's girlfriend's hanging backstage, waiting for the show to start. She's half the reason Kara wanted to come back to Nashville. You can't find true love in LA and you can't keep true love alive. Nashville has to work for all of us. Now that we've got money and we aren't scrappy little country kids playing in Honky-Tonk bars when we ought to study for the SAT, we all want something LA doesn't want us to have: a happily ever after.

Lord knows a bunch of drugged up, pimped out rock stars are probably doomed from the start. But I'll be damned if I don't give having a good life my best shot after the hell I've been through.

I work the guys up to a frenzy now that Kara's nervous strumming has become an organized, throbbing melody, "And when we're done here tonight, we don't stop partying until we've banged every sweet piece of pussy in Nashville, Tennessee."

Kara whoops loudly, even if we all know there's only one sweet piece of pussy she really enjoys. It's not like our fans know that the iconic southern belle likes women — possessive butch women. We all have our secrets. I know I have mine...

"Let's show Tennessee a good time, motherfuckers," I say.

All these years in L.A. and you still can't take the twang out of my voice. Especially when I say *Tennessee*.

"Woo!" Mickey cheers, necking back a Miller. Times like these I miss burying my face in a bowl full of cocaine and letting go. But I'm 5 years sober from coke, crack, liquor and meth. I have to let the natural high of getting on that stage take me over.

I can't be the guy I was when I hurt her...

I still don't remember her name, but fuck, I'll never forget her face. That dark-skinned, round face. I look for her in every crowd. I double-take every time I see a woman, dark enough to be straight from Sudan.

I imagine the contours of her body, which I can barely remember sober. I just have my imagination. The fantasy of the perfect girl.

The way she gripped me remains permanently etched on my mind. She'd been so sweet. So submissive. She fell into a villain's arms and I used her like a prostitute. She deserved better than cracked-out Seb'Jefferson. She deserved better than that punk ass Yannick.

You never stop working the 12 steps and I have unfinished business with Step 8. Make a list of all the people you have harmed and become willing to make amends. I am cursed to live with what I've done forever. She could have only been eighteen... she had to have been. It kills me to imagine that she might have been younger. That in the throes of a meth bender that involved coercing my producer to whore out his teenage girlfriend to me... I might have done what I did to someone younger.

I never knew what happened to her, and I never saw that

motherfucker Yannick again. Mickey does a bump and I fiddle with the chip in my pocket to avoid the triggers. To avoid *using*. Other guys might fuck with that shit and have fun, chill out for a while. I become a fucking monster. I become the guy who fucks a teenage girl after sticking a balled up fifty-dollar bill in her purse.

I *used* women. The more famous I got, the more of them I used. None of them wanted it less than *her*. Goddamn it. What was her name again?

We're ready to go on stage. I can hear the crowd and the natural high starts. Blood rushing past my ears. The thrill of performance. Mickey starts us off on the bass. Earl on drums. Kara on the guitar. The curtains aren't up and I can already hear the sounds of bras pelting at them. My trophies from all the women in America who would die for me. The curtain slowly rises and the heat pulses through me. *The best high on fucking earth.*

"Good evening, Nashville," I croon into the microphone and when they hear my Southern accent, they go *crazy*.

"How many of you believe in astrology?"

The crowd cheers.

"Which sign is the best in bed.... let me hear you scream...."

I hear Gemini faintly. Maybe Aries. I chuckle into the microphone and more women scream. There really isn't a better high than this. It's the only high that could keep me away from the powder. Music.

"I wrote this song *Aries* about a girl I loved... Sorry to all the other signs, but this one goes out to you..."

My baby's an Aries.
I like her red hot hair.
Her red hot tongue and her...

Yeahhhh

Three songs in, and I'm covered in sweat, still high off the music. After our set, we get off the stage and I'm pumped. *We made it.* Our manager steps out of the green room with a shit-eating grin on his face.

There's seriously no explaining how much I hate this guy. But he makes me rich. He makes himself richer, but I'm willing to accept that to be America's Southern heartthrob.

"Get your asses backstage, boys. There are hot and horny women here to meet *Rebel Blood*. Mickey, smile. Cut the crap. Earl, put the fucking lighter away. And Sebastian, try not to *grope* any of the fans this time."

"She asked for it. Literally. For her profile picture. How is that my fault?"

"I saw the damn blog post, Seb. Get your ass under control. I'm warning you. One more scandal and we *will renegotiate* your contract. Keep your ass in line."

I follow Mickey and Earl backstage and glance up, already planning to meet the fans with derision. I hate this part. The part where desperate lonely chicks act like they know you because of your job. I'd rather fuck them than smile at them and act like the guy they wish their boyfriend was. And then I see her. Well, I *hear* her friend first.

"Angie. You are not leaving. You march up to him and talk to him," a loud brown-skinned woman says, a distinctly adult voice over the hordes of high-lilted teenage debutantes desperate to meet us.

My gaze snaps over to the grown women. *Angie.*

That was her name. How the fuck could I forget? Then I see her. The night rushes back to me with all the details I thought I lost to methamphetamine years ago. Angie Victor. She's five years older and damn... she looks good.

She bursts away from the stage area as I make eye contact with her. Hell no. I don't care what my pussy ass manager has to say to me. I'm not letting that woman out of my sight. I follow her through the Emergency Exit.

"Angie Victor!" I call, rushing toward her. It's easy to hurry after women when you're 6'7". Her name rolls off my tongue so easily that my heart nearly jumps out of my mouth behind it. She's here. She's in Nashville. I never thought Yannick would let a girl like her go. She loved him too much and sick motherfuckers like that enjoy breaking a woman who loves that hard.

Her friend stops and stares at me, dumbfounded. Angie turns around. She folds her arms. Holy shit. She's prettier than I remember. Way prettier. Her body's perfect too. And her breasts are *huge*. Meg hurries toward me and says, "Listen, I don't care if you're famous but you need to know that you have a —

"STOP IT, MEG!" Angie screams.

"You tell him, or I will. He can't get away with doing this to you."

"Angie," I say, freezing. Every day in recovery I planned what I'd say to her if I ever saw her again and now she's at my show in Nashville of all places and my tongue turns into a damned cotton ball in my mouth and I feel like I've been bit by a rattlesnake. My blood is cold, and my skin tingles.

"You came to my show. You remembered me," I say. Suddenly, I feel all nervous, like she's the famous one. It's easier to be the famous one. I feel uncomfortable when women throw their thongs and bras at me, but most of the time, all I have to do is stand there. Now, I feel like I need to say something to her so she doesn't bolt, but I'm dumbfounded.

"She could never forget you," her friend Meg chimes in, "Seriously. She can't."

"Meg. Please. Leave us alone," Angie says, sounding seriously pissed off. I remember that look too, and struggle not to smirk.

Meg snorts and then goes back in through the emergency exit.

"Angie Victor," I repeat her name, promising myself to commit it to memory and suddenly feeling like a complete idiot.

"You're the girl," I finish, realizing I sound as stupid as a sheep.

"What girl?" she snaps, "You must have had hundreds of girls by now."

My heart races and I'm serious as a heart attack when I look at her.

"Maybe even thousands. But there's only one girl I'll never forget."

I'm surprised but I know that if I don't think fast, she'll slip through my fingers again and this surprise is heaven sent. One week back in Nashville and I've found her without even looking. Unfortunately, Angie apparently doesn't care much to see me. My comment makes her scowl.

"I'm sorry if I bothered you, Mr. Jefferson. I'm sure you're very busy with all your girls."

She turns to walk away from me, but there's no way in hell I can let her do that. I grab onto her arm and plead with her.

"Angie, wait. Don't go."

My heart pounds at the thought of losing her again. That moment of contact changes everything for me and I know that whatever I do next, I can't let Angie Victor go again.

I'll do whatever it takes to make her mine, even if I have to drag her kicking and screaming backstage. My grasp on her tightens.

3
FORGET ME

ANGIE

"I don't want to fuck up your life, Sebastian. The show was amazing. You're talented. Just forget you ever saw me."

I mean it. Now that I'm seeing him in person, the horrible night we first met (and had sex) rushes back to me. The things he said to me... and the way I came. I shouldn't have liked the dirty words coming out of his mouth or all of his talking about *black pussy*.

I bite down on my lower lip, willing myself to run away from him. I knew from experience he could overpower me if he wanted, and I'd stupidly sent Meg away.

"Can I get your number at least?"

"No, Sebastian. You can't."

"Okay. Listen, Angie. I'm sorry. I know it doesn't do a damned thing to undo what I did to you that night. But I've changed. And I'm sorry. I'm really sorry for everything I did."

"Right," I snap. "I heard the lyrics to your songs tonight. They're all about sex, cocaine, red heads you want to bang, breasts and money. I don't think you're any different. My friend dragged me out here tonight but it was a mistake."

"Why did you come? If it was such a mistake, why didn't you keep ignoring my existence the way you did the past 5 years?"

"I didn't *ignore* your existence," I huff at him.

How dare Sebastian insinuate that he's the victim of *me?*

"I tried looking for you. I thought about you, constantly."

"That doesn't flatter me, Sebastian. I'm not one of your little fans."

The derision in my voice appears to pierce him. Good. Now that I'm seeing him in person after all this time, I want to hurt the heck out of Seb Jefferson. I want to let him know that I'll never accept his stupid apology. And I'll never tell him he has a daughter.

"Answer the damned question, Angie. Why'd you come?"

"I got pregnant," I tell him. The words come easily because that's the truth.

He lowers his voice, platinum hair glimmering in the evening light, "I thought we took care of that."

"Whatever, Sebastian. I knew you'd react like this."

"You got rid of the kid, right?"

"Yeah. I *got rid of the kid,*" I sneer.

My heart races, but I don't want to tell him the truth. I won't tell him the truth and give him any power over Calypso's life. How could I forget he was such a damned scumbag?

He doesn't want a kid. Who the hell talks about a kid like that? Like something to get rid of. I want to punch the arrogant bastard in his smug face. How many fans will he have without that perfect jawline? What if I made those blue eyes black with a good punch in the face? Where would all of Seb's stupid groupies be, then?

He doesn't seem to notice my anger.

"Then you ain't got anywhere else to be tonight," he said, "Cool."

Great. I've backed myself into a corner. Meg appears again. Was this trifling hoe listening in?!

"She ain't going anywhere!" Meg yells. I flash her another glare and she emerges, shrugging. I scowl at her and she mouths, "Tell him later."

"Perfect," Seb says, "Angie Victor. I owe you a hell of a lot. May I interest you in a drink?"

"I don't drink," I snap at him.

Seb grins.

"Neither do I. But I can't take you for a coffee and I can't take you back to my place."

"There's a juice bar two blocks down!" Meg chimes in.

I turn to glare at her again, but she only winks and yells, "Bye, Angie!"

I snap at her, "You're leaving me?!"

"It looks like you've already got a ride home."

"Meg! Get back here!" I yell, chasing after her, but Meg threatens to tell Sebastian again and I can't have that. I let her go and I stand in the back parking lot, facing my worst nightmare. Sebastian. He's taller than I remember and way more muscular. I guess he's older too and I can see that on his face. He doesn't look like a hungry young man, all money and rage. He looks pensive and... deep. He looked like that while he was singing, too.

His music is awful, obviously, but it's impossible not to bob your head or remember the lyrics. And his voice... His voice makes me forget how much I hate him. But looking at him, our night together comes rushing back to me in painful, disturbing detail. He paid me for sex. He's a monster.

I turn to face Sebastian, loathing all over my face.

"Take me home," I snap.

Wait. I can't go home. Callie's at my mom's place, and I

need to pick her up before I go home. Just when I take my phone out to call her and weasel myself out of this nightmare situation, my mom texts me, and I glance down at my phone.

Meg explained. Have a fun night! Callie's already asleep. I'll take her to school tomorrow.

What the hell did Meg explain? Because she sure as shit didn't tell my mother about Seb Jefferson.

I shove my phone in my pocket to hear Sebastian crooning, "That your boyfriend?"

"I don't *have* a boyfriend."

"I don't believe that, Miss Angie," he says. "Pretty girl like you?"

I hate when he says my name. I roll my eyes, hoping he's totally turned off and hoping that he just brings me to my damn apartment.

"I got a vehicle parked at the hotel downtown... it's a bit of a walk if you don't mind," he says.

I try getting rid of him another way.

"What about the band?"

"Want to meet them?"

"NO."

Seb sticks his hands in his pockets and asks, "You ain't keen on Mickey Ford or Earl Wayne Jr.?"

He's handsome. I'll give him that. And he dresses well. Guys in Tennessee don't dress as well as guys in LA, but Seb has that perfect cool that's a little Lynyrd Skynyrd and a little Jim Morrison. Then I remember that scandal with Rebel Blood's website selling teddy bears wearing confederate flag t-shirts and I scowl deeply.

"I'm not keen on any of you good old Southern boys."

Seb sticks his hands in his pockets and if I didn't know better, I'd say he was nervous. Nervous around *me*?

"Let's go this way so we don't get mobbed," he says. His accent is still so strong. I never had a Tennessee accent.

He puts his hand on the small of my back, and I wriggle away from his grasp. Seb doesn't get to touch me. He hasn't earned the right. Even a hand on the small of my back is enough to get me nervous and worked up. Seb's touch is a threat.

"I thought about you all those years," he says, "I suppose you never thought about me."

I bite my lower lip and I know I have to lie through my teeth. How the hell can I tell Seb that I have to think about him every single day because when I look into my daughter's eyes, how the hell can I avoid thinking about her father? I shrug and feel grateful that I'm dressed in a totally not lusty soccer mom outfit. I don't want Seb to think I want him.

"Nope. My friend dragged me here."

"What are you even doing back in Nashville? Did you take my advice and get away from that scumbag?"

"Don't you dare," I snarl at him. Seb Jefferson has enough of an ego without taking credit because I left Yannick Reynolds. *Yannick sold me.* Yes, I left him. I might have been a dumb eighteen-year-old girl back then, but I wasn't *that* dumb.

Seb looks genuinely taken aback.

"I was joking."

"Yeah," she snaps, "I got that. Go ahead, call me a special snowflake."

"You may be special Angie Victor, but you ain't a snowflake."

I hate Seb. I hate his stupid accent and his stupid platinum blond hair. I hate his height. I hate his smile. I hate everything about him. But when I stand next to him, I feel *weird* about hating him. Like all the loathing I've bottled up for him is messing me up. And it's horribly and stupidly wrong.

"Am I taking you back to your place, then?"

"Do people like you even spend time in East Nashville?"

He chuckles and shrugs his big lumberjack shoulders. "I reckon they'd still welcome Seb Jefferson. Even now."

What he means is *especially* now. He can't take five steps outside without a camera flash going off. Right.

"Whatever," I say, "You can take me home. But don't expect me to be impressed by whatever douche bag car you've bought with all your millions."

"I've got several cars, Angie."

"Shut up," I grumble.

If Seb finds my complaints bothersome, he says nothing. What the hell is the point of this? I won't find my happily ever after hanging around Seb Jefferson. He's not Calypso's dad. He's her… sperm donor. And even if I were looking for a dad for Calypso — which I'm not — it wouldn't be a groupie-obsessed drug addict like Seb.

He reaches into his pocket and takes out a little coin. Before I can protest, he opens my hand and sticks the coin in.

"This is for you," he says, folding my fingers around it.

"Great. I don't want it."

I tip my hand into his. Seb's hand closes around mine and he squeezes it shut. Firmly. The contact from his hand makes my chest feel fluttery and gross. He uses women, and I know it. But I can't help the warm and tingly feeling where he's touched me.

"Please, Angie. Keep it."

He walks ahead a little and I refuse to open my hand to look at the weird ass coin he's just given me.

"Seb, I don't want it."

"We're only two blocks away."

"Sebastian Jefferson!"

"Quiet, woman? Do you want people to know we're back here?"

Woman. See? He's a denigrating prick. An asshole. An

idiot. And that stupid jawline doesn't work on me and neither does that sexy deep Southern accent. It's overplayed.

"Look at it," He says, and his voice becomes strained. "Please."

I'm not buying his tortured asshole crap.

"Do I look like I care?" I snap.

"Please," he begs again. There's something nice about hearing him beg. It feels like... sweet revenge.

Click here to order the book.
smarturl.it/prettylittlemonster

4

REMEMBER ME

SEB

SHE LOOKS at me like she ain't buying whatever I'm selling. Angie unfurls her palm and stares at my five-year chip. Her expression doesn't change. Five years of sobriety and she doesn't even give a damn.

I don't know what I thought would happen. I imagined this moment thousands of times. I imagined telling her she's the only reason I didn't end up overdosing in a bathtub somewhere.

She snaps, "What the hell am I supposed to do with this?"

Not the romantic answer I expected. I guess the problem with a fantasy is it's just that... the real Angie obviously hates me. She's still fucking beautiful, but I get it. She doesn't like my band. It's not my fault America's heartland is all about building walls and glorifying slave owners. I don't choose how they market Rebel Blood. I just like music and walking on the wild side. And when I came up with the band name, I also liked cocaine. A lot.

I stop in front of my "car" and face her.

"Throw it out for all I care," I tell her. "Point is, I got sober. I've been clean five years."

"You're a rock star," she hisses, "The only thing you're clean of is all sense of morals and dignity."

"Yes, ma'am," I tell her. One thing's for certain, despite all her put-on Los Angeles polish, Angie's a Southern woman through and through. A guy shows her money and class, all she wants to do is complain about morals.

"Don't you *yes ma'am* me!"

That's another thing about Southern women. No other women get my blood boiling like this. Maybe it's just her and her smart mouth. That's never failed to make me hard.

"Are you going to get in the truck?"

"*This* is your car?"

"Wish I were a little more city?"

"It's covered in mud. You're a *celebrity*. Shouldn't you have like... a Cadillac or something?"

Either she doesn't believe me or she's poking fun. Maybe Angie just doesn't know much about cars.

"It's the latest Ford F-150. It's brand spanking new with a lift and custom tires. It's my Nashville car."

"You are *so* annoying."

I pull the door open for her.

"Miss Angie."

She hesitates, like she doesn't know what the hell she's doing getting into a truck with a crazy asshole like me. I'm the guy who ruined her life. At least she doesn't look like she's doing too bad. I'm just as bad at ruining lives as I was at everything else back then.

But I've finally found her and if I have to drag her into the back of my truck, I'll do it. Luckily, Miss Angie doesn't force my hand.

She sits in the truck and relaxes her shoulders a bit. *I'm not a monster.*

"What are you doing in Nashville?" She asks.

"Bought a house. Trying to settle down."

She huffs and sounds disapproving or skeptical. Maybe both.

"Don't you prefer L.A.?"

"I prefer home."

I glance over at her, and she looks away.

"Whatever," she says, "It's a bad idea to go to my place. I'm totally going to regret this but... we should go to yours."

I can't ignore the instinctive tug in my chest. Excitement. There's a still a rush you get when a woman agrees to come to your place, even if you know she's a wildcat like Angie who would probably stab me to death before letting me get in her pants again. I know it's sick that's where my mind's going, but out of the millions of women obsessed with Rebel Blood, the only one who gets me going is this regular Nashville girl with her dark skin and her soft lips.

It would be my honor to bring her back to my place. To keep trying to impress her when she doesn't want to be impressed.

"Yes, ma'am," I say, sticking my tongue in my cheek so I don't grin too hard and scare her off.

She makes a skeptical face, but I drive her out to East Nashville. I never liked downtown much. Too loud. I can't think or write songs with a Honky-Tonk bar blaring music at all hours.

"Historic Edgefield," Angie grumbles, "Original."

"Would you prefer a penthouse downtown?"

Angie snaps, "I don't need a million dollar house to impress people."

I don't remember her being that harsh the night I met her. But she was in a predicament back then. I stop the truck at the end of the driveway. I don't want my assistant knowing I brought a girl back and I especially don't want her knowing I brought *the* girl back — the girl I've been looking for all those years.

I get ready to leave the truck so I can hold the door open for Angie. She reached out and touches my forearm. The contact repulses her because her hand darts away immediately.

"I'm not sleeping with you tonight. Got it? I know what you must think about me but I'm not... I'm not a prostitute."

"What are you then?"

She scowls and then snaps, "Right. Because one mistake makes me an eternal prostitute."

"Didn't mean all that."

"What did you mean, Seb?"

"I don't know anything about you," I point out to her, which only makes her scowl harder than before.

"What do you want to know? Because all you cared about before was—"

"Sex?"

"That wasn't sex," she snarls. "Don't you dare call what happened between us *sex*."

"I made you orgasm."

"That makes up for it, then? You can buy women like vases or million dollar houses as long as you make them cum."

"The house is actually six million dollars," I say, because I'm an idiot. A complete fucking idiot.

Angie glares at me from the side of her eyeballs, and her nostrils flare.

"I *hate* you," she hisses.

"I know. Want a tour of the house?"

Her shoulders relax a little. She glances over at the house and I can see straight through her good girl bullshit. It's a 6

NEW Series...

million dollar plantation home in a gorgeous historic part of East Nashville. It's a place I couldn't have dreamed up growing up dodging evictions out of double-wides. But it's nothing fancy by Los Angeles standards.

Fuck Los Angeles standards. That city gave me my first line of coke and more expensive addictions. The summer I gambled all our album earnings sticks out in my mind.

"I don't want to be here at all," Angie says.

I fold my arms and call the angry little lady's bluff. I like women who know their worth enough to make a fuss. Miss Angie doesn't scare me. She intrigues me...

"Why are you here, then? I didn't drag you here kicking and screaming."

"Because," she says, "I wanted to see how you turned out."

I don't think she's lying or putting up a wall this time. This is the closest I've come to getting to know the woman I...

Neither of us wants to admit what I did to her.

I want to reach out and touch her then, some dishonorable way of begging for forgiveness. I know that would only scare her. There's a rumble of thunder in the distance. I thought I smelled rain earlier but the big city has dulled every one of my country boy senses. Like I could show up in the country with platinum blond hair and a truck that cost more than my childhood home anymore. I gave up a normal life... for this home.

"I think I turned out pretty good," I say, earnestly.

Angie scoffs.

"Right. We'll see. How many groupies do you have crawling around that gaudy place?"

"*Gaudy?*"

"Only a white Southern man could buy a plantation and expect anyone to be impressed."

"Would you prefer I had a penthouse overlooking Nashville with black leather everywhere and naked women swimming in pools?"

She wrinkles her nose in disgust and I think I ought not to tell her that most of the top rock stars down here live like this.

"I'm only teasing, Angie."

She flinches when I say her name and I lead her through the columns onto the red brick pool deck near my side entrance. The lights are on in the pool and it's immaculate. I know she's blown-away, but she's also too damn stubborn to show how much this place impresses her.

I wish I could get her clothes off in the water, I think for a moment. Then I feel guilty for having those kinds of thoughts about her on account of what I did. I can't have her anymore. Not like that.

I press my thumb to the door and it opens with a warm voice saying, "Welcome, Sebastian."

"Yeah, yeah," I grumble, a flush in my cheeks that my talking door is proof to Angie that I'm an irredeemable bastard.

She steps into the kitchen and takes her shoes off respectably. If I still wore dirt-caked boots, maybe I'd do the same. But I don't, and it's mostly 'cause I'm looking at her. Those dark brown eyes dart around my kitchen, searching for whatever evil she thinks I'm hiding. If I ever was a pretty little monster, that ain't who I am anymore.

"No naked women in the pool," I offer awkwardly.

"Only because they're probably warming your bed," she grumbles bitterly.

"Come on this way, Miss Angie. I'll give you a brief tour."

She doesn't protest because deep down, I know she's impressed. She might scoff at the bedroom or make a little face at the jacuzzi in the bathroom, but most people would kill to live in a place like this. I know, because I was one of those people and then my music career took off and I got everything I wanted.

Every dollar. Every car. Every woman. I took everything I wanted until I ran out of people to hurt and started hurting myself. Drugs. Lots of drugs. Drinking. And being a damned fool.

We tour the downstairs but I'm too nervous to show her upstairs. That's where the bedrooms are and I don't know what I'll do to Angie Victor if I get her anywhere near a bed. I'd say anything to get between her thighs — and damn, I'd mean it. Her thighs have only gotten thicker and sexier over the years.

She's grown… and she's gorgeous.

"So where do you sleep?" She says haughtily. "Is there a coffin in a basement somewhere that you crawl out of?"

"No ma'am," I tell her, "I sleep in a bed just like everyone else."

I lick my lower lips because against my better judgment, the little guy downstairs has made a big decision. Tonight, I'm taking Angie Victor straight into that bed. Damn all my morals. *I want her.*

5

NEVER AGAIN

ANGIE

I KNOW I shouldn't have mentioned his bed the moment I say it. It isn't my fault that Seb Jefferson's house is *perfect*. I'll die before admitting it to him, but I can't help but want to squeal. It makes me forget that he's an utter pig.

The way he's looking at me makes me remember.

"Show me the bedroom, but don't get any ideas. I'm *not* one of your groupies."

"You keep mentioning," he grumbles, "The stairs are this way, Miss Angie."

"You can drop the good ole boy act," I snap. "Maybe your racist fans buy into that crap, but I don't."

"Racist? What's racist about my fans."

"Your entire band celebrates the confederacy."

He shrugs, which is so infuriating. Seb is ignorant.

"We celebrate rebellion, whatever that means to you."

"To most your fans, that's a time when black people were slaves. It's all about celebrating a horrific past."

"You ain't slaves anymore," he says, simply.

I glare at him and roll my eyes. He's not even worth my time. We're upstairs now and Seb pushes the door to one bedroom open. It's… a baby's room. I freeze. I know I need to get out of here, but for a moment, terror surges through me and all I can think is *Seb knows*.

"What's this?" I snap.

"The people who owned this place lost a baby, so they had to move. I was thinking about turning it into another studio. But I don't know. Maybe it ain't too late to find someone to settle down with."

"I'm sure you can buy a child bride like the other rich sickos you hang out with."

Seb snorts and laughs.

"You're real funny, Miss Angie."

"Whatever."

"You want kids someday?" He asks.

"I'm not talking about this with you. I only came here because…"

He folds his arms and stares at me, like he's been wondering why the hell I'm here too. But when I trail off, I realize he doesn't get it at all.

"Because… you're attracted to me?"

Oh. My. Goodness. How could I have ever believed that because he had a freaking baby room in his house that Seb wasn't just another asshole celebrity who thinks everyone with a vagina wants him because of his sheer awesomeness?

"I am *not* attracted to you," I snarl. "How dare you? Do you really think I look back on what you did to me with any type of fondness?"

"No," he says, honestly. "I don't. But… that night is the reason I got clean."

"Glad I could be a stepping stone in your personal growth journey," I snap. "Whatever. I'm leaving."

"I'll get my keys and take you home."

"No! I'll walk."

"You don't live close by," he says.

He's wrong, though. I live five minutes away from him and I realize that I'm *so screwed*.

I glower at Seb, and then we hear the rain. Classic Tennessee, raining when I want it to the least. That's the only thing I miss about Southern California. But I definitely don't miss the rent.

"It's raining. We can wait for the clouds to pass. I don't want you to go."

There's an urgency in his voice that terrifies me. Five years ago, we made a horrible transaction and now seeing him again, I want to hate him so badly. But he doesn't seem detestable. He seems... gentle. Firm but kind.

"I want to leave. Unless you want to add kidnapping to the list of things you've done that you should probably be in jail for."

"Does your husband like how bossy you are?"

"I already told you, I don't *have* a husband."

"Fine, what would your *fiancé* think if he heard you were at Seb Jefferson's house?"

"I told you, I don't have a boyfriend or a fiancé or a husband. I'm done with men. I'm never falling in love and I'm never giving another man an opportunity to screw up my life," I say to him, realizing I sound a little crazy and overdramatic.

I conveniently leave out the part where I don't want a man to screw up Calypso's life either.

"Is that what I took from you?" He says, meaning it so much that it hurts to watch him.

"I have to go," I say, and then I run like hell. Seb calls my name.

"Angie!"

I sprint down the stairs and push the doors open, running

straight out into the heavy rain. Damn, I'd hoped it was a drizzle. But it's an all-out rainstorm and the second I step onto the stones, I'm soaked. Nashville rain is heavy and my clothes are thin. The water soaks my wig, which now smells like the hairspray I used to stick the lace front down. Crap.

This is a hair emergency and worse...

I can hear Seb calling my name and I can't remember which way it is to the main road, so I take off down one path and end up behind the house. If I can hide from him, maybe he'll head back inside and I can find the main road.

I don't want to be with Seb for another second. I step in some mud and shriek as I can't pull my shoe out. My sneaker treads are all worn from long shifts at the restaurant and not enough money to get a new pair. Clumsily, I slide forward and yelp again, falling straight into Seb's arms. They're firm. Really firm. I grab onto his forearm without realizing what I'm doing. His hands move to my waist. He grabs hold of me before I can face plant in the mud and then pulls me to my feet.

Seb fixes his aquamarine eyes on me. I remember staring up at him from the crowd and thinking about what it would be like to have him meet my gaze. No sane woman could resist that. Maybe that's why he made me orgasm. Yeah, I still remember that orgasm five years ago. It's not like I date or have many more orgasms to look back on.

When I look into his eyes, I think maybe I'm not totally broken. Maybe Seb is really just that sexy and magnetic, that I could know he's a monster and still feel... his chest. His firm chest. According to the gossip blogs, he has knew tattoos too. Tattoos that no one has ever seen.

Why the hell am I thinking about Seb's tattoos?

He pulls me to my feet and whispers, "Careful, Angie."

His voice is so deep. My legs wobble and I tell myself it's the mud nearly causing me to slip again. It's definitely not

Seb's voice melting me like butter. He's getting wet now too from the rain and it's getting harder to keep my distance from him. His scent overpowers the hairspray smell sliding down my neck. He smells like sweat and cologne. Really expensive cologne. He might dress all casual but one whiff, and it's clear that Seb is rich.

Really rich. I feel embarrassed by my thin, wet clothes and the way my body presses against him. I swallow and try to will myself to pull away from him. He's holding my waist and pulling me against him like I belong there. Seb smells like he's been on stage all night, but also like pine wood and leather. He wears a *lot* of leather. I can't stop thinking about his smell. So I'm not really thinking at all, just standing there, stupidly pressed against him while he holds me.

I shouldn't be anywhere near someone as dangerous as Seb.

He'll destroy me.

"Let me go," I whisper, "Please..."

"You're just as beautiful as that night," he says, "And I'm sorry I hurt you. Don't give up on men because of me."

He's officially hugging me now.

"Let me go," I whisper. "I'm sorry I bothered you, Mr. Jefferson."

He nods, rain soaking his platinum blond hair against his neck. I realize I'm bracing myself against his chest, my hands feeling his warmth. We're close to doing something that my lips keep telling him not to do. He releases his hand from my waist, but I keep mine pressed to his chest.

"One kiss," he pleads. "I just want... one."

"I can't kiss you," I whisper.

"Then don't," he says.

He leans in and kisses me. I hate how good it feels. The rush is immediate and sugary sweet, blasting all my senses awake. We're kissing in the rain with wet clothes clinging to our bodies and our hands are all over each other. Sebastian's hands are back on my hips and he grabs me closer to him.

"One more, Miss Angie," he whispers. "One more..."

I pull away from him and shake my head. I have to be strong. My heart hammers in my chest and my body suddenly remembers that this is dangerous. Everything about Seb is dangerous, and I'm putting my daughter in danger just by letting him touch me.

"No. No... we can't *ever* see each other again."

6
ALWAYS

SEB

I GET her a towel and get her in the truck. She won't tell me where she lives, which is probably smart. But I have no intentions of letting Miss Angie go. I drop her off downtown, even if I suspect she doesn't live anywhere near downtown.

She tried to run home, so she must live close. I pull my car two blocks down before I get out and some kid says, "Holy shit! That's Seb Jefferson!"

I take the hat off his head and walk off, ducking behind a bus station, leaving the kid with a good story or another way to slander me in the press. I don't give a damn anymore. I have another purpose... Angie Victor.

Predictably, she calls that pretty loud-mouthed friend of hers to pick her up. I write the license plate number before heading home. You don't grow up in Tennessee the way I did without knowing your fair share of cops. You don't know any cops without knowing your fair share of dirty cops.

I call my cousin Bobby Ray and give him the license plate. Meg Nigel. She's a hotshot lawyer with a social media profile designed to project professional success. She posts a picture at her best friend's bar five weeks ago and now it's sitting on my phone — Angie's exact location.

Stalking her ain't exactly the way to prove I'm a changed man, but you'd be surprised how lonely and boring it is to be famous. I keep to myself when I ain't with the band. I usually hang with Kara, but she's taking a break from all of us because of the Mickey incident. Our bad press puts her at risk of having her sexuality exposed.

But I can't show up at this bar alone, especially as I don't drink anymore, so I guess I need to get the band together for a *Rebel Blood* night on the town.

Kara politely declines my invitation. Mickey's too high to say no to a Friday night adventure. Earl Wayne Jr.'s visiting someone up at Brushy Mountain State Penitentiary, but promises he'll be back in time for a party. Friday. That's four days away. Four days of practice, four days of songwriting. I can write another song about her. Who am I kidding? All my songs are about Angie. And before Angie, they were all about her, too. I just didn't know it yet.

On Friday, I wake up at noon after a late night of meeting and greeting fans plus a meeting with our shit-head manager where he lectures me some more about the incident. Yes, I spit on a few fans. I did a lot of stupid shit when I was high as a kite. Fame gets to you. It fucks with you. Other people forget you're human and you forget they're human too.

Starting the day without an eight-ball means I have to work for my pleasure. Two hours of strenuous exercise. One of these vegetable shakes. And a bunch of shit that only rich folks bother with. Rich folks like me. My house bustles with staff by seven a.m. I hate it. I prefer being alone, but since we're doing a small tour around Tennessee, keeping everyone paid while I write the album, I have to keep the house running.

NEW Series...

I can't write with all those fucking people around, so I lock myself in my study, put my headphones on and strum.

By the time I'm ready to meet the boys at Angie's bar, I've written four songs about her. Good songs, but none of them good enough for the radio with all the cussing and talking about her pussy. Those are the best rock songs — the ones that don't make it to the pussy ass American radio.

Fuck being nervous about Angie. I'm a superstar and I dress like one. Black leather pants. Loose silk shirt. Cowboy boots. My cocky fuck-you Seb Jefferson smile. Angie Victor ain't getting away from me so easily tonight.

Mickey's been at the bar for an hour by the time I get there. He's drunker than a skunk on a Sunday and there's a little blood on the corner of his left nostril. It breaks my heart that I'm probably half the reason he's on coke. He makes me feel guilty for getting clean, but he also makes me want to punch him in the stupid fucking face.

"She recognized me," Mickey slurs as I approach the table, fuming.

"Did she run off, you idiot?"

"Oh, she's spitting mad. She told me to call you and tell you not to show your sorry ass in her bar."

I sit down, scowling at Mickey. The worst part about idiots is they never know how dumb they are. Mickey's worse than an idiot. He's a drunk idiot, with eyes so freaking blue that most women look past his bullshit. But that idiot's the reason I had to dye my hair platinum.

Label says with the blue eyes, we look too much alike. I get a hairstylist turning me into David Bowie and he gets to be a normal man. I can't complain too much — I make triple what he does from everything we do. I'm the star...

Before I can tear into Mickey for being a goddamn idiot, Earl Wayne Jr. strolls in. *I told this motherfucker to keep a low profile...*

All 6'7" of him sticks out like a sore thumb. Cowboy hat. Giant buckskin jacket. Jeans as blue as the sky over the Ozarks. Orange boots with mink skulls on the tip.

"Hey, hey, hey! It's Earl Wayne Jr. Let's get a round of shots on the house," he yells.

I don't think people from this part of town are too keen on *Rebel Blood*, but Earl offering the round of shots leads to pleasant applause — the type of applause that motherfucker lives for. It sucks that my best friends both wish they were the center of attention like I am, and I hate it. The lead singer. The man behind the music. The man with a target on his back.

My face doesn't belong to me. It belongs to everybody. Earl and Mickey think they want this, but it's a cursed way to earn a living.

Earl's massive order draws her attention, and Angie comes out from behind the bar, looking prettier than the first day I saw her. Prettier than when I touched her in the rain. Her hair's different now. It's curly and tied up in a red scrunchie. I like my women natural and holy hell, Angie Victor looks natural.

Earl sits at the table and starts talking bullshit about a bet he made with a singer down in Memphis. I don't give a damn about his story, because I'm stuck on Angie. Perfect fuckin' Angie. Her hair sticks to her neck with sweat.

She's wearing black leggings that hug her curves, especially her ass. Her practical sneakers are worn so thin, I don't think they've got soles left. She's wearing a low-cut v-neck t-shirt with nice breasts sitting in them.

Another server brings our drinks and I barely thank her because I'm looking at Angie who finally notices me looking and scowls. She doesn't want me here. Bars in Nashville *pay me* to show up, but Angie doesn't want me anywhere near her bar. I can tell from the look on her face. Too bad.

NEW Series...

I want to see how she turned out too.

A thin layer of sweat on her forehead and the bridge of her nose makes her look gorgeous... like she's just had a fresh romp in the hay. I lick my lips as Angie approaches, even if she's spitting mad. She'll *always* be the sexiest woman I've ever seen.

And I don't care if she's mad... as long as she gets her sexy ass over here.

Click here to learn more.

EXTREMELY IMPORTANT LINKS

JAMILA JASPER
Diverse Romance For Black Women

Turn the page for a **FREE** book download

EXTREMELY IMPORTANT LINKS

ALL BOOKS BY JAMILA JASPER
https://linktr.ee/JamilaJasper
SIGN UP FOR EMAIL UPDATES
Bit.ly/jamilajasperromance
SOCIAL MEDIA LINKS
https://www.jamilajasperromance.com/
GET MERCH
https://www.redbubble.com/people/jamilajasper/shop
GET FREEBIE (VIA TEXT)
https://slkt.io/qMk8
READ SERIAL (NEW CHAPTERS WEEKLY)
www.patreon.com/jamilajasper

Extremely Important Links

JAMILA JASPER
Diverse Romance For Black Women

MORE JAMILA JASPER ROMANCE

Pick your poison... Delicious interracial romance novels for all tastes. Long novels, short stories, audiobooks and more. Hit the link to experience my full catalog:

FULL CATALOG BY JAMILA JASPER:
https://www.jamilajasperromance.com/books

PATREON

7 SEASONS OF SERIAL CHAPTERS
NEW serial chapters published WEEKLY on my Patreon. Read all six seasons of *Unfuckable* (Ben & Libby's story)...

For a small monthly fee, you get exclusive access to over 375 episodes of my first completed serial as well as access to the current ongoing serial, *Despicable*.

Patreon

Patreon has more than the ongoing serial…

⚡ INSTANT ACCESS ⚡

- NEW merchandise tiers with **t-shirts, totes, mugs,** stickers and MORE!
- **FREE paperback** with all new tiers
- **FREE short story audiobooks** and audiobook samples when they're ready
- #FirstDraftLeaks of Prologues and first chapters **weeks** before I hit publish
- Behind the scenes notes
- Polls and story contribution
- Comments & LIVELY community discussion with likeminded interracial romance readers.

LEARN MORE ABOUT SUPPORTING A DIVERSE ROMANCE AUTHOR
www.patreon.com/jamilajasper

ABOUT JAMILA JASPER

Jamila Jasper is an Amazon bestselling author of African American women's fiction and romance novels. She writes contemporary interracial romance novels with gut-wrenching plots, titillating alpha male bad boys, and strong female main characters from diverse backgrounds — from London, to Atlanta, to Kampala. In her free time, Jamila enjoys hiking, spending time with her cat and salsa dancing. Use the icons below to find Jamila Jasper on social media. Use the hashtag #JamilaBWWM and post the Jamila Jasper book you read online for a social media shoutout!

- facebook.com/bwwmjamila
- twitter.com/jamilajasper
- instagram.com/bwwmjamila
- amazon.com/author/jamilajasper
- bookbub.com/authors/jamilajasper

THANK YOU KINDLY

Thank you to all my readers, new and old for your support with this new year. I look forward to making 2021 an INCREDIBLE year for interracial romance novels. I want to thank you all for joining along on the journey.

Thank you to my Patrons.
Join the Patreon Community.

Sydney, Phia, Sharon, Charlotte, Assiatu, Regina, Romanda, Catherine, Gaynor, BF, Tasha, Henri, Sara, skkent, Rosalyn, Danielle, Deborah, Kirsten, Ana, Taylor, Charlene Louanna, Michelle, Tamika, Lauren, RoHyde, Natasha, Shekynah, Cassie, Dreama, Nick, Gennifer, Rayna, Jaleda, Anton, Kimvodkna, Jatonn, Anoushka, Audrey, Valeria, Courtney, Donna, Jenetha, Ayana, Kristy, FreyaJo, Grace, Kisha, Stephanie E., Amber, Denice, Marty, LaKisha, Latoya, Natasha, Monifa, Alisa, Daveena, Desiree, Gerry, Kimberly, Stephanie M., Tarah, Yolanda, Kristy, Gary, Janet, Kathy, Phyllis, Susan

Made in the USA
Middletown, DE
03 November 2022

14107554R00187